Praise for *The Move*

'Dark and gripping, this tale is perfect for snuggling
up with by the fire with a glass or two of wine'
Closer

'A dark and foreboding tale of a rural dream gone wrong;
of what can happen when we try to paint over the cracks'
Sunday Post

'Felicity has the reader gripped when she explores
unhealthy relationships based on insecurity and
delusion. She writes with a raw realism'
Adele Parks, *Platinum*

'Tense and tightly plotted'
Woman

Felicity Everett grew up in Manchester, lived, worked and raised her family of four in London. In 2014 she returned from a four-year spell in Melbourne, Australia to live in Gloucestershire. After an early career in children's publishing and freelance writing, she published her debut adult novel, *The Story of Us*, in 2011. Her second novel, *The People at Number 9*, was published in 2017.

Also by Felicity Everett

The Story of Us
The People at Number 9

FELICITY EVERETT

the
move

ONE PLACE. MANY STORIES

HQ
An imprint of HarperCollins*Publishers* Ltd
1 London Bridge Street
London SE1 9GF

This edition 2020

1
First published in Great Britain by
HQ, an imprint of HarperCollins*Publishers* Ltd 2019

ISBN: 9780008288419

MIX
Paper from
responsible sources
FSC™ C007454
www.fsc.org

This book is produced from independently certified FSC™ paper
to ensure responsible forest management.

For more information visit: www.harpercollins.co.uk/green

This book is set in 11.2/16.5 pt. Sabon

Printed and bound in Great Britain by
CPI Group (UK) Ltd, Croydon, CR0 4YY

For my family
(sorry about the sex scenes)

1

It was a miracle. I had navigated the town's one-way system without taking a single wrong turn. And this had to be the right road out because I'd just passed Tesco Express, which I remembered Nick telling me was the last chance to pick up a pint of milk before you hit bandit country. As the houses petered out and the last streetlight of the town dwindled to a pinprick in my rear-view mirror, darkness fell like a cosh across the windscreen. I flicked the headlights onto full beam and turned the radio on. The syrupy late-night jazz made me feel like a character in a film. I imagined the panning shot, following my little car along the contours of the valley – the heroine, driving with trepidation into her new life. Nick had wanted to come up and fetch me, but I'd told him no. I didn't want to be mollycoddled. Not any more.

A dilapidated signpost reared up from nowhere and, unsure whether I had read it right, I made the split-second decision to take the turn-off anyway, pitching the Renault downhill into a tunnel of green. Branches closed over my head and the hedgerows rattled the sides of the car, their abundant spring leaf-growth a sickly green in the halogen. I followed the lane through all its labyrinthine twists and turns and was starting to wonder whether I might after all have gone wrong, when I came to the derelict barn that marked the start of the hamlet. The cottage was around the next bend. With a surge of relief, I pressed the accelerator, saw – too late – a brief flash of orange in the headlights, braked hard, felt a dull thud; drove on.

'I think I hit a fox.'

I stood on the doorstep, trembling. This was not the homecoming I had planned.

Nick pulled a sympathetic face. 'I didn't even *see* it.' I could feel my voice starting to break. 'I thought it was a branch, but it can't have been because look…' I raised my palm to show him a rusty smear of blood across it.

'It wouldn't have felt anything,' he said briskly, 'I wouldn't worry. Come here…'

He drew me over the threshold into a welcoming hug, but I held myself a little aloof, torn between the gut-melting desire his presence still, in spite of everything, evoked and a reluctance to sully his pristine clothing with my bloody hand.

'What if I only injured it?' I fretted. 'It might not even be dead…'

'Come on, Kaz…' Nick said, with slight impatience, 'this is the countryside. Foxes are ten a penny here. The farmers hate 'em. You'll be a local hero.'

He tilted my chin upwards with his knuckle and pressed his mouth on mine and I forgot about the fox and let my lips cling to his as if it were the kiss of life, which, in a way it was. When at last he signalled, with a volley of little kisses and a cancelling stroke of his finger across my cheek, that it was time to stop, I sighed, and turned to the room for the first time.

'Wow!'

I had only seen the cottage once for half an hour after the vendor had moved out, leaving the ghostly silhouettes of her mock-Regency furniture on walls that needed a lick of paint. They had had the lick of paint and more. Oak floorboards gleamed in the lamplight. Fat church candles flickered on the deep sills of the curtain-less windows. Familiar items of furniture mingled with new ones I didn't recognize. The place looked like a photo-shoot for *Ideal Home*.

'You've been busy,' I said.

'I wanted it to be nice for you. You don't mind that I chose things without you, do you…?'

He stooped slightly and looked into my eyes.

I shook my head with an amused grimace. Why should I mind about *that*? For the past four months, I had barely been able to choose what clothes to wear, what meal to eat, what TV channel to watch. I don't think I was going to have a hissy-fit about whether he'd gone for Buttermilk or Dimity on the skirting boards.

'That's lovely,' I said, nodding towards a scuffed leather armchair.

'Local antique shop,' Nick said smugly. 'It's the real deal, not one of those naff reproduction ones. Would have cost twice as much in Shoreditch.' I had to suppress a smile at my alpha male husband's unexpected knack for home-making. He had even had the rug cleaned. Or perhaps it just looked better in front of the rustic wood-burning stove than it ever had beside our ugly Victorian fireplace at home. I needed to stop calling Trenchard Street home. *This* was home now.

I struggled to subdue a wave of nostalgia for our old life. We never got the house right, in nineteen years. It had been a mish-mash of stuff – my parents' teak dining table surrounded by Nick's Swedish wishbone chairs. Nick's carefully chosen abstract artworks jostling my folksy wall hangings. We didn't see eye to eye about décor but somehow between his minimalism and my clutter we created a home. I'd preferred it when we'd just got together and the place was full of toys and IKEA tat, but as the boys grew up and Nick started to entertain his clients, good taste began to prevail. My quirky Mexican candelabra disappeared, to be replaced by a tasteful stainless steel job, and the Klippan sofa ended up in a skip. Yet the more our home became Nick's home, the less *at* home he seemed. Funny that. I sometimes wonder if I was too much of a pushover. Perhaps he'd have respected me more if I'd put up a fight – stuck to my messy ways. Because things had got pretty messy anyway.

I glanced again around the open-plan cottage – glow of firelight over lime-washed walls, stacked logs and plumped cushions; a background scent of something grown up and aromatic.

'What do you think?' Nick asked.

'I love it!'

He made to kiss me again, but I waved my bloody hand at him, more cheerfully this time, and he took me by the waist and steered me towards the kitchen. Here too, he had judged things perfectly. Belfast sink, maple work surface, slate grey Aga, concealed spotlights. And running along the back wall, a triptych of dormer windows, sleek dark mirrors, behind which lurked who knew what. I watched the reflection of my hand-washing in their black panes, foaming suds carrying away a wisp of pink under the state-of-the-art mixer tap. Nick handed me a threadbare tea towel – the one from way back, featuring ham-fisted portraits of Ethan and all his Year One classmates. I dried my hands, taking care not to sully the corner featuring the giant-headed alien that was our son, then rearranged the cloth with satirical precision over the hanging rail of the Aga.

'I'm surprised you let *this* stay,' I said, indicating the old-fashioned four-door oven.

'It's a little piece of history,' said Nick. 'I'm not a complete philistine.'

'I could have sworn it was brown.'

'I had it re-enamelled.'

'You did not!'

'Don't you like it?'

'No, I *do*.' I clutched his forearms eagerly and felt him tense up.

'The colour's gorgeous. It's just... *you* re-enamelling an Aga.'

'Not literally me.'

'Even so...'

'The estate agent was really helpful. Recommended local people. The grey was her idea...'

I bet it was, I thought. I bet she had you on speed-dial. I'd met her once myself – Marnie – sugar-coating on a will of steel. Boob job. I had to stop thinking like this.

Nick handed me a glass of champagne and we clinked rims.

'To us,' he said.

He held my gaze, his eyes full of remorse. I wanted to tell him it was OK; that I had forgiven him. I welled up and he turned away, perhaps in shame, perhaps in exasperation. I watched him bend down to put the bottle back in the fridge, his shirt riding up to reveal the ragged birthmark on his lower back. I could have traced the shape of it with my eyes shut.

'We'll never live it down, you know,' I said, straining after the playful tone of our earlier banter. He stood up again.

'What?'

'Us. Here with... *that*. I jerked my head towards the Aga. Wait till Dave and Jude see it.'

'They'll be jealous as fuck,' he said. 'They'd kill for a place like this. London's over.'

'Hmmm,' I said.

'They *would*,' he insisted. 'They're miserable. Jude hates her job. Dave only stays for Arsenal. If they hadn't re-mortgaged they'd move out in a heartbeat. They're in denial.'

I smiled doubtfully, wondering if it wasn't Nick who was in denial. Moving to the country had never been part of his game plan. He used to come out in a rash if he had to stay in a gîte for a week when the boys were young, so the idea that he'd suddenly become a convert was a bit of stretch. Still, a fresh start had been called for and this one was as good as any.

'Why shouldn't we live somewhere nice?' he continued, bullishly. 'Not that Jude and Dave will admit it's nice. They can't afford to. Not even to themselves.'

'Nick!' I laughed, incredulously. 'They haven't even got here yet.'

'They don't need to. I could see it in their eyes when I showed them the brochure. You poor bastards, they were thinking. Forget about having a life. It'll be tribute bands down the Corn Exchange for you from now on. Good luck with multiculturalism. Good luck with buying a gram of coke.'

'You don't do *coke*.'

'I know, because *I* don't need to blot out the misery of my desperate urban existence. That's what I mean. Denial.' He seemed to notice, at last, that he'd been ranting, and had the grace to look a little sheepish.

'Anyway,' he brightened, 'Shall we do the tour?'

I followed him up the open tread staircase, gratified to see that he'd given my blue slipware bowl pride of place on the landing window ledge. I touched it for luck on my way past.

'Study,' he said, standing to one side so that I could put my head round the door. 'Had to double up some of the books.'

I nodded and backed out again.

'Bathroom,' he announced unnecessarily.

'Nice mirror,' I said in surprise. 'Where'd you get that?'

It was an ornate antique French job – not Nick's style at all. It hung opposite the claw-footed cast-iron bath, making the otherwise poky room look bigger and grander than it had any right to.

'It was here when we looked round,' he said, frowning, 'don't you remember?'

'Oh yeah,' I said quickly, 'So it was. It just looks much better now you've done all this...' I waved vaguely at the freshly painted walls.

'She charged me over the odds for it really,' he said with a shrug. 'Not my scene, but I remembered you liked it...'

'It's gorgeous,' I said, resting my cheek on his shoulder, 'thank you.'

Nick inclined his head towards mine, and the tarnished mirror made Siamese twins of our reflection. He planted an absent-minded kiss in my hair, and I counted the seconds until he broke away again.

*

The first time he'd kissed me, I'd needed to come up for air. I suppose it wasn't completely unexpected – he'd been giving me the eye ever since our bit of banter at the bar earlier in the evening. And every time he'd looked across at me, I'd had to look away quickly and pretend I hadn't been ogling him back. I'd been telling myself the classy-looking blonde on his table might just be his date, not a permanent fixture, but I knew in my heart I was kidding myself. He had 'married' stamped through him like Brighton rock. It had got to that time in the evening when they put the lights down and cranked up Whitney, so rather than be a wallflower, I'd scrounged a ciggie off someone at my table and ducked outside. I'd been scrabbling in my bag for some matches, when his lighter flared by my cheek.

'Oh, right, thanks,' I said.

He lit his own cigarette and, crossing one arm over his midriff, propped the opposite elbow aloft and smoked it as if smoking were its own art form.

'So...' he said, after a while.

I glanced sideways at him, cursing my lack of small talk.

'... Lunch next week.'

It wasn't even a question.

I raised a quizzical eyebrow, hoping to convey much. That I was not the pushover he thought I was; that I was not into married men; that I might, in fact be busy next week.

I had only just put the cigarette to my lips when he leaned across and took it off me, tossing it, along with his own into the parched grass around one of the pegs securing the marquee. For a second, as his lips met mine, it occurred to me that the whole lot could go up. I didn't care.

*

'Shower's a bit rubbish,' Nick said now, stepping away from me just that bit sooner than I'd hoped. 'Like being pissed on by a gnat.' He demonstrated what looked to me an average flow. 'I think we should get a bigger head.'

I imagined us in the steamy cubicle, water thundering down, hair plastered to our cheeks, bodies entwined...

'OK,' I said.

'And last but not least, the master bedroom,' he said, opening the door with a flourish.

I cast a greedy eye over the bed, which seemed to stretch like a small continent between the threshold of the room and the wide sash window on the gable wall.

'Great view to wake up to,' Nick said.

'I remember.'

I did have a vague recollection of a wooded hill rising gently from behind the house, but I wasn't sure whether I had seen it in the pages of the brochure or in real life. It had been a big selling point, the hill.

'His 'n' hers hanging, like you wanted.'

He opened the doors of the built-in cupboards, in which every conceivable category of possession had its niche, from sportswear to handbags, jewellery to hats, the advantage of this approach being that the rest of the room retained its pared-down, monastic charm; the disadvantage, that the opening of the doors forced us back against the side of the bed, making it difficult to remain upright. In another life, we might have reached for one-another's hands before falling back, like felled trees, onto the pristine duvet.

'I know it's small...' Nick said.

'No, I like that about it.'

'... But it's got everything we need.'

'The blind's nice.'

'And if we just get in the habit of putting stuff away...'

I thought of our bedroom in Trenchard Street. The Lloyd loom chair, buried beneath piles of clothing, the dressing table, so cluttered with beauty products that I could barely reach for my hairbrush without causing a tsunami.

'Definitely.'

'Aren't you forgetting something?' I said, as he made his way back down the landing.

'Am I?'

'Ethan's room?' I said, with a perplexed smile, my foot poised on the bottom step of the attic stairs.

For an instant he looked confused.

'Oh, yeah. Go and have a look if you want.'

'Aren't you coming...?'

He shrugged and followed me up.

The door stuck a little as I pushed it open, breaking the seal of the fresh paint. I switched on the light and a bare forty-watt bulb illuminated a spartan space, empty except for two single beds and a cluster of unopened packing cases.

'Singles?' I turned to Nick with a bemused look.

'I thought that'd be more practical,' Nick said, evasively, 'in case…' He gave me a defensive glance.

'In case *Gabe* wants to stay,' I supplied. A pained look crossed Nick's face.

I should not have sounded so grudging. Gabe was Nick's son. The fact that he was pushing thirty and had just bought a flat of his own, courtesy of a whopping loan from his father should not, I supposed, preclude him from feeling welcome in our house. Surely Ethan should take priority though? It must surely still be *his* room, not 'the boys' room' or 'the spare room'. It would be hard enough persuading our disaffected young son back to this sleepy hamlet after his gap year, without making him feel like a guest. I don't know what I had expected. Blue and white striped walls? A miniature basketball net? Ethan was nineteen now. A man. All the same, the emptiness, the *sterility* of the room could not have contrasted more starkly with the care Nick had lavished on the rest of the house.

I thought of Ethan's old room in London. It had been a health hazard, the way teenage boys' rooms often are – you went in holding your breath and hoped you could retrieve the five mouldering coffee mugs from under the bed before you had to gasp for air. It had accumulated grunge the way a bat cave accumulates guano, his interests over the years evidenced in layers, like relics in an archaeological dig, from Harry Potter to Stormzy, ammonites to condoms. But beneath the rank whiff of adolescence and the deliberate affronts to political correctness, I had always been able to detect the little boy he had been – not just in his football trophies or the dog-eared Pokemon cards at the back of a drawer, but in the clean, underlying tang of goodness.

'Oh well,' I said, coming out of my reverie, 'if he gets himself a girlfriend, I suppose we can always push the beds together...'

I turned around to find Nick gone. How long had I been standing there? Two minutes? Ten? Had he left because I'd offended him or had he merely got bored of waiting? I felt a flutter of anxiety in my stomach. How graceless I'd been; how boorish to pick holes because the furniture wasn't just so in every room. He'd gone to so much effort everywhere else; made such a beautiful job of it.

'Nick?' I called anxiously, hurrying down to the first-floor landing.

'Better get a move on if you want some of this fizz,' he called back, his tone friendly and relaxed.

'Coming!'

I clattered down the last flight of stairs, relieved, chastened, grateful.

2

I rose up from sleep like a deep-sea diver. For a few seconds I had no idea where I was, and then I heard footsteps and the clink of crockery on the landing and I remembered. I kept my eyes closed until Nick had entered the room and set the tray down on the bedside table, I don't know why. When I opened them, his face was an inch from mine, moving in for a kiss. I feinted to spare him my morning breath, and his lips landed on my cheek instead. *His* breath smelled faintly of garlic from last night's meal and of his occasional tobacco habit and of Nick, which was the part that always slayed me. Perhaps mistaking my fastidiousness for lack of interest, however, he had already crossed to the window and raised the blind.

'There you go,' he said, turning to me proudly, 'what do you reckon?'

I squinted into the sunshine, waiting for the dazzle of blue and green to resolve itself into a view. The hill was actually two hills, a greater and a lesser one, rising up from the land like the uneven breasts of a sleeping giantess. Bright green foliage covered the lower slopes, but the peaks protruded, nude and straw-coloured as if the effort of rising so high had sapped them of fecundity. Above, a single pillowy cloud hung in the turquoise sky as if on wires.

'It'll do,' I said, turning to pick up my teacup.

'Fuck off!' Nick gave me an incredulous grin and I smiled back mischievously. For the first time since my arrival I felt connected to him. This was how it used to be – easy banter, insults even. The ruder we were to one another, the better things were between us. He had courted me in obscenities, but for months now he'd been treating me like his maiden aunt and for months I'd been feeling like her.

I threw off the duvet and went to stand beside him, slipping my hand warily around his waist. He slung his arm over my shoulder in comradely fashion and we contemplated the scene together.

'It's lovely,' I said, 'I love it. Well. Done. You.' I punctuated each word with a kiss, lingering on the last one as a pretext to inhale his scent.

'Yeah, well,' he said smugly, 'it was a no brainer really.'

I hooked my thumb over the waistband of his pyjama bottoms, and pretended not to notice him tense up. He turned and nuzzled my shoulder and, taking this as permission, I threaded my fingertips after my thumb. It felt like vertigo now, my desire – I could barely breathe. With a more or less convincing growl of lust, Nick made a lazy grab for my breast and I gasped with surprise and then, as his touch became more sensual, with gratitude. Pride left me now, and need took over. I manoeuvred myself in front of him, spread my palms wide across the windowsill and tilted my buttocks up and back interrogatively, as if posing for the world's least imaginative pornographer.

'All right then,' he muttered, his voice thick, at last, with lust.

I didn't look round, but waited for the first frisson of pleasure as his hands shucked my nightdress up over my hips, then the unbearable hiatus as he readied himself, the anticipation seeming to stretch out until the precise moment when fear that he would do this thing was perfectly balanced against dread that he might not. And then he was in me and I could no longer look at the view, because he had one hand on the crown of my head, pushing it down, and the other on my waist, for purchase, and all the disorientation and humiliation of the past was briefly, joyfully obliterated in the disorientation and humiliation of the present. My forehead juddered against the glass and he withdrew, flopping down on the bed with a faint harrumph of satisfaction. I stayed standing – limbs a-tremble, skin aflame, everything above the waist alive and energized, everything below numb and remote, yet still retaining the memory of pleasure, as an amputated limb retains the memory of an itch.

I leaned my forearms on the windowsill and took in, once again, the view beyond. It had a calming, almost soporific effect – the blueness of the blue, the greenness of the green, the emptiness of the landscape. Except it wasn't quite empty, I noticed now.

'Hey. There's someone on our hill!'

Nick peered after my accusing finger.

'It's not *our* hill,' he said, laughing. 'It's a local beauty spot. People go up there all the time. I shouldn't think he copped much of an eyeful, if that's what you're worried about.'

I squirmed. I don't know what I'd thought – certainly not that we owned it, but perhaps that we might have privileged access. A foolish idea, come to think of it, so I tried to make a joke of it, tapping on the window and calling out in my best cut-glass accent, 'I say, you there! Get orf our land!'

By coincidence, the hiker chose that moment to start heading down. Nick was delighted.

'There you go. Breeding will out. You're a natural. Rounding up the peasants, keeping down the foxes. I told you you'd take to country living.'

Foxes. Oh God. I felt again the slither of tyre on gravel, the dull thud, the dread and minutes later, as my hand skimmed the moulded plastic of the bumper, the certainty of what I had done. I thought of the poor beast's stiffening carcass decaying somewhere under a hedge. I glanced down at my fingers, half expecting to see blood on them.

A two-tone chime sounded downstairs, startling me. I stared at Nick and for a moment he stared back, equally flummoxed. Then his face cleared.

'It's the door. You'll have to go.' He nodded apologetically towards his still semi-erect penis.

'Oh God!' I grabbed my dressing gown, wiping my soiled fingers on a screwed-up tissue in the pocket as I hurried downstairs, desperately hoping it wasn't a neighbour or anyone on whom I needed to make a good impression.

I needn't have worried. A courier was peering impatiently through the mullioned windows of the front door. I opened it with an apologetic smile and he thrust a large square box into my arms and handed me an electronic pad to sign, almost taking my eye out with the stylus in his haste to get away. The package was light but bulky and addressed to Nick. I tried not to speculate. Let him have a life. Let him take delivery of a parcel without it being pawed and scrutinized by his mistrustful wife. But then I noticed the company logo.

I raced back up to the bedroom, and did a silly little jig.

'I know what this i-is! It's my thermocouple, isn't it?'

'Bloody hell!' Nick muttered bitterly. 'Three weeks they've had to deliver this and they pick the day after you arrive.'

'I'd have thought that was when you'd want it to come...'

'Well no, I was planning on having things ready for you, to surprise you.'

'The kiln, you mean?'

'Better than that. Come on, I might as well show you now.'

'Show me *what*? What are you up to?'

He picked up the package in one hand and yanked me up off the bed with the other.

'Where are we going?'

He galloped me down the stairs, only letting go of my hand when we reached the kitchen, so he could unlock the back door. He was still wearing pyjama bottoms and his feet were bare but he strode up the garden, past the pond and the vegetable patch – a man on a mission.

'Nick!' I hurried after him, half anxious, half excited. 'What's the big—'

But he had disappeared, squeezing through a gap in the yew hedge I hadn't even known was there. With some trepidation I followed him and found myself in a hidden dell, surrounded on all sides by shrubbery. In one corner loomed what at first glance looked like a tree house: a timber structure with a shallow-pitched roof, all clean lines and Scandinavian simplicity. Three floor-to-ceiling windows gave onto a narrow veranda, which was raised on stilts to clear the steeply sloping ground in front, while the back nestled into a bower of mature shrubs. Timber steps led up from the scrubby lawn to a glass-panelled side door. It was utilitarian without being cold, rustic without being hokey. I knew Nick hadn't built it himself – he could barely put up a shelf – and I doubted he had even had much of a hand in designing it, but he had gone out of his way to think about what I would like and found someone to make it, and that, well… that was a kind of miracle.

Speechless, grinning, I shook my head as I followed him up the steps and through the door, which slid open with a satisfying rumble. It was hot inside. Dust motes swirled in the light. There was a smell of timber and fresh paint and the sound of a bluebottle flinging itself stupidly against the glass.

'So yeah, this is it,' said Nick, with quiet pride. 'Your studio.'

I stood beside him surveying the view down the garden and beyond to the valley, and slipped my hand into his.

'You didn't need to do this.'

'I wanted to.'

'Trying to get rid of me so you can have the house to yourself?'

There was a pause. The temperature in the room seemed to drop a degree or two. I'd meant it as a joke, but it was too soon; too near the knuckle.

'That's right,' he said, stretching his lips into a grimace.

'I'm kidding. I know why you did it and I'm touched, honestly I am. Nick, I absolutely love it.'

'It's the other view,' he said briskly. 'The one you don't get from the bedroom. Or from the house at all, come to that. It faces south-east, so it gets the sun nearly all day.'

I glanced around the room and nodded my approval. He seemed to have thought of everything – my wheel and kiln were there of course; also a wedging table, a glazing area, a sink, metal shelves for work in progress. Only...

He saw the brief frown cloud my features.

'What?'

'No, nothing.'

'What have I got wrong?' he asked wearily. 'I thought I'd got it all covered. If you knew what I spent to get the floor reinforced for that beast over there...'

He nodded towards my kiln, cold and inert without

its thermocouple, but soon to be the beating heart of the enterprise.

'I love it. Honestly, there isn't a single thing I'd change.'

'Oh, but there *is*.'

'It's trivial,' I shook my head, 'I'm sure there's a solution.'

'A solution to *what*?' he smiled through his exasperation.

I could have kicked myself. I had done it again. He had spent a fortune, but more importantly, he had invested his *time*, taken advice, thought through my methods – thought of *me*. And I had rubbished it with a moment's tactlessness.

'It's just…' I pulled a rueful face, '… Well… it's lovely that it's a sun trap and I love all the light. Only, with the clay – it can dry out so easily. I could have done with a damp room or at least a bit of shade, or cool somehow. I'm sure we can think of something though…'

He walked over to the kiln and stood with his back to me, drumming his fingers on its surface. One two three four, one two three four. I hovered nearby, mortified.

'I'm sorry, Nick.'

'It's fine.'

'No, I've been… I'm such a…'

'I just wanted to get it right. To *make* it right.' His voice was tight.

'You have… you are. Please, Nick, stop beating yourself up. It's time to stop now.'

I went over and laid my cheek against his bare back. He didn't move. His skin was cool and clammy. I wrapped my arms around him and held on, trying to warm him up.

3

'Funky, or elegant? What do you reckon?'

I held up an Ikat print tunic in one hand and a grey linen dress in the other. Jude reclined further on the bed, the better to appraise both outfits from a suitable distance.

'I'd go with that,' she said, leaning forward and swatting the dress, 'the other one looks a bit "eccentric potter".'

'Oh, cheers, Jude…'

'No it's nice, and everything, it's just… I'm not being funny, Kaz, you've got to be careful living in a place like this.'

'What's that supposed to mean?'

'Well, we had a little nose round the town on our way here – it's very cute, but…'

I jutted my chin, defensively.

'… Also, let's face it, a bit Middle Earth.'

'It isn't actually,' I said hotly. 'That's just the touristy bit. There's quite a decent commercial gallery that you wouldn't have seen because it's tucked away. And there's a craft beer place and an art trail twice a…'

'Don't take it so personally,' interrupted Jude, laughing, 'it's just where you live. It doesn't define you.'

I looked at Jude in her Agnès b. shirt and her expensive haircut and felt a faint twinge of... what? Not dislike, surely? One could not dislike one's best friend, who has stuck by one through thick and thin, particularly thin. Irritation, then. Yes, Jude could be irritating. Dave too. They had made fun of the Aga, as I knew they would. Dave had started humming the theme tune to *The Archers* and talking about milk quotas in a funny accent. But then the four of us had gone on to enjoy an evening of drunken camaraderie. Dave had brought coke 'for old time's sake' and everyone had done a line except me. I was tactfully discouraged. There was a lot of repartee about what Dave insisted on calling 'the Auld Neighbourhood', even though he's not Irish and it was in Hackney. Mutual friends were shot down in flames for their hypocrisies and pretensions. I found myself wondering what kind of jokes Dave and Jude made about us behind our backs, although to be fair, we had not really been joke material of late. Not unless you had a very sick sense of humour, anyway. It was a fun evening all the same and for a couple of hours, in the glow of the fire and the embrace of the wine, and to the strains of a mellow soundtrack provided by Nick's music app that told you if you liked that, you might also like this, I started to see how I might become a person again, a friend, a *wife* even.

But that had been last night and this was tonight and the grey linen dress looked try-hard with the wedge heels that Jude had suggested, yet frumpy when dressed down with Converse, so I had abandoned it in favour of a drapey sweater and jeans. It had been a warm day and the sky was still blue, but a bank of pinky-grey clouds was scudding up the valley on a brisk evening breeze. The fairy lights that Nick had rigged in the trees around my new studio were swinging alarmingly, and smoke was swirling from the barbecue like a malevolent genie released from its lamp.

Jude and I stood on the grass, arms hugging our bodies and sipping our wine, while further down the garden Nick was greeting some early arrivals, his tone jovial and not a little strained.

'This reminds me of my sixth birthday party,' I muttered in Jude's ear. 'My mum invited the whole class and I hid in my bedroom and refused to come down.'

'Let's not talk to them,' Jude said. 'Let's just get wasted and dance on the patio.'

I gave her an anxious glance.

'Relax,' Jude patted me on the shoulder, 'I'm kidding.'

Already, Nick was shepherding an elderly couple up the garden path towards us: the man, white-haired and slightly stooped, in a houndstooth jacket and slacks; the woman ruddy-faced and beady in a polyester two-piece.

'Darling,' Nick said (he never called me darling), 'these are our next-door-but-one neighbours, Jean and Gordon from Prospect Cottage. Jean, Gordon; meet my wife Karen and our very good friend Jude.'

I shook Jean's papery hand, then Gordon's surprisingly soft one.

'*Jew*, was it?' bellowed Gordon, his face contorted with

what I hoped was curiosity, but feared might be something worse.

'Ju*de*,' said Jude, with a beaming smile, 'short for Judith.'

'Ah...' said Gordon, with a hint of relief.

'But I *am* Jewish, as it happens,' said Jude, 'on my mother's side anyway, which is how it works. All that wandering in the desert. I suppose they couldn't be sure who the father was, so they made it matrilineal.'

'I see,' said Gordon, with a faint look of distaste.

'Anyway,' Jude said breezily, 'I'm about to get a top-up. Can I bring you something to drink...?'

'A light ale for me and Jean'll have a tomato juice,' Gordon said.

Perhaps Jean would like a Mai Tai, I felt like saying; perhaps she's in the mood for a Sex on the Beach. I caught Jude's eye as she headed off towards the makeshift patio bar.

'Grab me another beer will you, Jude?' Nick called after her. 'On second thoughts, you won't have enough hands, I'll come with you.'

'Nick...' I protested, but they had gone and I was marooned, clutching my glass, as tongue-tied and awkward as if the new guests were some glamour couple from Islington, not our septuagenarian neighbours from two doors up.

I turned back to them with my best hostess's smile. 'Have you... lived here long?'

Jean turned deferentially to Gordon.

'How long is it, dear?'

Gordon raised his eyes heavenwards.

'Nineteen sixty-seven we moved in,' he muttered as if this were a topic of conversation he was tired of rehashing.

'Nineteen sixty-seven, that's right,' Jean nodded fondly, 'because we got a television and that lady won the song contest in her bare feet.'

Gordon muttered to himself and drifted off to weigh up the vegetable patch.

'Goodness, that's a long time!' I said, with a forced smile.

Fifty years in this one spot. Fifty years married to Gordon. I felt a gloom descending and I wasn't sure if it was on Jean's behalf or my own. Would I find myself reminiscing at some future date on my own half century spent in this obscure little corner? The hedges growing higher every season, the trees growing taller, the wonky signpost finally falling off so that not even Jude would be able to find me?

'We moved in with Gordon's mother, after his father passed away.'

'Right,' I said.

'And by the time she passed on I was in the family way, so it made sense to stay in the house.'

'How lovely!' I said, thinking the opposite. 'It must be so nice to have that sense of continuity. Do your children still live nearby?'

'Oh no, dear, Peter's in Dubai and...' she lowered her voice, '... Gordon doesn't see eye to eye with our daughter, so we don't see her any more...' her tone was wistful '... or the grandchildren.'

'Oh, what a shame,' I said with a sympathetic pout, 'it's such a lovely spot for little ones too.'

Who was I kidding? Prospect Cottage was every estate agent's nightmare – a blight on an otherwise desirable hamlet in which the average property prices had doubled in a decade. Its mellow stone frontage had been pebble-dashed over and the portion of its front garden not turned into hard-standing for the couple's Honda Civic, was dominated by a vast Leylandii, whose one benefit was that it obscured a fuller view of the ugly uPVC porch which Jean and Gordon had filled with gloomy, Triffid-like houseplants. Neglect, the consequence of its owners' advancing years, had been the property's only saving grace, allowing its hedges to grow tall and shaggy, ivy to rampage up to its sagging eaves and moss to spawn on wall and outbuilding alike, softening its ugly profile into an irregular dark green carbuncle.

'... They know who their granny is though,' Jean continued now, the chirpy optimism in her tone more heartbreaking by far than despair, 'I never forget their birthdays. Send 'em a postal order every year, on the dot.'

A postal order, I mused, was that still a thing?

'That's nice,' I said doubtfully.

Jean gave me a wistful smile but as we both glanced across to where Gordon was still glowering at the kale, it died on her lips, and I looked away embarrassed. Over her shoulder I could see a young couple making their way down the lane, he carrying a bottle of champagne, she a Kilner jar trimmed with gingham. Behind them trailed two little girls in flouncy dresses and Alice bands, each clutching a small bunch of garden flowers. I squeezed Jean's arm by way of 'excuse me' and her eyes met mine in mute appeal, as if there was more she had wanted to say to me.

'Douglas Gaines,' said the newcomer, pumping my hand warmly and handing me the bottle. 'And this is my wife Imogen.'

She was a woman for whom the term pretty might have been coined: snub-nosed, blue-eyed, smooth-haired, with a mouth neither too big nor too small. She wore a fitted cotton dress and an angora cardigan over her freckled shoulders.

'Courgette chutney,' she said, thrusting the Kilner jar at me. 'Last year's, I'm afraid, but it keeps for ever.'

I juggled the champagne, the Kilner jar and my half-empty glass before finding a precarious equilibrium.

'Thank you so much.'

Douglas ushered the two girls forward.

'And *these* two monkeys are Honour and Grace. Say "hello", girls.'

'Hello,' they chimed, thrusting their bunches of wilting flowers at me.

'Oh! Sweet.'

I made an awkward grab for one of the posies and the jar of chutney slipped from under my arm and smashed on the path.

The faint babble of conversation stopped and there was a brief silence, before someone – it must have been Dave – filled it with ironic applause.

Slowly, I took in the tableau of horror – the green gloop on the path, studded with shards of inch-thick glass; the spatter of chutney up the legs, and yes, on the dresses of Honour and Grace; the expressions of polite dismay on the faces of their parents.

'God! Oh God. I am so sorry. I'm such a…'

Grace (or was it Honour?) started to cry while her braver sister cast a silent malevolent spell on me. Whatever she was summoning – pustules, incontinence, lameness, it couldn't have been worse than the agony of standing there for what felt like decades, apologizing on a loop, while the Gaineses' smiles grew ever more strained.

'You've met the wife, then?' Nick appeared from nowhere, clapping a matey hand on each of their shoulders, and looking from Douglas to Imogen and back again with an expression of such pop-eyed satirical enthusiasm that they had no choice but to laugh. Even I managed to crack a smile – my roguish husband, whose insults were taken for compliments, whose sins masqueraded as misdemeanours – always on hand with a ready quip.

'She made it herself,' I murmured, woefully, in Nick's ear. He bent down to appraise the spilled chutney before sticking his finger in an uncontaminated bit and licking it ostentatiously.

He grimaced.

'Lucky escape if you ask me!'

There was a moment of silence while the assembled guests digested the audacity of his remark, then Imogen turned on him an expression of scandalized delight and batted his sleeve and Douglas emitted a complicit snort. Jude handed me a dustpan and brush and ushered the little girls towards the kitchen. I heard her promising them Coke, crisps and stain removal, in that order. Day officially saved.

More people came. A friendly couple called Ray and Min who ran the B&B and overhauled vintage motorbikes in their spare time, followed by a plump Scottish woman, Cath, mannish of dress, unfussy of demeanour. She explained which house she lived in and I must have looked surprised. It was the picture-perfect cottage with roses round the door, which I had imagined might belong to some apple-cheeked matron and Nick had insisted was more likely a lucrative holiday let. Cath was a garden designer, she told me, and whilst her own garden reflected her old-fashioned preference for lupin and hollyhock, she had paid for it by designing minimalist gardens for city types who didn't give a shit about plants but cared very much that she'd won two silver gilts at Chelsea. I smiled at that.

Things were getting almost buzzy now. The local farmer dropped in, accepted a glass of wine, offered us a discount on his organic beef and asked us to like his Facebook page before heading off to move the yearlings to their summer pasture. Then came an interesting pair, young and arty-looking with foreign accents and I got quite excited until Min took me to one side and explained, in embarrassed tones, that they were guests at the B&B, who hadn't quite grasped the protocol, and thought it was open house. I didn't mind. They bulked out the numbers and brought down the average age of the guests by a good couple of years. I even had a slightly stilted discussion with the woman about the merits of the Swedish education system, only to be told later by Jude that they were Dutch.

As twilight fell, a couple of rackety youths looked in, who seemed to know everyone, but only hung around long enough to eat a burger apiece and down a couple of beers, before heading up the lane towards the local pub. Nick muttered 'freeloaders' under his breath, but I didn't mind – I liked their swagger and their air of entitlement and the way they came and went, like the weather. I could almost fool myself they were mates of Ethan's – that we were a family again.

It was only when the four of us were clearing up at the end, trekking back and forth from garden to kitchen with glasses dangling between our fingertips, making cheery remarks as we passed each other on the path, that it occurred to me that Jean and Gordon must have left without saying goodbye.

4

I slept in the next morning. I could hear the murmur of voices downstairs, the chinking of cups and smell bacon cooking. For a while I pretended to myself that I was still asleep. I couldn't face it. The laughter, the chitchat, the morning-after discussions, during which my progress would be monitored, my rehabilitation assessed and scored. But Jude and Dave were leaving today, and I knew that if I let them go without saying goodbye, I'd only regret it. I struggled into my dressing gown, ran my fingers through my hair, glanced into the mirror to reassure myself I still had a reflection, and then made my way along the landing, slowing as their voices came within earshot. I could tell from their hushed, confidential tones that they were talking about me. I stopped, one hand on the banister, and listened.

'… I just think you have to be so careful,' Jude's voice – low and serious, '… It *might* be therapeutic, but it might be too soon…'

'Yes, I haven't forgotten, thank you,' Nick interrupted tersely, 'and of course I'm not going to push her. I'm not an idiot. Only the psych said, career aside, it could be a good outlet… a safe space…'

'Don't you think this should be her safe space? Here, with you? In your house?'

I clattered noisily down the rest of the stairs.

'So yeah, no... I suppose the neighbours aren't exactly what you'd call cosmopolitan,' said Nick, and I marvelled at his ability to turn on a sixpence, 'but their hearts seem to be in the right place and it's not like we need any more friends as such... oh hi, darling. Come have a coffee.'

'So yeah, Kaz, we were just saying. Not a bad gaff you've got here,' Dave pitched in, with uncharacteristic tact.

'The neighbours seem friendly,' added Jude. She shuffled her chair along to make room for me.

'Well, we hardly know them yet,' I reminded her, holding out a mug so that Nick could pour the last of the coffee into it.

'The B&B woman seemed nice. *Normal* anyway,' said Jude.

'You'd have to at least pretend, wouldn't you,' put in Dave, 'running a B&B.'

'*I* quite took to Cath,' I said.

'The er... big woman?' said Jude.

'The lesbian,' Dave said, in a satirical whisper.

'Is that how we identify women,' asked Nick drolly, 'by their size or their sexuality?'

'Works for me,' said Dave.

'Anyway, yeah, *Cath* was nice,' I said.

'Better keep an eye on the missus, Nick,' Dave said.

'She's promised me some fuchsia cuttings,' I said to Jude, ignoring him.

'Eh-up!' Dave slapped the table.

'Shut up, Dave,' said Jude wearily.

'Shall I fry you an egg, love?'

Nick leaned across the table and touched my hand. I watched his fingers caress mine and felt the warmth of his touch, but the two phenomena seemed unrelated. I smiled at him and shook my head.

'What about the Fotherington-Farquars?' Jude nudged me, her eyes round with suppressed merriment.

'They're called Gaines,' I said with an admonishing smile. 'They were all right, I thought. Especially considering I dropped her chutney.'

'*Chutney though!*' Jude rolled her eyes.

'What's wrong with chutney?' I said, laughing.

'She'll be joining you up to the WI next,' said Jude with a sulky smile.

'She will not.'

'My God, their kids are precocious,' Jude said, changing tack. 'You should have heard them when I was trying to get the stains out of their dresses.' She put on a high drawly voice. '"I don't think it will come out completely because Mummy's chutney has turmeric in it and turmeric is used as a dye in India."'

'Yep, you're right,' I muttered, 'spawn of the devil. Remind me to sneak round after dark and kill their ponies.'

I didn't know why I was being mean to Jude. Because she was going home, I suppose; because she was leaving me here.

'Don't be like that,' she said. 'I'm not saying they're not nice people. I just can't see you hanging out, that's all.'

'Yeah well, I didn't *hang out* with our neighbours in Trenchard Street, did I? I hung out with you.'

The truth of this statement – its emotional heft – silenced us both for a moment.

'Come home!' Jude said, pouting. 'We *miss* you.'

Nick winced and Dave threw Jude an exasperated glance.

'Not *home*, obviously,' Jude backtracked, '*this* is home. And a very homely home at that. Much nicer than… well every bit as nice as… Anyway, you know what I'm trying to say… Oh Christ, when you're in a hole, eh…?' She looked in slight desperation from Nick to Dave and back again, then leaned forward and patted the back of my hand. 'Take no notice of me, babe. I'm just being selfish. I want what's best for you. You know that… as long as I still get to see you once in a while and you promise not go off with old Vita Sack-of-potatoes up the road, I'll let you keep your little bit of paradise. How about that?'

I rolled my eyes, not trusting myself to speak.

'Well, it *is*,' Jude insisted, waving toward the window as if I had challenged her, 'it's paradise. Look at that view. A person could never get tired of…'

'Jude, I'm not a child!' I snapped. 'We're not here for the view as you very well know. I wish to God you'd all just…' I put the back of my hand to my mouth and focused hard on the tufts of meadow grass waving their own strange semaphore message through the kitchen window.

It was awkward after that. Too much politeness about the order in which showers should be taken, too much willingness to strip beds and take taxis to the station, rather than put us to any trouble. An onlooker might have mistaken us for casual acquaintances, rather than friends of twenty years' standing. I felt the old feeling returning, the fish tank feeling, as though I were behind glass, moving more slowly than everyone else through the wrong element. I watched Jude check the train times on her phone and had to fight the impulse to snatch it off her. Don't leave me here! I wanted to say. Take me back to London with you. Only take me in a time machine back to before the silences and the evasions and the sudden lavish treats. Back to a houseful of noisy adolescents pissing off the neighbours and a busy social calendar, back to a pair of perky tits and a husband who occasionally wanted to fondle them. Back to the sound of sirens and the smell of chicken shops; back to rubbish in bus shelters and busted sofas on street corners; back to reality.

I heard the rattle of Jude's suitcase wheels on the landing and felt, for a moment, overwhelmed with despair.

By the time we were loading our guests' luggage into Nick's new Range Rover, the mood had lifted a bit.

'Nice light environmental footprint you've gone for here, mate,' Dave said sarcastically.

'He's just jealous,' said Jude, as if we didn't know.

Nick smirked and switched on the ignition. Then, half joking, half in earnest, he turned the sound system on full blast, slid down the front windows and roared up the lane with Nirvana riffling the hedgerows like a cyclone. He had taken three blind corners at breakneck speed, to the anxious hilarity of his passengers, when, rounding the fourth, a Transit van loomed out of nowhere. Brakes squealed and we were flung forward in slow motion, collapsing like puppets against the leather seats.

'Shit!' Nick killed the music and we sat in shock for a moment, watching the bonnet of the Transit vibrate. I thought we must have hit it, but leaning out of the open passenger window, I saw that it was juddering, not due to any impact, but because it was held together mainly by rust and gaffer tape.

Not that the van's shaven-headed driver seemed much mollified by the lack of physical damage. Seeing him glare down at us through his wrap-around reflective sunglasses, I shifted uneasily in my seat.

Nick raised a hand, acknowledging fault, and then, with his trademark insouciance, gestured towards a passing place a few yards behind the Transit, into which the other driver might easily reverse so that the two vehicles could pass each other. The youth continued to stare at us, his neck pulsing beneath a terrifying-looking Celtic cross tattoo. He gripped the steering wheel and worked his jaw.

'Dude's off his head,' muttered Dave.

'I think you'd better just back up,' I said.

'Oh, come o-o-on!' said Nick, slapping the steering wheel in frustration. 'He's only got to reverse three yards and I can get past him. What's he even doing round here anyway? Goon like that.'

'Big problem in the countryside apparently,' Dave said, 'nothing else for them to do.'

'I'll give him something to do…' muttered Nick ominously. All the same he looped one arm around the back of my head rest, rammed the car into reverse and with his gaze fixed on the rear window, accelerated recklessly around corners and up and down undulations in the road, until we were almost back at the cottage. Then he tucked in beside a drystone wall and waited.

All was quiet except for the sound of birdsong and a branch tapping out a rhythm on the roof and for a moment it seemed the van might have been a figment of our imaginations. But just as Nick was losing patience and seemed ready to pull out again, it came jerking and squeaking around the bend and the exaggerated slowness of its approach made me nervous. I squinted into the Transit's windscreen, but the sun glanced off it, turning it into a vast silver rink, the only sign of life inside the slow back and forth of a talisman dangling beneath the rear-view mirror.

'Uh-oh,' Nick murmured, and his voice sounded suddenly small. There was a pause. A light breeze stirred the nettle patch. I could hear my heartbeat in my temples. Then a cacophonous roar, a squeal of tyres, a skitter of pebbles. I shut my eyes and braced for the impact… and braced… and braced… and then, warily, opened them again.

'Jesus fucking Christ!' hissed Nick as the van accelerated away in a cloud of filthy exhaust fumes, leaving the Range Rover unscathed.

'What a cock!' said Dave.

Jude and I laughed with relief.

Nick put the Range Rover in first gear, his hand trembling slightly on the gear stick, and accelerated away at even greater speed than first time round.

'They don't tell you about twats like that in *Country Life*, do they?' Dave called, over the sound of rushing air and roaring engine.

'Yeah, well, he's not a local,' Nick said, defensively. 'Probably just some blow-in, staying off the main roads so he doesn't get pulled over.

But it was too late. Our country idyll was exposed for the sham it was. There was no time, now, to prove to Dave and Jude that you could actually get a decent coffee in the town, or to take them accidentally-on-purpose past the stylish gallery, where I hoped I might eventually sell my work. It was too late, anyway, after the run-in with Crazy Van Man and last night's collection of oddball neighbours to convince myself, let alone my sophisticated urban friends, that this was any place to live. You only had to look at the two station platforms, the up line and the down, to see that anyone with any taste or *savoir-faire* was heading back up to the smoke, whilst the down was populated by what Ethan would scathingly term 'randoms'.

The train was pulling in. Jude enveloped me in a perfumed hug.

'Thanks,' she said, 'it was a blast. Great place, kiddo. Just, you know… give it time.'

She gently peeled my knuckles off the collar of her denim jacket and picked up her case. Nick and Dave did some manly back-slapping and then our visitors were on the train, moving down the carriage, mingling with the other passengers so that they could no longer be distinguished one from another, only from those left behind.

5

'The clay will find you out,' my ceramics tutor used to tell me and it was true. In my beautiful new studio, the clay found me wanting. It wasn't its consistency: Nick had taken my plea to heart and found me an old fridge, which, unplugged, made the perfect storage facility. It wasn't any of the practicalities: I had ironed out all the little teething troubles that had arisen from his misapprehensions about my practice. The awkward configuration of tool store, worktable and wheel had been corrected and I had rescued an old piece of formica from a skip which made an ideal glazing surface. The kiln was up and running.

It was, if anything, too perfect. I didn't feel equal to it. I'd got used to working in the utilitarian strip-lit basement of Trenchard Street, where anyone over five feet seven had to stoop. Needless to say, at six feet one, Nick had not visited often. It had always been 'the basement' never 'the studio'. The wheel, worktable, kiln and shelving had been squeezed in alongside extraneous junk. By the end, despite Nick's repeated promises to help me sort it, a proliferation of finished pots were jostling for space with garden chairs, bags of jumble and Ethan's outgrown toys. It had suited me – the informality of it, the sense that my work was provisional – only one step-up from Play-Doh. Underground, unseen, I had somehow felt freer to explore unseemly things, primeval things. That's how teddy bears and gingerbread men came to wield axes on my pots; how rag dolls went topless in badly applied lipstick; how hearts and bootees, tampons and butterflies, condoms and cupcakes became ubiquitous tropes. Almost by accident, I had developed a style. Not that I'd known it, until, thanks to Jude, I was offered a show in a posh West End gallery, written up in their catalogue as a feminist ceramicist. They mean lady potter, I'd said, and we'd laughed.

Here, though, was a fresh start. If I couldn't rediscover my muse up here among the treetops, with the clouds scudding and the birds singing, and the zinc gleaming and the kiln humming, where could I? This place was light and open, an eyrie, from which, eagle-like, I should be able to soar.

I tried to sneak up on it, to let habit take over – feel the weight of the wet clay between my palms, the sense of possibility. I got the treadle going, centred the clay, mind in neutral. I dunked my hands in water, braced my elbows on my knees, pushed down with my thumb, not too hard, just hard enough, to let the pot flare, rise, grow. It was a living thing, the clay on the wheel; close in too fast, squeeze too hard, show it anything but tenderness and it would fly away. I came near a few times; felt it live, held my breath... lost it. I made a couple of pots that morning. Serviceable vessels, both of them; many a potter would have finished them, glazed them, fired them. Not me – I didn't want these lame, damaged specimens that would sit on a shelf unable to sing.

Into the bin went the latest abortion, and I stood at the window, staring out at the garden, wondering if my best work was behind me, or if I had just believed the hype.

Stir crazy, I headed back to the cottage, knuckles rimed with clay. I would make us a coffee, I thought – talk things over with my husband, take him into my confidence. Befriend him. Take your time, he would tell me. There's no pressure. You've been through a lot.

Slipping through the gap in the hedge, I caught sight of him through the living-room window. He was pacing back and forth with the phone clamped to his ear. Something about his demeanour – the tight lips, the furtive expression – gave me pause. He was probably just buying time, I told myself; negotiating an extension on that Fitzrovia job. He certainly seemed to be negotiating. Surely it was work, not...

Panic rose in my chest. I found myself clenching and unclenching my palms; trying to drive back the feelings of doubt, of worthlessness. I turned around on impulse and went down the garden path. Closing the gate behind me, I began heading up the lane towards the woods but soon changed my mind. I did not want to brood alone in the shade, I wanted to strike out into sunshine, put myself in the way of human contact; reassure myself that life was good and people generally well-meaning. I wanted to make a friend. Turning back, I strode briskly past the Gaineses' house, and slunk undetected beside the overgrown hedge of Prospect Cottage, telling myself I would look in on Jean another day when I was feeling more robust. For now I needed harmless chatter, tittle tattle, laughter.

My pace slowed again as I drew level with Min and Ray's B&B, with its cheerful hand-painted sign. People who ran B&Bs must be sociable types, mustn't they? And Min seemed like she might be friendship material. I had seen her the previous week, getting out of her car with a yoga mat under her arm. We had waved at each other. But today the gravel driveway in front of Min and Ray's had two strange cars on it and the sign said 'NO VACANCIES'. The whirr of a strimmer could be heard in the back garden. Now did not seem like the time.

That left Cath, whose house, whilst much less forbidding than the Gaineses', was set back above the lane, its front door accessible only via steep stone steps, the very effort of climbing which would undermine any claim I might make to have been 'just passing'. A shame because Cath seemed perhaps the likeliest candidate for friendship among the locals I had so far met.

I walked on past the ruined barn to the edge of the hamlet, where I turned right at the fork in the road, picked my way over the cattle grid and headed up the hill.

It was steeper than it looked, and I had to stop halfway and hold on to my thighs. Down at the bottom, a car door slammed and a dog-walker shouted, 'Bailey! *Come* to heel!'

I turned, curious. Perhaps Nick and I should get a dog,

I thought, though the beasts I used to see in the park in London frightened me to death, with their barrel bodies and their bared teeth. This dog seemed a different proposition – a setter or something. I could just see its tail, waving like a pennant, between the cattle trough and a clump of nettles.

I moved off again, pushing hard into the balls of my feet as the sandy path climbed higher and then petered out. Now my sandals slithered on flattened grass, making my climb even more difficult. I glanced up. The summit was still a good distance away. The house would be visible now, if I looked, but I had already decided that the sight of it should be my reward for reaching the top. A breathless scramble past a couple of scrubby bushes and I was there. My chest heaved and my lungs burned but I felt exhilarated; even more so when I turned round to take in the view.

I gazed first into the far distance, where beyond the town, the estuary glinted through a cleft in the hills like a shucked snakeskin. The sky was overcast, except where three broad beams of sunlight burst over the valley, turning it an improbable emerald green. Hedgerows divided the fields into geometric shapes I couldn't name and tangles of woodland camouflaged the lichen-coloured farms and houses, the only signs of modernity an occasional solar panel or the swish of a car along the road into town. It was as lovely as a picture on a calendar and just as unreal. Slowly, I allowed my gaze to track back down the lee of the valley, past the manor house, the stand of trees, the sagging roof of the barn and at last to what I must call, for want of a better word, *home*.

I was standing now where the hiker whom I'd suspected of spying on us had stood and I was relieved to see that from this distance you couldn't really make out in any detail what was going on in the house – only whether lights were on or off (they were off), whether smoke curled from the chimney (it didn't), whether there was anyone moving about in the rearward facing rooms. There was.

Nick was in the bedroom; the vague flicker of movement somehow still identifiable as my husband. And then a second flicker which I couldn't account for, unless… no, surely not? I shaded my eyes with my hand and squinted. It must be a trick of the light. But no, *two* silhouettes stood side by side, their heads seeming to touch, like figures in stained glass. Blood rushed in my ears. I felt sick. Not this. Not again. I slumped down on the grass. Could it be *her*? Surely not. He had promised me that was done with. He had promised. Someone else, then? Another one. Some floozy from the local pub; a neighbour, maybe? Perhaps he was addicted. Perhaps I was. Yes, that was it. I was making this happen. It was my fault.

I heard a faint keening, like the rise and fall of a car alarm several streets away, and it took me a moment to understand that I was making the noise myself. Climbing unsteadily to my feet, I focused again on the blankness of the bedroom window, of *my* bedroom window. There was no one there now. They were gone, or perhaps just out of sight. The glass looked as dark and impenetrable as a lake, from which something ugly might or might not briefly have surfaced.

I felt wetness on my knuckle and recoiled in surprise as the woman's red setter bounded joyfully around my knees.

'Get down, Bailey!' the young woman called, panting up to me and grabbing the dog's collar.

'It's all right, he won't hurt you, he's soft as anything,' she gasped. 'Just not very well trained. He's my sister's dog.'

They said people looked like their dogs, but this woman looked like her sister's dog, which seemed an odd coincidence. She was tall and rangy, with thick auburn hair pulled back in a ponytail. She was wearing the inevitable Barbour jacket, but she wasn't a country type, I could tell. No one round here wore make-up to walk a dog.

'Oh no, yeah, I'm not scared, it's OK,' I said, willing myself to keep looking at the woman and not to glance back at the house.

'Oh good,' said the woman doubtfully.

'It's steeper than it looks, that's all,' I said, putting a hand to my chest.

'Tell me about it,' said the woman. She waffled on about preferring the gym to the great outdoors and how poorly trained the dog was and whether or not in the countryside you could get away with not scooping the poop. I was in the fish tank again, watching her mouth moving, but hearing only whale song. The woman cocked her head curiously, but having no idea what she had just said, I muttered something vague and turned away. The next time I looked, she was heading back down the hill, holding the dog on a short leash. I glanced at the house and felt something like grief rising in my chest.

I waited, in a state of agitation, until she had got far enough ahead that there could be no risk of my catching up with her, and then I began my own descent, galumphing down the hill sideways, knees trembling, breathing ragged, my eyes aching with pent-up tears. I jumped the last foot from the bank onto the lane, and turned my ankle as I landed. It was as much as I could do to limp my way across the cattle grid without crying. I was hobbling homeward as fast as I was able, when the dog woman's Fiesta came by. Shrinking into the hedgerow to let it pass, I caught my T-shirt on a bramble and had to wrench myself free. Droplets of blood bloomed on my arm and trickled down, blending with the clay dust to turn my wrist pink. I rubbed it to a lurid smear, then hurried on, trying to adopt a jogger's pace so as not to look like what I was – a deranged harpy running home to catch my husband in an act of infidelity.

'Oops-a-daisy!'

A firm hand gripped me by the shoulder and I stopped short, panting and staring wildly into a face so huge and ruddy and friendly, with its abundance of chins and laughter lines that, if it weren't for a whiff of Lily of the Valley and an absence of facial hair, I might have taken Cath for Santa Claus.

'Oh God! Sorry, I'm so sorry.'

She had a recycling box perched on one ample hip, most of its contents now slewed into the gutter.

'Not to worry,' said Cath. 'Do me good to get down there. You were going some, though, what's the hurry? And did you know you're bleeding?' She swivelled my forearm to show me. 'Why don't you come in and we'll put a...'

'I can't!' I said, a little wildly. 'It's very kind of you...' I tried to moderate my tone, and attempt a normal person's smile, '... and I really would love to come and have a chat another time, but I've got... I'm... expecting a delivery!'

'Oh, OK,' said Cath with a doubtful smile. She bent down effortfully to pluck an empty whiskey bottle out of the gutter. 'Be sure your sins will find you out,' she said, waving it aloft, but I was already speeding away.

It was the last push now, past the B&B, past Jean and Gordon's, up the killer slope, muscles like water, heart hammering, and at last I could see the cottage. I stopped dead. The Range Rover had gone from its parking place. I felt sick. Bile actually came into my mouth. This was it, then. The worst. I looked across the fields to the main road. They could only have left minutes ago. Christ, he must have nerves of steel. How long had I been out? I'd lost track. If only Cath hadn't wittered on so... They'd be nearing the town by now. It was only ten minutes the way Nick drove. I could see them in my mind's eye – staring straight ahead, smelling of perfume and sex. A discreet goodbye at the station, a screeching U-turn and Nick would be on his way back, a packet of fags or a newspaper tossed onto the passenger seat for an alibi. I'd have to be quick...

I ran up the garden path, high on adrenaline. The door was unlocked. I scanned the living room wildly. The TV was tuned to *Sky News* and muted. An empty coffee cup sat on the arm of the sofa. I sniffed the air like a wild animal but the pleasantly smoky scent of the wood burner was all I could discern. I took the stairs two at a time. The bedclothes were tumbled. Yanking back the duvet, I scanned the bottom sheet for stains, but that proved nothing. They probably did it standing up. They were probably doing it when I saw them from the top of the hill. My stomach clenched at the thought. I hurried to the bathroom and flipped open the pedal bin, but found only my own panty-liner, cringing around its smear of discharge. I felt a pang of self-disgust. No wonder Nick went elsewhere. I let the lid clang shut and returned to the landing, glancing this way and that, at a loss what to do next. I stood like a sentinel at the front window, clutching my elbows to stop myself from trembling. I could see the road in the distance, stitched in and out of the undulating landscape. I squinted hard but the passing cars were too far away to identify their colours, still less their makes. Any one of them could be Nick's. Soon enough I would hear his wheels crunch on the gravel, the expensive clunk of the driver's door. I could not afford to be like this when that happened. I would go back to the studio, I decided; play dumb. Yes, that was it. I'd keep the upper hand. Stay in control.

I went downstairs, through the kitchen, out through the unlocked door. I could do this. Past the pond and the vegetable patch. I could do it. Through the gap in the yew hedge, across the grass, up the steps.

I closed the door behind me, inhaled the warm,

wood-scented air. I pressed my palms on the cool zinc of the work surface and took a few deep breaths.

An angry buzzing noise made me jump. I cast around in a panic, failing at first to recognize the vibration of my mobile phone, which I had switched to silent and slid into the pan of the old kitchen scales I used to weigh out my clay. I snatched it up, just as the buzzing stopped. Nick. Nine missed calls.

6

'So next time,' Nick slapped me between the shoulder blades in comradely fashion, 'she's going to tell me before she heads off into the wide blue yonder, aren't you, my little vagabond?'

I laughed awkwardly and scuffed a stone along the footpath.

'I should've thought one could go for a stroll in broad daylight without prompting a house-to-house search,' said Cath drily.

'Yeah fair play, I probably overreacted,' Nick admitted. 'But we're new round here, and she's got form...'

I cast Nick a hurt sideways glance.

The Fleece was in sight now, and I was feeling apprehensive. Nick and I were not really pub quiz types, but Ray and Min had invited us and the other team members were the Gaineses and Cath, so to turn it down would have seemed rude. Here was a chance, anyway, to prove that I was more than the hopeless klutz who had dropped Imogen's chutney and knocked Cath for six. Here was a chance to get to know our neighbours better and get a feel for the wider community. So I had accepted Min's invitation, had touted Nick's encyclopaedic knowledge of world capitals and premiership football; had delved into my purse on the spot for our share of the entry fee, even though Min assured me we could pay on the night. And now it *was* the night, and if I could have turned and run, I would have.

It was, as Nick had promised, 'a lovely boozer', the sort of place you came across on holiday and never shut up about when you got home – leadlights and roses round the door and locals playing dominoes in the snug. It had been a sticky day. A pearl grey sky was stretched tight as a drum skin over the valley. Around the trestle tables out front sat hikers who had popped in for a pint at four and never left. Inside, the air was warm as beer, and there was a friendly atmosphere. Being a fundraiser for a nearby hospice, the quiz night had attracted, besides the regulars whose special pewter tankards hung above the bar, a cross section of village society. There was a table of scruffy-looking eccentrics with loud, entitled voices – 'Old money', Nick told me under his breath – and a gaggle of blokes by the bar in windowpane checks and designer jeans, whom I could see for myself were 'new money'. There was a gang of rugger-buggers competitively downing pints and on the other side of the inglenook, a table of book-club cougars with highlighted hair and expensive casual wear. The vicar was there, and the local poet in his sailor's gansey. There was a horsey contingent and a hippy contingent and a gaggle of underage youth from the town, conspicuous by their desire to fly under the radar. Yet even these shifty sixteen-year-olds looked more at home than I felt.

'I've a book of local walks I can lend you,' Douglas Gaines said to me as we ducked under a beam and made our way toward a table 'reserved' for us with a scribble on a folded napkin. 'There are plenty of them and most of them are way-marked, so it's really quite hard to get lost.'

'Oh, I wasn't lost,' I started saying, 'I just went up the hill behind our—' Nick gave me a look. 'But yeah, that would be lovely.'

'So, what's everyone drinking?' My husband reached for his wallet. With one ear on Douglas's friendly prattle, I watched him stroll to the bar and catch the barmaid's eye ahead of his turn – classic Nick. He'd done the same to me the day we'd met – cut me up in the queue for the bar. Not that he remembered it that way. In his retelling, he'd swept me off my feet. Banter, cocktails; never looked back. Does it count as queue jumping, if the person in front of you is invisible? Because I don't think he even saw me at first. I was next in line and then suddenly, I wasn't. It was only when I muttered 'be my guest' under my breath, that he turned round, fixed his unfeasibly blue eyes on me and said with his mile-wide, fair cop grin, 'And what'll *you* have…?'

I watched him tip the barmaid now, and barge his way back to our table with a tray of drinks, somehow contriving to have the people on whose toes he trod apologise to *him*.

There was a whine of feedback, and an amplified *phut* as the landlord tapped the top of his mic.

'Am I on?' he said, and everyone clutched their ears.

'Evening, ladies and gentlemen,' he said, once the volume had been adjusted, 'welcome to The Fleece charity pub quiz. And you *are*. Welcome to it. Boom, boom. No, seriously, I hope you've got your wits about you and your phones switched off – yes, I'm talking to you, Dave Sullivan. Is he in, Dave? Where are you, you cheating bastard…?'

'Just kidding, folks. It was all a misunderstanding, wasn't it, Dave? Half a day in the stocks and he saw the error of his ways. A-n-yway, ladies and gents, for those of you who *do* want to play by the rules they're very few and very simple. Just like our regulars…'

The landlord continued his banter while his wife, a glamorous redhead, distributed the quiz sheets.

'Who's going to be captain?' said Ray.

'Do we need a captain?' Imogen asked.

'Just someone to write down the answers and adjudicate if there's a difference of opinion,' Douglas suggested.

'God help them!' Min muttered with a wry smile.

'Well, I know literally nothing about anything so…' I started to say.

'Here,' Cath reached for the clipboard, and I wasn't sure whether she was exasperated at our team's indecisiveness or my self-deprecation, 'I'll be captain.'

'OK,' boomed the landlord, at last. 'A nice easy round to get you started: visual arts.'

Nick caught my eye and gave me a little nod of tacit encouragement. I felt a twinge of anxiety.

'Which artist painted *The House of Doctor Gachet at Auvers?*'

A collective groan went up.

'What's the matter?' shrugged the landlord, all injured innocence. 'Come on, folks, this is kindergarten stuff. I'll repeat the question. Which painter…'

'Auvers…' said Nick, tapping the table urgently with his fingertips. That's ringing bells. Come on, Kaz, we know this…'

He glanced at me and I shrugged stupidly. Auvers, Auvers. It didn't mean anything… and then all of a sudden, it did.

Sunlight slanting through stained-glass windows onto sand-stone pillars, the patter of Ethan's five-year-old feet as he ran towards the votive candles, hand outstretched, Nick's intervention; tears, a scuffle. My outrage. 'He's only little.' His furious hissed response, comparing English children unfavourably with the mythical French ones who will sit through a five-course dinner without a peep. We made up afterwards. He bought Ethan an ice cream and me a pretty postcard – a painting of the exterior of the church, drooping like a circus tent against an inky sky, a nun making her way into the foreground down a cobbled path, her eyes downcast. It could only have been by one artist.

'Van Gogh!' I all but shouted.

'Oh.' Imogen Gaines bit her lip in amusement. 'I was just about to say Cézanne.'

We smiled at each other politely, neither of us wanting to contradict the other, each of us equally sure she was right.

'Could do worse than listen to Immie, people,' Douglas Gaines murmured, 'she does have a first in art history...'

'Oh well, in that case...' I backtracked. 'Only I thought... isn't Cézanne more Provence?'

'I'm putting Van Gogh,' Cath said, and that was that.

'Question two,' said the landlord and the buzz of conversation died down again. 'By what name was the actor Archibald Leach better known?'

'Oh, that's an easy one,' said Ray.

Cath raised her eyebrows enquiringly, pen poised.

'Tell 'er, Min.' Ray gave his wife an affectionate nudge.

'I don't know,' Min said.

'You *do*,' he insisted, 'Archie Leach. Bristol-born. One of your mum's favourites.'

'You see, this is what he does,' she said to the rest of us.

'What?' Ray affected innocence.

'You make a big production out of it. You know very well I haven't a clue. You're just spinning it out to make yourself look good.'

'How does asking you for the answer make me look good?' he protested, but he'd been rumbled, and his wry smile told us he knew it.

It was nice to watch them play out this charade, the back-and-forth, the faux exasperation, obviously masking a deep affection. They were an unlikely couple, he a grizzled biker of sixty or so, she at least ten years his junior, genteel and pretty in skinny jeans and pumps. She was the last person you would expect to ride pillion, yet I had seen the two of them myself, more than once, roaring round the lanes on their Ducati, locked together in leather like a pair of mating cockroaches.

'I could do my impression…?'

'Please don't,' said Min, wincing, but Ray was already in character, setting his jaw and knitting his brows, his accent pitched halfway between Hampstead and Hollywood.

'Juday! Juday! Juday!' he said and even I knew it was supposed to be Cary Grant. The whole pub erupted.

'All right over there, giving the game away,' said the landlord sternly, 'I'll be docking you points if you're not careful. Question three. What was the name of the exhibition mounted by Charles Saatchi at the Royal Academy in 1997, which launched the careers of the so-called YBAs?'

'Sensation,' said Nick, quick as a flash.

'So it was,' Douglas Gaines nodded. 'That was the one with the cut-in-half shark and the fried egg how's your father, wasn't it? Miracle they got away with that garbage, looking back…'

'Oh, I don't know,' said Nick, 'I thought the shark was pretty cool. *The Inability of the Living to Contemplate Death*…'

'*The Physical Impossibility of Death in the Mind of the Living*,' Imogen corrected him. I watched Nick bridle and then look at her with fresh eyes.

'Whatever,' he said with a wry smile. 'Iconic artwork anyway.'

'So everyone says,' Imogen replied, tilting her head archly. 'But hardly an original one. I think Holbein said it better in *The Ambassadors.*'

Nick made a 'get you' face; it was both grudging and admiring, a look that signalled a re-evaluation. He had given me that look once...

*

'... I'll have a margarita, if you insist,' I'd said and then spoiled the effect by blushing. It was hard not to be seduced by Nick's easy charm and studied dishevelment, tie already yanked to half-mast. He hadn't turned a hair, to give him his due. Just took the hit – which was generous as only the beer and wine were on the tab – it being my boss's third wedding. The order took ages, especially the margarita, as the barman was really only used to pulling pints. By the time he'd poured it with great ceremony and added the straw, Nick was holding out a twenty a little impatiently between his middle fingers. He paused for a second while I took the first sip, more, I think, to satisfy himself that he had successfully charmed me than because he really cared if I liked it. If I hadn't been a bit squiffy from the lunchtime reception, I probably wouldn't have had the nerve, but I made a bit of a meal of it, tilting my head from side to side, narrowing my eyes, swallowing...

'Not bad,' I said, 'a bit light on the triple sec…'

'Ah,' he said, still bantering, still eager to make good his escape, 'isn't it always the way?'

'Not in Tijuana,' I said.

That was when he'd given me the look; the look he was giving Sloaney Imogen now. 'Hello…' it seemed to say, 'you may be of interest after all…'

*

'Didn't it all start decomposing,' Cath said breezily, 'the shark? You'd be mightily pissed off, wouldn't you, if you'd paid squillions for an original Damien Hirst and you ended up with a nasty wee bit of muck in a tank.'

'He had to remake it, actually,' Imogen said. 'There was a bit of hoo-hah about whether he could call it the same thing, despite it being, essentially, a whole new artwork, but he claimed that being a conceptual artist, the *idea* of the work was more important to him than the physical expression of it, so…' she shrugged prettily and there was an awed silence. I remembered then that it was Cézanne and not Van Gogh who had painted *The House of Doctor Gachet at Auvers*.

'Only right they beat us, really,' Douglas Gaines declared as we ambled homeward at closing time. 'What with that chap's mother being a patient in the hospice; lovely for him to be able to take her the cheque. It brings a lump to my throat just thinking about it.'

'We gave them a run for their money though,' Nick said. 'Narrow margin.'

I could feel my cheeks colouring in the darkness. Nick had never been a good loser, especially when pipped to the post by a bunch of posh boys. And it had been the rugger-buggers who'd won the day, confounding expectations with their in-depth knowledge of meteorology, roman numerals and the lyrics of the Spice Girls.

'Well, if anyone's to blame, it's me,' I said. 'We might have won if I'd listened to Imogen.'

'Nonsense,' Min called over her shoulder, 'you did brilliantly.'

'Hardly matters now,' muttered Nick.

'Of course it doesn't,' agreed Douglas Gaines. 'The main thing is we raised the money and had a good time. At least I did. Haha.'

'Oh yes, it was *fun*,' Imogen agreed. 'I love it when the village comes together. It doesn't happen often enough. We should do that Auction of Promises we were talking about, Douglas. Get the marquee up while the weather holds.'

As the road curved away from the village and the footpath narrowed, we transformed ourselves from a tipsy rabble into a more or less orderly procession, with those who had had the foresight to bring torches lighting the way for the rest. The air was thick with a coming storm, so that even the occasional gust of fume-laden air from a passing car brought welcome relief.

'So tell me,' said Cath, weaving a little, 'what did you reckon to the Village of the Damned?'

'Yeah, not bad,' I said, hedging my bets, 'I mean, they're not exactly soul mates, but they seem a decent bunch, on the whole.'

Cath snorted.

'What?' I said, but she shook her head mysteriously.

'My lips are sealed,' she said.

'Do you not go up the pub much then?'

'Not really,' she said. 'It's all right on a night like tonight, but it can be a bit cliquey the rest of the time, if you get me...'

I thought I probably did.

'So what *do* you do for entertainment?' I asked, boldly.

'Oh, I'm not much of a party animal any more,' Cath replied and a wistfulness seemed to come over her. 'I'm happy enough with my seed catalogues and a box set these days...'

I was about to probe further, when she stopped and sniffed the air.

Up ahead, the others had congregated at the point where the road broke out of the woods and started to curve along the valley's edge.

'They're waiting for us.' I hooked my arm through Cath's and urged her into a comical jog, which became less comical and more sheepish as we got nearer and saw that the others had not, in fact, stopped to wait for us, but to gaze in consternation across the valley.

'Shit!' mouthed Cath.

'Is that a fire?' I said, dumbly as if any other phenomenon could be responsible for the sparks shooting up into the darkness above the treeline and the sky glowing dirty pink.

Only now did the *douf douf* of house music and the stutter of a strobe light impinge. This was not pyromania, then, but recreation.

'It isn't the first time,' Ray said grimly. 'And they'll be going till three if it's the same mob.'

'What is it, some kind of rave?' I asked. I could imagine Ethan's withering sarcasm, 'Some kind of *rave*, Mother?'

'Just kids,' Cath patted my arm, 'summer solstice. Nothing to fret over.'

'All the same,' said Douglas Gaines, 'you wonder what their parents are thinking.'

'Good job we've no guests this weekend,' muttered Min.

'It's not the noise that worries me,' grumbled Douglas Gaines, 'it's the destruction of habitat. They moan about the Hunt, this lot, but they don't think twice about the havoc they're wreaking with their fires and their rubbish and their bloody racket.'

As if to underline his point, a stuttering bile green laser lit up the sky, prompting a burst of joyous ululation from the revellers. With much tutting and head-shaking, we moved off again, clambering over a nearby stile and down the muddy path that came out near the old barn, lately a repository for several abandoned and burned-out vehicles. The air of camaraderie that had united us after the pub quiz was replaced now by one of disapproval and righteous indignation, to which I found myself instinctively resistant. For all the selfishness of the revellers, there was an energy to their hedonism that I found beguiling. It seemed life-enhancing and visceral, a sybaritic two-fingered salute to everything about the English countryside that was staid and safe and depressing – the tea shops and the kagouls and the olde-worlde typefaces; the Miss Marple prettiness of it all.

We kept up a desultory chat for a while, but the closer we got to the hamlet, the more the music reverberated within the hollow of the landscape, so that, parting company, we had to time our farewells to fall on the off-beat or go unheard. Only Cath, waving a cheery goodbye and staggering slightly as she hauled herself up the steps to her house, seemed assured of a good night's rest.

7

It must have been the silence that woke me; I lifted my head off the pillow and thought for a minute I'd gone deaf, it was so profound. You wouldn't think it possible to fall asleep to a pounding techno beat but apparently it is. *Douf, douf, douf* for hours on end – coming up through the foundations of the house, making the floorboards leap, making my chest thud until *douf, douf, douf* was who I was. And now it had stopped, and it took me a moment to recognize that the soft *phutt phutt phutt* that had replaced it was not tinnitus, but the sound of raindrops falling on the window.

Nick would have tried to put a stop to it hours ago if I'd let him. When two a.m. had rolled around and the rave had shown no signs of stopping, I'd had to plead with him not to storm up there. He was furious, hopping round the room with his foot jammed into the wrong leg of his jeans in his haste to get dressed; muttering about the selfishness, the sheer fucking *irresponsibility* of it. I'd been frightened then, not so much of what the kids might do to Nick, but of what he might do to them.

I still winced recalling the night a few years back when Ethan had had a party. 'A few mates,' he'd said. 'Over by midnight,' he'd said. We'd come home at one, to a blue light slicing the terrace and a world-weary copper placating irate neighbours. We'd had to barge our way through dodgy-looking youths to get into our own house. Stopping for a second to usher a green-gilled young woman towards the downstairs toilet, I'd lost sight of Nick and the next thing I'd known there was a full-scale brawl going on in the living room – nothing to do with the gatecrashers as it turned out, everything to do with my husband attempting to eject his youngest son through the (still closed) French windows. The look on Ethan's face has stayed with me – a mixture of hurt and vindication; as if he had expected no better from his father, but had nevertheless hoped, even as he pushed at the boundaries of Nick's goodwill, to be proved wrong.

Tonight, though, the offenders were strangers, we were the aggrieved party and as furious as Nick undoubtedly was at the disturbance, I could tell his heart wasn't in it.

'It's not worth it, Nick,' I cajoled him. 'They'll have stopped by the time you get up there.'

I offered him my noise-reducing headphones and after a last brief rant, he'd climbed back into bed and gone out like a light.

I, on the other hand, had lain staring at the ceiling, eye-balls itching with tiredness, trying and failing to wrestle my body to sleep through half-remembered meditation techniques. And the moment I started to drift off, or so it seemed, pandemonium broke out again, closer at hand this time. Engines revved, whoops and catcalls rang out; faintly at first, then building to a crescendo as the convoy passed through our hamlet and away. I glanced anxiously at Nick. His eyelids fluttered, but he didn't stir. In the grey dawn light, his face looked improbably handsome, like the death mask of a boy pharaoh – thick, dark brows; long Disney lashes; the arrogant curl of the lip. I leaned in, felt his breath on my cheek, let my lips hover over his, imbibed his scent, his essence; wished I could have him; wished I could *be* him; got too close. He grunted, smacked his lips, rolled his head the other way and I retreated, lowering my head contritely onto the pillow, hands folded beneath my cheek.

The next time I woke, the room was bright, but I could barely keep my eyes open. Nick was speaking to me, his face close to mine, his tone urgent.

'... So you're going to have to drop me or I'll miss my train. And then you need to ring the garage and get them to come and look at the car. Call me later and I'll tell you where to find the paperwork. Kaz. Kaz?'

'Wha – why? Where will you be?' I felt panic rising in my chest. I could smell Givenchy on him. He was dressed for work.

'Look, I know it was a rough night last night, but I've got to make the nine twenty-three and I need you to get up *now* and drop me. I'm sorry, love, but the Range Rover's got a fucking flat.'

'Uhuh? OK then, just let me…' I scrambled out of bed and searched around for yesterday's clothes. 'Did I know… about this meeting or…?'

He sighed.

'Oh yeah,' I lied, 'no, I did, I did. You'll be back tonight, though, right?'

'I won't be back if I never bloody get there.'

I stalled twice at the junction, and at the third attempt, pulled out so fast in front of a speeding Tesco delivery van that Nick had to brace against the dashboard.

'Sorry,' I said, 'I'm just not used to the… sorry.'

It seemed as though I'd barely hit thirty, before we had joined a school-run tailback on the outskirts of the town.

'Fuck's sake…' muttered Nick under his breath.

'Don't worry, we've got five minutes,' I reassured him.

'I might be quicker walking…' He reached for the handle of the passenger door but just then the traffic started moving again.

We pulled into the station forecourt with two minutes to spare.

'So yeah, the garage,' he said, leaning in to give me a peremptory kiss on the cheek.

'Where will I…?'

A horn sounded behind me.

'I'll call you,' he said.

Driving back, the valley felt sluiced through with freshness. A washed-out sky leaked watery sunshine into the brook, which had transformed overnight from a sluggish brown trickle to a gush. Despite the lack of sleep, I felt energised – ecstatic even. The day stretched ahead of me, long as a decade. I couldn't remember when I'd last felt so free, or, for that matter, so capable. I would sort the flat tyre, spend some time in the studio; marinade the steaks I'd just bought from the organic butcher as a treat for Nick's return.

On the way into the hamlet, I met Min and Ray in their Jeep and pulled over to let them pass. Ray wound down the window, so I did likewise.

'Get any sleep?'

'A bit.'

'Well, you needn't worry, they'll not be back. I spoke to the Old Bill this morning and they're going to get a Cease and Desist order. That means court if they try it again.'

I must have looked surprised.

'Oh, I'm all for a bit of fun, don't get me wrong,' Ray held up his hand, 'kids need to let off steam. We used to go up there ourselves back in the day. Bit of wacky baccy and a ghetto blaster…'

Min raised an ironical eyebrow.

'… But you can't be having amps and lights and all the rest of it, it's taking the Mick.'

I nodded in agreement, then, unable to think of any further small talk, shrugged and smiled and started to wind up my window, until Min signalled me to stop.

'What are you doing Thursday?' she asked. My mind went blank. What might we be doing, other than what we were always doing these days, clopping around our Wendy house in our too-big shoes, cooking pretend meals on our pretend Aga, fooling no one.

'I'm… pretty sure we're free.'

'Come and have something to eat. We've some other friends coming who we'd like you to meet.'

I welled up a bit then. Who cried at a casual dinner invitation?

'That would be lovely,' I said and even through the meniscus of tears I could read Min's sympathetic smile; appreciate the tact of her businesslike, 'Good!'

I noticed Ray glance in his rear-view mirror. Another car needed to pass. He gave me an apologetic wave and drove on.

Outside the cottage, the Range Rover was sagging lopsided on the gravel like a drunken penitent. I poked the tyre doubtfully with my toe. It was completely flat. A thing that size would cost a fortune to replace. I made straight for the study, not allowing myself even a glance towards my studio on the way up the path. Plenty of time for that once I'd got the important stuff out of the way.

The paperwork wasn't where I thought it would be. Nick was usually so methodical. House stuff in the house compartment, work stuff in the work compartment, car stuff…

apparently nowhere. I rummaged through the desk, trying to stay focused on the task in hand, resisting the temptation to pry and probe. What, for instance, was this brochure for a hotel and spa in Hertfordshire? Four-poster beds. Nine-course tasting menu. Was it a souvenir? Somewhere he had taken *her*? Somewhere he might still be planning to? No. It was over. I believed him. Trust. Trust was my watchword now. I closed my eyes, took a breath. I had just put my hand on the car warranty when the phone rang.

'I was literally about to ring them…'

'No need,' Nick said, 'it's sorted.' His tone was friendly and relaxed. He was in First Class, I could tell, lording it with his laptop open and a complimentary tea. 'Turned out I had the details in my phone. He should be with you any time and I've paid up-front, so all he'll need from you's a signature.'

'I think I can manage that.' I gave a long, silent exhalation of relief.

'And Kaz…?'

'Yeah?'

'Sorry I was a twat.'

I stopped for a moment on my way downstairs to take in the view from the landing window. Last night's storm seemed to have swept all that was heavy and baleful out of the valley, leaving it clean and fresh and new. Every cloud looked as though it were blown across the sky by a fat-cheeked cherub, every gentle breeze left its shower of apple blossom. I could scarcely believe now, watching a distant car meander along the road into town, that just a few days ago I had stood here in a state of delusional jealousy. To think I had been daft enough to work myself up over some phantom lover whom he'd have had to teleport into our bedroom for the timing to be even remotely plausible. I felt ashamed now, that I'd been *that* unhinged *that* recently, especially after all the effort he'd put into my recovery and the commitment he was demonstrating to our marriage now – stepping down from the board at work so he could work part time, selling the house he loved, moving away from all our friends, leaving London, where, despite all his protestations, I knew he'd much prefer to be.

I went downstairs and tuned the radio to the music channel that Ethan had got me into. Then I started unpacking the shopping. I'd cheated on the salad, buying a washed and ready-to-serve one, which I could just dump straight in a bowl. Nick wouldn't know the difference and I might even have time to throw a pot before he got back. I made the marinade myself, but I forgot to secure the lid on the blender and it pebble-dashed the work surface with Worcestershire sauce and parsley. I didn't really mind, though. Everything seemed different today. Auspicious. The way the sun bounced off the rows of white brick tiles and the cow parsley nodded amenably in the field beyond. I'd been projecting so much onto this place, I realized, when actually it was a blank canvas. I could choose how I led my life here, just as I'd choose how to shape my clay.

I leaned over the sink to wipe a smear of marinade off the window, and noticed, once again, a lone figure on the hill. I stopped and squinted, suppressing a faint pang of anxiety. Then I saw he had a dog with him and I relaxed.

I peeled the muslin off the clay. It looked tired and dry and lifeless and another day I might have lacked the will to take it on, but today I was its equal. Whacking it hard with the heel of my hand I emitted, in spite of myself, a cathartic grunt of joy. Before long I was thrusting and turning, turning and thrusting, the clay reviving in my hands. It was coming now – that sheen and glow that meant it was ready to throw. I felt excitement swing up from the pit of my belly.

The throwing of a pot is always an adventure, its precise shape, size and finish in some mysterious way beyond the potter's complete control, however skilled she is. I loved this about it and I'd struggled hard enough in learning my craft to consider the making of a serviceable vessel a minor triumph in its own right. As I'd become more skilful, though, the pot had become a means to an end, rather than an end in itself – a three-dimensional canvas on which to experiment with sgraffito, wax resist and inlay techniques.

It was this experimentation with form and decoration, rather than any conscious desire to innovate or shock, which had brought me a degree of success, and even, dare I say it, notoriety. The pots had become my journals – three-dimensional scrapbooks on which I had doodled away, not realising until they stood hardening off on the shelf, how much I had inadvertently revealed of myself, their nursery pastel colours at odds with what my dealer insisted on calling their 'subversive' subject matter.

My dealer! That had been a turn-up. I still had to pinch myself. I'd given Jude a sneak preview one night after dinner when we'd had a few drinks and she'd nagged and nagged me until I'd let a friend of hers take a look. A friend, it turned out, who just happened to co-own an art gallery off Cork Street. An exhibition had been scheduled – eighteen months hence, *because, darling, there was admin to be done, catalogues to be written, insurance to arrange...* How we had giggled, Jude and I, at the purple prose they had put in that catalogue.

KAREN MULVANEY – REDEFINING SPACE. CONTEMPORARY CERAMICS AND THE CONCEPT OF 'SHE'
THIS STARTLING DEBUT FROM ONE OF BRITAIN'S MOST EXCITING CERAMICISTS EXPLORES THE INTERFACE BETWEEN ART AND CRAFT, FEMINISM AND FUCKING...

I had laughed, but secretly I'd been thrilled. I had followed my heart; made work from a place I didn't even understand, never really thinking of an audience, and yet I had found one. Had been about to find one, anyway...

I had no desire to revisit those themes now – couldn't have if I'd wanted to. That person was gone; shattered along with the pots themselves. The only thing my new work would have in common with the old was that it should not be utilitarian. The *form* of the pot – its integrity as a vessel, the way it handled would be crucial, but only as part of a bigger picture. For a while now, I'd been thinking about a series of pots inspired by the landscape here – by its gentle undulations and mysterious random carbuncles; ancient burial mounds, some of them, or so I'd been told. I wanted to create a sort of installation – an artwork, where the meaning came not only from each individual pot, but also from its relationship to its neighbour. I envisaged an army of pots, as uniform in size and shape as the vagaries of throwing would allow, the small variations between them becoming the warp and weft of the bigger design, so that the whole took on the contours of a landscape. It was a huge undertaking, and open-ended. Who knew when I should consider it finished, or what I would do with it when it was? But it excited me. What could be more appropriate for a woman with a newly empty nest than to fill her empty days creating a landscape of empty vessels?

So it was with some trepidation that I centred my freshly wedged ball of clay on the wheel and curved my palms around it. Trance-like, I moved my foot on the treadle, watched the clay start to spin, containing it in my hands, exerting only enough influence on it as to reveal the pot within. The sun slanted through the window, dust motes shimmered at the edge of my vision. Magic happened.

And then a car horn blared in the lane and my pot spun itself into an ellipse and collapsed.

I swore, first at the noise, and then at myself for forgetting about the breakdown man. I ran down the garden, dangling my wet grey hands in front of me like a zombie.

'Coming! I'm coming,' I called.

'I was just about to give up on you,' he said, grumpily. 'I went up the 'ouse, but I couldn't get no answer. Can't leave without a signature or I don't get paid.'

He nodded at the replacement tyre. I could smell the aroma of new rubber from where I was standing.

'Sorry,' I said, putting my scribble where he indicated.

'We'll try and look after this one,' I said, despising myself for wanting to placate him. 'My husband tends to get a bit *Top Gear* behind the wheel of that thing.'

'Nothing to do with the way he's driving it, love,' said the man, grimly. 'Someone's 'ad a go at that.'

8

I talked myself down over a mug of tea. It could have been an accident. The breakdown man was an arse – the type, I could tell, who enjoyed putting the wind up women. The way he'd said the words 'vandalised' and 'slashed' – rolled them around his tongue – had been creepy and I'd been glad when he'd driven away in his stupid truck with its 'Honk if You're Horny' sticker.

If it wasn't an accident, it was last night's partygoers. That much was obvious. I'd heard them come whooshing out of the woods like flotsam when the rain came. You didn't need to be Sherlock Holmes to figure out that a bunch of bored yokels, high as kites on who-knew-what, might want to stick it to the Man on their way home. But if it *was* them, they'd not have stopped at ours. They'd have done a job lot.

I left my tea half drunk, washed the clay off my hands, and headed out to the lane. The only other cars I could see were Cath's unassuming Kangoo van – hardly a red-rag to a class-warrior – and Jean and Gordon's Honda marooned on the hard standing in front of Prospect Cottage. I was squinting at it, weighing up whether it was the car or the house itself that was lopsided, when the front door opened a crack.

'Oh, hello,' I jumped guiltily, seeing the pale face peering out, 'I didn't mean to bother you…'

Jean stepped outside. She was wearing an old-fashioned nylon housecoat over her day clothes and her hair stood out around her head like a dandelion clock. I approached her with what I hoped was a reassuring smile. 'It's Karen from two doors along. You came to our housewarming…?'

'I know, dear,' she said, but I wondered if she did. She seemed vague and disoriented, quite different from the beady-eyed seer she had seemed that night.

'I expect they kept *you* up all night too?' I said.

'Who?' she looked confused.

'Did you not hear that mob in the woods?'

'Mob?' she repeated, pulling the door to behind her now, with a nervous backward glance.

'It went on till nearly four,' I told her, 'and then this morning, surprise, surprise, we've got a flat tyre. Bit of a coincidence… Well, you shouldn't jump to conclusions, I suppose, but that's what the garage man said when he came to fit a new one. Vandalism, he said.'

'Vandalism,' she repeated in a whisper and I wasn't sure whether she was awestruck or simply trying to recall the meaning of the word.

'Well, that's one possibility, but I didn't mean to worry you – just thought I'd check whether it was only our car and it looks like it was, so that's great. Great for you, I mean. Not so great for us, but you know, not the end of the world…'

'Jean?' Gordon's voice was like the crack of a bullet and Jean flinched as if she'd been hit. She stepped back into the porch and with an apologetic shrug, made to close the door.

'Anyway, if you *do* happen to find anything amiss…' I said, putting my hand against the glass to stop her. I felt suddenly alarmed as if my visit might have repercussions for her once I had left.

'Jean!'

We both winced this time and Jean all but scrambled for the inner door. I was on the point of turning away when her face loomed briefly again through the crack. She paused for a second as though daring herself to speak. Then changed her mind and was gone.

I found Cath in the garden, ankle deep in manure. For a woman who'd made hard work of a leisurely stroll back from the pub, she seemed an agile gardener. Despite the fag clamped between her lips and a certain amount of grunting, her spade sliced through the muck in rhythmic fashion. Even I, a novice in the garden, could recognize the effort that must have gone into transforming this arid patch of ground into a fertile bed of rich loam.

'Well, if it isn't the second Mrs De Winter!' she said, ditching the fag when she saw me approaching and propping herself on her spade. I smiled doubtfully. 'I'm about due a coffee break. Care to join me?'

I followed her down the herringbone brick path, geraniums frothing, cabbage roses swinging in her wake. Her garden seemed to be everything she wasn't – lush and blowsy and feminine. I loved it.

She hoiked her boots off at the back door, and, seeing me bending to remove my own shoes, she tutted, and told me not to be daft. The kitchen, like the garden, was organized chaos – seedlings sprouting on window ledges, dog-eared cookbooks bowing a timber shelf. She had a good eye, I thought. The table and chairs, though rustic, had the patina of proper antiques and a cabinet of to-die-for vintage crockery took up most of one wall. I sat down on the old church pew in front of the window, and leaned back on a needlepoint scatter cushion embroidered with the words 'Team Cunt'.

'Well, I know what you mean,' said Cath, when I shared my concerns about Jean and Gordon's marriage, 'he's a bit of a sergeant major type, for sure, but they're a different generation, aren't they…?'

'Well, I don't know,' I said, doubtfully. 'He seems like a tyrant to me. Her children don't get on with him either, she told me…'

Cath looked taken aback.

'I never realized they had any,' she said and I wondered whether Jean had just been feeling unusually chatty on the night she and I had met, or whether she had singled me out for her confidences on purpose. I shivered, and thinking it was the draught from the open door, Cath pushed it to with her foot.

'Ah well,' I said, taking a slurp of coffee from my Clarice Cliff cup, 'just have to keep an eye, I suppose.'

'Aye,' agreed Cath, and soon we were chatting innocuously about fruit trees and badgers and parking headaches, both here and in London. She told me how a parking ticket had led to a chance encounter with a TV producer, which had in turn led to a regular gardening slot on daytime TV. I gave her a potted (and sanitized) history of my life in London and had a good old moan about Ethan and Gabe and how tricky things could be with stepsiblings.

She told me about the excitement there had been in the hamlet when the SOLD sign had appeared outside our cottage.

'... Then nothing happened for ages, and when they delivered the skip, Min and Ray just went,' she nodded grimly, 'holiday home.'

'Why?'

'Oh well, you know, no one'd moved in, even though it was perfectly habitable and there's all this expensive work being done – John Lewis deliveries. The usual signs...'

She narrowed her eyes shrewdly and I bit my lip in mock contrition, even though I had nothing to feel contrite about, not in that regard, anyway.

'... But then Min buttonholed Nick on the lane,' Cath went on, 'and he told us *you* were moving here. Cue rejoicing.'

'Rejoicing...?' I said.

'Well, relief, anyway. And of course, speculation, because we'd met Mister, but where on earth was Missus?'

I closed my eyes against a rush of memories…

*

… a bright room, the smell of plug-in air freshener overlaying a less pleasant institutional tang of disinfectant and nylon carpet. Breeze from a child-locked window stirring vertical blinds, the chains between them tinkling like Buddhist bells. A single bed and next to it on the bedside table, a plastic jug filled with water and a plastic-wrapped plastic glass. A paperback book, its spine unbroken, and a copy of *Grazia* still pristine. The creak of the plastic-covered mattress beneath me, as I lifted my head off the pillow, and squinted at the hazy figure entering the room.

'Hello, Karen,' she'd said, and it was as though she was speaking to me from twenty leagues deep, through breathing apparatus, 'I've brought your medication…'

*

'… High-powered job; foreign travel, power suits,' Cath was saying when I zoned back in. It took me a moment to register that she was describing the woman they'd expected me to be.

'We decided you'd sweep in at the last minute and tell Nick you hated the kitchen tiles and he'd have to change them…' she chuckled.

'You must have been sorely disappointed when I turned up!' I said.

'Relieved, my dear, relieved.'

We talked about books after that and cooking and about our neighbours, guardedly at first and then less guardedly. Her take-off of Douglas Gaines had me weeping with guilty laughter. At last, when she was rolling her seventh consecutive cigarette, she told me about her girlfriend Annie, who had died of ovarian cancer.

'Oh, don't look like that,' she said, seeing my face grow solemn. 'She'd have hated that. Wee lassie packed more life into her thirty-eight years than I'll get if I live to be a hundred. She'd have cracked you up. She did me...' she shook her head fondly, 'the mouth on her...'

And seeing the expression on Cath's face, I thought for one mad shameful moment that I'd willingly die right there and then if I thought Nick would remember me with a look like that.

'What do you miss most about her?' I asked timidly. She threw me a quick glance, as if weighing up whether our brief acquaintance could bear the burden of such intimacy, then pulled on her cigarette until it was down to its cardboard filter, held the smoke in her lungs for what seemed an age, and exhaling, said, 'The person I was when I was with her.'

Cath looked down in apparent surprise at the dimp between her dirty fingertips and with a smile and a shrug, pushed it into the soil of a nearby plant pot.

'Damn!' I said, glancing at the clock on her kitchen wall. 'My clay'll be rock hard!'

Even then, she kept me for another ten minutes quizzing me about my pottery project and it wasn't until I was back on the lane that I remembered I hadn't asked whether *her* car had been tampered with. Then again, it didn't seem so important any more. So what if someone had slashed Nick's tyre. Shit happened. I knew that better than most. But I knew now I had someone to turn to when it did. I had a friend.

I caught the clay just in time. It was starting to dry out but I ladled palms full of water onto it and set it spinning again. Once I had coaxed it back to life, I thrust my thumb gently into its slippery centre and hollowed it gradually, lovingly, into a bulbous vessel, about ten inches high and eight in diameter, tapering to a slender neck. It wouldn't have made a vase because it would barely have fitted three blooms. It wouldn't have made a storage jar, because you'd never have got anything in or out. It was a pot to no purpose, a pot of nothing – just as I'd meant it to be.

Holding my breath, I rotated the wheel very gently and slipping the wire under the base, carried my pot, balanced precariously on its bat, over to the drying rack. It was a humble thing really, a prototype, but already I was itching to make another. I reached for my phone to see if I had time. I expected it to be two thirty – three at the latest. It was twenty-five to six. No wonder I felt faint – I'd had nothing to eat all day.

I dialled Nick's number, puzzled not to have heard from him already. It clicked straight to voicemail and I hung up quickly before the familiar message could kick in. 'Nick Mulvaney here, can't get to the phone right now. You know what to do.' No, I didn't know what to do, that was the problem. What were you supposed to do when a recording of the voice you woke up to every morning still turned your guts into a smoothie? OK, so he was on the tube. That was something. I summoned the train timetable to my mind's eye. He'd most likely make the 6.04 from Paddington.

I glanced down at my clay-streaked jeans and gave my underarms an experimental sniff. I could just about get the dinner on, have a quick shower and still be at the station in time to meet him.

Heading back to the cottage, I almost tripped over a plant pot upended on the flagstones near the front door, a casualty of the wind, I assumed. Roots and earth had collapsed through the cracked terracotta and my little olive sapling was snapped in two. This morning I'd have seen it as an omen – clear proof that the forces of nature, the elements themselves – were conspiring against me. Now, it scarcely registered. I swept the debris to one side, so Nick shouldn't have to walk through it, and made a mental note to re-pot it tomorrow.

The kitchen was a mess. I'd meant to get back to it sooner, but the day had got away from me. The sink was full of washing up and the compost bin had attracted a swarm of flies, which were taking it in turns to dive-bomb my dish of marinating steaks. I could have sworn I'd put it in the fridge. I frowned, trying to think back through the labyrinth of the day's events, but it was hazy and unreachable as all my memories seemed to be these days. I knew what Nick would say, 'It's those bloody happy pills,' but that wasn't it, I was sure. He hated that I was still taking them because they were a reminder of my mental fragility, which he loathed not only because it was inconvenient and embarrassing, but also because he felt responsible for it. I'd tried to tell him it wasn't that – that Jude got brain fog, too. That it was a common side-effect of the menopause. Anyway, it scarcely mattered now. What mattered was getting my shit together.

I knew I ought to have rinsed the meat under the tap and started again with a fresh marinade, but Nick could get tetchy if dinner was late.

What the eye didn't see, I thought, and covered it with a clean tea-towel.

By the time I'd got things ship-shape and put some spuds in the oven it was six forty-five. I had just enough time to shower and get glammed up before I went to meet him. I awarded myself a small glass of wine for being a good and sane lady for a whole day and took it upstairs with me. Stopping off on the way to turn on the shower (it took an age for the water to run hot), I went into the bedroom, stripped off my filthy clothes and dialled Nick's number again. I liked the idea that he would pick up in a carriage full of commuters, his tone, inevitably curt and impersonal, and that I should be here, alone and naked. I imagined saying his name, telling him what I'd like him to do to me when he got home. I swayed my hips a little, in time to the ringtone, thinking of his hands on me, inside me...

Voicemail *again*.

Oh well, the signal could be dodgy until you cleared Reading...

All the same, I was beginning to get the familiar nag of anxiety, of distrust. I fought it back, took another sip of wine, jabbed out a quick text message: '*Cant waIT to see you whaT tine meet train? XOXO,*' and pressed 'send'.

By now steam was billowing out of the bathroom. I propped the phone on the bathroom shelf where I should see it flash if he rang and stepped into the shower. Hot water thundered on my head and the alcohol took its effect. I felt faint, but pleasantly so – as if I were being purged. I bent down to reach the shampoo and was overcome with dizziness. Squatting there in the shower tray, trying to summon the energy to stand again, I felt a dragging sensation in my inner thighs and looking down, saw a red tadpole swim out of me and elongate into a dash, a line, a strand, before being whisked away in an eddy of water. Damn. Nothing for five months and the one night it really mattered, this...

By the time I was soaped, shampooed and rinsed, I couldn't see out of the shower at all. I made a porthole with my fist in the steamed-up glass and cursed when I saw the message alert on my phone. I stumbled out of the cubicle and snatched it to within an inch of my face.

'Sorry babe, fuck up with the bid. Back tomorrow now. Call you in the a.m. X'

It seemed then as if it had always been inevitable. As if Nick's text had been waiting in the ether and I had somehow willed it into my inbox through my own neediness and fear. I went through to the bedroom and stood at the window, hugging my towel around me, watching the sky turn gradually from sapphire to cobalt to navy, my pale reflection in the glass growing more visible with each subtle change of hue until by the time dusk had fallen, I could see myself almost as if in a mirror – rats' nest hair dribbling water onto slumped shoulders, eyes like craters in a greyish moon. However hard I tried to keep up, it seemed Nick would always be one step ahead.

Here I stood, where *they* had stood, arms entwined, heads touching. Except that they hadn't. I had conjured the whole thing from fear, from dread; from a sense of unworthiness. Just as I was doing now when I thought of them clinking glasses at the Malmaison, or romping in a four poster at that Hertfordshire Spa – the images so vivid I might have been watching them on TV. This was the rat-run of the mind; the obsessional thought-maze that the psych had warned me about. This paranoia, not Nick, was the problem.

I lowered the blind and plopped down on the end of the bed as if someone had cut my strings. I'd like to say what I felt was despair, but it wasn't even as powerful as that. It was a nothing feeling. As if I didn't exist; as if I shouldn't exist. As if I were in the way. The temptation to crawl under the duvet and write the evening off altogether was overwhelming. But I'd left candles burning downstairs and the steak was still out on the work surface. I should eat. Self care. That was important. That had been the 'take-away' from all that expensive therapy I'd had. How could I expect Nick to love me if I didn't love myself?

I didn't bother to change out of my dressing gown, but put a comb through my hair so I shouldn't feel too much like an inmate. The house felt suddenly huge, downstairs a very long way away. Rivulets of water dripped off my wet hair and down inside my robe. Glancing in the landing mirror as I passed, I looked blurred and insubstantial – transparent, almost. I wondered if I might actually be dissolving. Is personhood contingent on place? Because here, now, in this house where I didn't belong, I felt like a ghost. The night felt more real than I did. It leaned in now, breathing its heady scents through the open window – sweet perfumes of nicotiana and stock but beneath them, the rotting reek of silage. It was as if a monster had dined on human flesh then freshened its breath with a parma violet...

Telly. That's what I needed. Canned laughter, adverts. I switched it on. The news. I picked up the remote to change the channel and then felt bad and left it, turning up the volume so that I could hear it in the kitchen, the reporter's voice plummy and compassionate. 'Rashida lost three family members in the raid…'

At least now I didn't have to do any driving. I could take the edge off. I sloshed some wine into a fresh glass, took a slug, lit the gas and put the griddle pan on it. I hoiked one of the baked potatoes out of the oven, tossing it from palm to palm, then dumping it onto a plate, next to a handful of salad. The pan shimmered with heat. I stabbed the smaller of the steaks with a fork and was lowering it in when I noticed what I thought was a thread from the tea-towel clinging to it. I made to pluck it off and it moved. A closer look revealed three, four, five such threads, wriggling over the surface of the meat. Bile came into my throat and I flung the steak back into the dish beside the other one, the surface of which, I could now see, was alive with tiny maggots. By now, the pan was smoking filthily. I grabbed its cast iron handle and had moved it to the back burner before my brain registered the searing pain across my palm. I stared down, bewildered and then thrust my hand under the tap. Water bounced back in my face and at the same moment, the smoke alarm went off. I groped my way to the back door and flung it open, wiped my eyes on the sleeve of my dressing gown and then, standing on tiptoe, stabbed at the alarm with my outstretched finger. Just as the kitchen alarm peeped its last, the one in the living room kicked off.

The noise was an assault now, an affront to the holy darkness that shrouded the house, a siren telling the world that a madwoman lived here, who couldn't keep a steak fresh, let alone a marriage. I was starting to panic. Water still clung to my eyelashes, blurring my vision and the urgent screech of the alarm seemed to fluctuate wildly in pitch and volume. It felt like the outward manifestation of my own inner turmoil and I wanted it to stop. It was too high to reach on tiptoe, not quite high enough to make it worth fetching a chair. I flung myself repeatedly at the off button, jerking and flailing with each attempt, so that my reflection, glimpsed side-on in the black window pane, pop-eyed with effort, dressing gown gaping, resembled a corpse bouncing on a gibbet.

The alarm raised a last chirrup of protest and then stopped. Gradually the bland burble of the TV reasserted itself – its volume though loud, still a murmur to my poor deafened eardrums. The MacLennan family from Leicester had saved a grand total of fifteen pounds sixty-eight by replacing their favourite food brands with own-brand substitutes. Mum and Emma seemed thrilled to have got the household budget back on track. She was wearing skinny jeans and a SuperDry T-shirt. She looked nice. *So* nice, so normal, so comfortable in her domesticity that I wanted to cry, but I knew if I started I wouldn't stop. I had just collapsed, exhausted, on the sofa when I heard the back door close; not slam, as if blown by a gust of wind; *close,* as if shut behind a person entering.

9

In the moment it took to register the sound of the back door closing, certain among the day's events – the slashed tyre, the upended plant pot, the mysteriously peripatetic steaks – came back to me like emblems in a half-forgotten dream. It seemed obvious in hindsight that they had not been the annoying coincidences I had persuaded myself they were, but deliberate acts of sabotage – calling cards, no doubt – for the visitor who had just walked into my kitchen without seeing any need for stealth.

All my life I had rehearsed my response to theoretical moments of peril – in my imagination I had saved Ethan from vicious dogs, disarmed knife-wielding rapists and wrestled suicide bombers to the floor. But now that a stranger had walked into my remote country cottage to do me harm, I was paralysed. I sat, frozen on the edge of the sofa while my heart tried to batter its way out of my rib cage and my breathing came so fast and shallow that I thought I might faint. My eyes panned across the room in what felt like slow motion, seeking a weapon. Candle on window ledge, DVD box on floor, magazine rack, *logs in basket!*

I slid off the edge of the sofa, prostrated myself across the hearthrug and felt around in the basket until my fingertips closed around a log of suitable diameter. Then, shielded by the alcove, I clambered to my feet, weighing the log in my hand. I didn't even feel the bark chafe my scorched palm, I was too intent on its heft, its potential as a weapon. The blood was pulsing in my ears, but for the first time all day my mind was focused.

I could see him now through the open door. He was going through my handbag, which I had left on the kitchen table. He seemed untroubled by the possibility of being caught, an observation which did not give me much comfort. I skirted the room, back to the wall, blessing the fact I was barefoot, blessing Nick's thoroughness in getting the floorboards relaid and waxed, so that not so much as a squeak gave away my approach. I was behind the kitchen doorframe now. Peeping round, I could see the back of his hoody-clad head, bent over my purse, his fingers riffling through it. I took the last three steps at a run, raising the log above my head so swiftly that I heard the displaced air whoosh in my ear, and if he hadn't looked up at the last moment, if I hadn't caught a glimpse of his face, reflected in the window – the startled eyes, the sunken cheeks, the elfin chin...

'Jesus, Mum, what the fuck!' he wheeled round, his face ugly with disbelief.

'Ethan! Oh my God. Oh my God. Oh my Jesus God!'

I dropped the log and pulled him close, overcome with relief and joy and remorse and the consuming desire to bury my face in his hot unwashed scalp and breathe in my own genes, my own kind, my child, my love. He raised his arms and broke angrily out of my embrace.

'I mean, what the *fuck*? You could have *killed* me. You're supposed to be better. Dad said you were *better*!'

'No, darling, I *am*,' I protested, with a manic laugh that was never going to help my case. 'It's just – Daddy's not here and I wasn't expecting anybody so I just – well, I know it seems bonkers, but there's some funny people round here and I thought...'

I saw the expression in his eyes.

'... I don't know *what* I thought. I can see now I was being ridiculous, but honestly, sweetheart, as far as *I* knew you were in Chiang Mai. Why didn't you tell us you were coming back? I'd have met you at the airport.'

'Why didn't I *tell* you?' he said, his face contorted with incredulity. 'I've been trying to fucking tell you for forty-eight hours. I ran out of money, like four days ago. I owe this Australian girl three hundred quid for my flight and I sent you about twenty WhatsApps. Why don't *you* look at your frigging phone, would be a better question.'

'*WhatsApps?*' I said, frowning and patting my dressing gown pocket.

'It's too late *now*, Mother,' he said, rolling his eyes. 'There's a cabbie out front waiting for his fare. It's seventy-two quid and his metre's still running, so...'

He tipped the contents of my purse onto the table and started raking through the small change. I handed him my credit card.

He slept in our bed that night, and I took the sofa. I couldn't bear to put him in the attic. If I'd known he was coming, I'd have made it a bit more welcoming, but it was as cold and inhospitable as the first night I'd moved in and I was ashamed even to show it to him.

'So tell me all about it,' I said to him the next morning. We were sitting at the kitchen table, Ethan tousle-haired from sleep, in a Singha beer T-shirt and tracksuit pants, his skin tanned and glowing, except where a new tattoo on his bicep had formed a scabby crust. Ethan paused in his task of forking the last strawberry onto a portion of home-made waffle, and fixed me with a sardonic stare.

'Which bit?' he said.

'All of it,' I said, 'I *missed* you. We both did. Come on, buddy. Look at this place...' I waved a weary hand at the impossibly lovely landscape beyond the kitchen window, '...*dullsville*. Let me live vicariously through you. That's what we have children for.'

'*Dullsville*, Mother?' Ethan said with a pitying smile. 'It was good,' he said, 'mostly. Phuket's a bit of a tourist trap, but the north is nice. Very spiritual.'

Now it was my turn to smile.

'What?' he said.

'No, nothing…' I said, then, unable to resist, 'Is that where you got the tatt?'

'Please don't.'

'What?' I asked in all innocence.

'Try and be down with the kids. It's embarrassing.'

'Sorry,' I said, a little hurt. 'What is it anyway?'

'It's Sanskrit,' he said. 'It means, "my soul honours your soul". Some shit like that. This girl made me get it.'

'The Australian girl?' I said, keeping my voice light, despite a flutter of disquiet.

'No, a different girl.'

I smirked.

'So your soul doesn't honour her soul any more?' I said.

He put down his knife and fork.

'Can you not?' he said.

I held my hand up.

'Sorry. Sorry. So… how was the accommodation? Was it backpackers' hostels?'

'Yeah, mainly. But Thailand's so cheap you can stay in hotels…'

'Till you run out of money…'

He gave me the look.

'Sorry.'

'Mum, I'm not a kid any more. I've been living independently for eight months. I've been to two different continents and six different countries and I'm not done yet, so…'

'You're not home for good then?' I couldn't keep the dismay out of my voice.

He looked at me and then, pointedly, around the idyllic country cottage I was privileged to call home.

'Are you serious?' he said.

'No, I just thought… it's not long till term starts. Wouldn't it be a good idea to save up a bit? Get stuck into your reading list. You don't have to stay *here*. I'm sure Jude'd…'

'I'm going to defer for another year,' he said, quickly and determinedly, as if he had rehearsed this speech. 'There's a lot more I want to do. I just need my flight money. This girl can get me work on her stepdad's fruit farm in Queensland.'

'The girl you owe money to?'

'Yeah, but she'll sub me for a bit.'

'Oh, I'm not sure that's a good…'

'It's none of your business!' he snapped.

I bit my lip and stood up, snatching his empty plate away, not wanting to well up in front of him. I washed his plate in silence, glancing over at him from time to time. He was picking his tattoo scab disconsolately. My boy. My blood.

'I hope you brought me your washing!' I said brightly.

He was right. A good parent trusted their child. They didn't tie them to their apron strings. They sent them out into the world with their blessing, Australian girls notwithstanding. Australia – how far away was that? Five thousand miles? Ten? How many times a year would I be able to visit if he settled there? Would my grandchildren have Australian accents?

'I've only got what's in that,' he jerked his head towards

a smallish backpack. 'I could do with some new stuff, actually…'

I refrained from asking him what he had done with the rather pricey lightweight rucksack we'd bought him before he set off, or its prolific contents. I imagined it was even now winging its way to New South Wales courtesy of Kylie or whatever her name was.

'We might run to a new pair of jeans…' I said.

'Not from round here though, right?' he said guardedly. 'I'll get them in London.'

'There's a Mark One in town,' I said, 'they do a nice line in stone-washed denim for twenty-five quid a pop.'

He looked at me as though I'd suggested running him up a pair out of some old curtains.

'Gotcha!' I said, pointing at him and laughing.

His face broke into a grin and for the first time since he'd arrived we were our old selves. Me and Ethan. Ethan and me.

'Is this a private party or can anyone join in?'

I started guiltily as Nick appeared through the back door.

Ethan stood up. I was so conscious of him shuffling from foot to foot behind me while I submitted to Nick's rather over-zealous kiss that I forgot to sniff my husband for another woman's perfume. When Nick had relinquished me, Ethan stepped forward and the two of them executed an awkward man hug.

'Bad penny, eh?' Nick said, with a slightly forced joviality.

'Thought I'd pop back and say hello,' said Ethan.

'Doesn't he look well?' I said to Nick.

'Very well,' agreed Nick, 'no sign of jet lag. What time did your flight get in?'

'Sore point,' I interjected quickly, 'he had to get a cab back from the airport.'

'Christ,' said Nick, 'what did *that* cost? Wasn't there a coach?'

Already I could feel it. The tension.

'It was my fault,' I said quickly. 'He'd been sending me messages and I didn't pick them up.'

'Why didn't you try me?' Nick asked Ethan, sounding a little hurt.

Ethan shrugged.

'I assumed you'd be together... You live together, right?' he added, pointedly.

'Yeah. I was in London, though,' said Nick. 'Had to stay over. Bitch of a deadline on a bid... So, yeah,' he raised his hand, offering Ethan a commiserating high-five, 'I could have come for you...'

'Wouldn't have done to miss your deadline,' Ethan said and leaving Nick's hand hovering in the air, he left the room.

'What's up with him?' Nick said disconsolately.

'What do you think?' I said.

'Christ!' Nick said. 'It's been months. I thought I might be off the naughty step by now.'

I gawped at him, astonished; in *awe*, almost, that he could make light of behaviour that had ripped through our marriage like a tornado.

Had Nick forgotten how our home had been afterwards? Me bursting into tears over nothing. Ethan pushing the boundaries like mad and Nick responding with the maturity of a toddler. Once, I remembered standing in the kitchen doorway, horrified, watching Nick trying to stuff cornflakes into Ethan's mouth, having retrieved a not-quite empty packet from the bin, which Ethan had disposed of in a sulk claiming his father hadn't left him any. Had Nick forgotten how, for months on end, the air had vibrated with hostility, aggression and shame?

'I could murder a coffee,' Nick said.

'I'll make some fresh.'

'So you weren't on your own after all?' he said, jerking his head towards the ceiling.

'No,' I said, 'I nearly crapped myself when he turned up out of the blue. I was cooking this steak that I'd bought for dinner…'

'*Steak*. Nice.'

'… Well, *not* so nice actually, but that's another story… anyway, the smoke alarm goes off, and I burn my hand and I'm freaking out so much I don't hear the bell, and Ethan's got a cab waiting…'

'Yeah, how much *did* that cost?'

'Oh well, fifty quid or so…'

'Jesus!'

'Anyway, Ethan comes in through the back door, which I'd left open because of the smoke and I think he's an intruder. You know who I thought it was? Remember that

freaky guy you had a face-off with in the lane that time…
Anyway, I get a log, right…'

Nick was looking pointedly over my shoulder at the coffee machine. I shut my mouth abruptly, swallowing the lump that came in my throat at his seeming indifference. Would it have cost him so much to hear me out?

10

'So who are these people again?' Ethan asked, as we made our way down the lane to Min and Ray's house.

'Our neighbours, obviously,' said Nick.

'You don't have to stick around, love,' I told Ethan. 'Just stay for a drink to be sociable, and then you can make your excuses.'

'Why can't he stay for dinner?' said Nick. 'It's not like he's got anywhere to be.'

'Well, it won't be much fun, will it,' I reasoned, 'stuck with a bunch of old fogeys chewing the fat?'

'Sounds fucking depressing when you put it like that,' said Nick.

'Don't be mean,' I said, with a reproachful smile. 'Min's gone to a lot of trouble. I'm sure it'll be lovely for *us*.'

As we approached the porch of Min and Ray's house, the motion-activated light clicked on, bathing us in its chilly interrogative beam. I could see the muscle flexing in Nick's cheek, Ethan chewing his lip nervously. I clutched the bottle of wine in both hands and plastered a smile on my face as the door opened.

'Evenin' all,' said Ray. He was wearing jeans and a faded Grateful Dead T-shirt stretched over his pot-belly. His straggly grey hair was hooked behind his ears.

'Hello there,' I said, 'I hope you don't mind us bringing Ethan along. He's just back from his gap year.'

Ethan closed his eyes briefly.

'All right, mate?' Ray greeted him with a manly handshake-cum-shoulder-clasp.

'Is that your bike?' Ethan jerked his head towards a vintage Norton parked a few feet away on the drive.

'One of 'em,' said Ray. 'Into bikes are you?'

'Yeah, me and a mate hired a couple of Hondas in Cambodia. Got a bit of a taste for it.'

'Honda's not a bike,' Ray said scornfully. '*That's* a bike. Play your cards right I might take you for a spin later.'

'*That'd* be cool!'

'Oh, I'm not sure that's a good...' I started to say but Nick flashed me a warning frown. I was surprised. It wasn't like him to be protective of his son's masculine pride. Against my better judgement, I banished from my mind all visions of twisted metal and butchered flesh and kept quiet.

'Oh dear, are we early?' I asked, as Ray showed us into the deserted living room. It was a curious mixture of good taste and eccentricity. Oak beams, exposed brickwork and a baronial-style fireplace were domesticated with warm lighting, squashy sofas, and all manner of throws, rugs and wall hangings. I couldn't help wondering about the collection of Victorian taxidermy on the sideboard, though – a startled-looking squirrel stared out beadily from its glass coffin, a pair of greenfinches hovered for all eternity under a dome and strangest of all, a trio of fancy moths, wings outstretched, impaled on slender wires, resembled a tiny crucifixion. By the time I had taken in a vintage Wurlitzer jukebox in an alcove and – this at least should have come as no surprise – an expensively framed but hideously kitsch airbrushed poster of a motorbike hanging over the fireplace, I had warmed more than ever to our hosts.

'No, you're not early,' Ray reassured me, with a friendly pat on the arm. 'Fashionably late, actually, unlike some people…'

Cath had just walked in from the kitchen, wearing a natty electric blue suit and carrying a tray of drinks. She put it down on the table.

'*I've* been earning my keep,' she said. 'Potatoes don't peel themselves, you know.'

'You look nice,' I told her, going for an awkward air kiss.

'Ach, away with you,' she said, blushing furiously. 'Here, try some of this. If you like it there's a bottle in the kitchen for you.'

She poured me a glass of fizz and I took a sip. It was delicious – fragrant and light with a lovely alcoholic kick to it.

'Home-made elderflower champagne,' she said, proudly. 'Mmm! Nick, you should try this, it's amazing.'

Cath waggled the bottle at him.

'I'll stick to beer, thanks,' he said.

'How about you?' Cath peered round me at Ethan.

'Gosh. Where are my manners?' I said, yanking him in front of me and remembering, just in time, not to smooth his hair as if he were still in Year One.

'Cath, this is Ethan, my... our son. Ethan, this is Cath – she's the most *amazing* gardener.'

To his credit, Ethan did not recoil from my touch, nor betray the monumental boredom he must, I imagined, have felt on being introduced to a middle-aged horticulturalist. In fact he acquitted himself rather better than his father, who stood gazing vacantly around the room as Cath regaled the rest of us with gossip from the green room at *Gardener's World*. It wasn't until Ray had answered the door to the next round of guests that Nick seemed to remember his manners, which might have had something to do with the fact that one of them was a striking brunette wearing a tan leather dress and an armful of bangles. Cath was still chatting away, but I kept losing the thread now, as I watched this woman thrust her hip at Nick and fiddle self-consciously with her hair. The husband wasn't bad-looking either, though he wasn't my type. He was short, with owlish specs, a linen scarf wound bandage-like around his neck and a head of unruly grey curls. I could see Nick sizing him up as the three of them chatted, mentally ascribing him a position in the pecking order a few rungs down from Nick's own. The miracle, from my point of view, was that a couple who looked like this should be running a gallery in an undistinguished little town like ours instead of in Manhattan's East Village. Along with some of the other recent developments in my life, Ethan's return, my tentative friendship with Cath, the excitement I felt about my new art project, it seemed – notwithstanding the woman's enviable glamour and the fact that she was all but throwing herself at my husband – to augur well for our future here.

Min came in from the kitchen, spectacles perched on her head, apron tied about her waist and a large glass of wine in one hand. She told Ray off for not putting any music on and then did the rounds of her guests offering olives and pistachios, making proper introductions that skilfully drew out the things we had in common, without seeming forced or formal.

'I was just telling Luca and Melissa here,' Cath told me, 'some jakey's taken up residence in the old barn across the way.'

'Jakey?' I repeated dumbly.

'A tramp, a vagrant... sorry,' she put on a genteel English accent, 'a homeless person.'

'Oh dear!' I said, then realising that my dismay might be misinterpreted, 'that is... it can't be very easy, can it? Living rough... out here?'

'Must everyone live the conventional life then,' Luca challenged me, with a mischievous glint in his eye. 'In his little house with his little car and his little computer?'

'Or *hers*,' Cath put in, pointedly.

'No, of course not,' I said with a combative smile, 'but I

wonder if you'd be so "live and let live" if you had someone sleeping rough at the bottom of *your* garden.'

'I like to think I'd be pretty relax,' said Luca. 'Society is never going to fit every square peg into a round hole. Maybe this person, he's happier than any of us?'

'Och, sentimental nonsense,' Cath insisted. 'Do you know the stats for premature death among the homeless? Because I'm from Glasgow...'

'... But this guy's not shooting up heroin in a doorway, is he? He's living close to nature. He lights a fire, he shoots a rabbit, he gets the aglio trigono from the woods, he has a feast. Maybe it's us who are the fools with our mortgage and our online shopping from Waitrose...'

'I wish...' muttered Cath.

'What's ahlee-oh treegono?' I asked, seizing a chance to move the conversation on to a less contentious footing. Luca warmed to his theme: wild garlic, apparently, and abundant in the woods round about, as were edible mushrooms. He'd take me foraging, he promised. 'Early one morning, when the season come around.'

'What's this,' Nick wandered over, 'foraging with my missus? Not sure I like the sound of that.'

'Oh no, it's not what you think,' Luca laughed nervously. 'Foraging mean taking food from nature... living off the land.'

'I know what foraging means, pal,' Nick said, giving Luca's shoulder a playful punch, 'I'm not an idiot.'

There was a slightly awkward pause before Ray topped

up our wine. Then we all clinked glasses and the conversation turned to more innocuous chitchat about the pleasures of the country versus those of the town, the superiority of Italian cuisine to all others and the unaccountable preference of the English for warm beer.

Min called us through to the kitchen for the first course, prompting exclamations of delight at the charm of their shabby-chic décor – the retro lighting, bentwood chairs and the weathered metal advertising signs for Fry's Chocolate and Shell Gasoline.

An hour into the evening and we could have passed for a group of old friends. The wine helped, of course, and the informality of the set-up – the scrubbed pine table, arrayed with Min's home-made Middle Eastern meze, which soon had us leaning across one another to hand around bread, scoop dips and snatch fat olives from the bowl with barely a by-your-leave. I was, I realized to my surprise, having a good time. Cath was on excellent form, Ethan appeared to have bonded with Ray, and Luca it turned out, shared my love of early twentieth-century British pottery and knew a great deal about it.

It must have been the elderflower champagne, because I'd only had one glass of red with dinner, when Melissa asked me about my work and before I knew it I'd gone into a little too much detail.

'… An installation, I think you'd have to call it,' I heard myself say. 'The theme? Gosh, well, I don't know. Barrenness, I suppose.'

'Barrenness?' she wrinkled her nose prettily.

'Yes,' I said, a flush rising up from my neck, 'the end of reproduction.'

I sensed Nick bending a worried ear in my direction from across the table.

'And if that sounds wanky, I don't care!' I reached for my glass and took a defiant swig. 'That's what's on my mind. I say on my mind, but I barely feel I've *got* a mind sometimes and that's part of it too. I don't know where *you* are with all this, Melissa... but if I'm honest, I'm finding it all pretty bloody awful – no pun intended.'

'Oh, I can't *wait* to shut up shop,' she said, 'but I'm afraid it's a few years off for me. Mind you, I've never wanted kids, so it's all felt like a messy waste of time. Maybe I'd feel differently if I'd put my body to good use!'

She laughed disingenuously and I glanced across at Nick, who was looking at her as if he thought she had put it to exactly the right kind of use. I wondered if he would look at me like that if I got myself up in a leather sheath and too much lipstick and decided he would probably just laugh.

'Anyway, I shouldn't jinx it by talking about it,' I said. 'I've barely thrown a pot yet, but seeing as my generous husband has laid out a small fortune on a fabulous new studio for me,' I reached across the table and caressed his fingertips, 'I feel I should make the most of it.'

Nick allowed his hand to lie inert beneath mine for a moment and then extricated it to reach for a hunk of bread. I wasn't sure quite what I'd done wrong, whether it was the over-sharing of my ideas, their crassly feminist nature, or perhaps even the fact that I had undercut them by turning into a simpering wifey at the end of my awkward little speech. Maybe he just wanted to keep his options open vis-à-vis the voluptuous Melissa. Maybe he just wanted to keep me guessing.

'Well, it sounds like a wonderful concept,' said Luca, plunging gallantly into the awkward silence, 'and especially for being inspired by the locality here, it would be amazing if you would consider perhaps for *us* to take a look?'

I shrugged awkwardly.

'There isn't much to look at yet.'

'Ah no of course, but at your set-up at least. Your work space,' Luca beamed. 'We have a little art trail that we organize each year.' His eyes were bulging with enthusiasm now, his curls bouncing around his spectacles like bed springs. 'We could put you on the map in your new locality, so to say...'

'*Speak*, darling, so to speak,' Melissa corrected him wearily, 'and Karen hardly needs *us* to put her on the map. She's very well established already. We're fans,' she added, turning to me with a sycophantic smile.

'Of mine?' I said doubtfully.

'Oh sure,' Luca said. 'Your "She" series kicked ass, man. We wanted to buy a piece for the gallery, but your dealer said there was nothing available.'

He shrugged and looked at me, as if expecting an explanation.

My hand, clutching the serviette in my lap, seemed to

have gone into some kind of spasm. My mouth opened and closed like a goldfish's. The conversation at the other end of the table tailed off.

'Ah well, yes, I had a…er… there was a bit of an…'

'Some of the pots got damaged,' Nick interrupted suavely, 'and no one wanted to put their hand up. Legal nightmare…'

Ants swarmed in my head. I could feel the heat of the spotlights, see the grey gleam of the gallery's concrete floor, hear my own voice howling…

*

I'd been pacing up and down ever since I'd arrived, minutely adjusting my pots on their plinths to show them to their best advantage. They'd been so long in the making; I didn't want any detail to be missed. I knew what people were like once they got a glass of champagne in their hands; friends, critics – even collectors – would just stand there gassing away, more interested in the Cork Street gossip than in engaging with the work.

'You OK on your own for twenty minutes if I pop out and buy a pair of tights?' Claudia Fussell had said at six o'clock.

'No problem,' I told her, 'Nick's due any time.'

'Oh and before I forget…' she opened a drawer, took out a couple of envelopes and handed them to me, '… fan mail I assume…'

The first envelope contained a congratulations card from my old tutor at art college. I hadn't seen him for eighteen years. He'd made a massive impression on me, but I didn't think he'd even known my name. I got a lump in my throat reading it.

The second envelope must have been hand-delivered. There was no address or stamp, just my name scrawled in an unfamiliar female script.

I was still staring at it in a daze when Nick breezed in a few minutes later.

'Well hello, Mizz Karen Mulvaney, how's the interface between Feminism and Fucking coming along?'

I looked up and watched the facetious smile die on my husband's lips. His eyes moved quickly from the letter in my hands, to the discarded envelope on the floor, and back to my face.

'Something wrong?' he said, all bogus innocence.

'You lied!' I hissed.

'Karen?' he said, warily.

'That one-night stand? The one you regretted with every fibre of your being?'

My voice was bitter and sarcastic but with a catch of tears. I thrust the letter under his nose, too close for him to read, before dashing it to the floor at his feet.

'Seems like she didn't get the memo, Nick. She seems to think it was a four-year affair.'

'Karen, Karen, *listen...*' Nick's voice was low and urgent, 'whatever she's told you, it's not true; she's unhinged.'

He took a step towards me and reached for my hands. I

knew if I let him touch me I was lost, so I turned and grabbed one of my pots to ward him off.

'Karen, love, please don't...' Nick's voice was quiet, pleading. 'This is crazy. There's no need.'

He made a sudden movement and I thrust the pot out at arm's length, like a madwoman dangling her child over a cliff, eyes glistening, throat clotted with tears, weight shifting slightly from foot to foot.

'No need?' I nodded towards the letter on the floor, 'What about that? Four years! Four fucking *years*!'

The pot was heavy in my hands, the glaze slippery...

'It's not what you think. You're making *way* too much of it. Don't do this, Karen, don't punish yourself. Oh, sweet Jesus!'

I let it drop and it smashed on the floor, shards flying everywhere.

I didn't even glance at the wreckage, just kept my eyes locked on his, while my hand groped for the next pot.

'You're waiting for Ethan to go to uni,' I said, nodding towards the letter, 'that's what she says. You're going to do right by your son, and then you're leaving your sham of a marriage and going to her.'

'Not true! Not *true*! Kaz, she's a fantasist. She'd say anything. Hell hath no fury, you know that...'

I toppled the next one. He had to duck out of the way to avoid getting hit. He was cowering now, clutching his head. It was good to feel powerful...

I wasn't even listening now. He was begging, tears in

his eyes, dodging from plinth to plinth, trying to intercept me, but I was on an adrenaline high; living for the smash, living in the moment of destruction, wrecking everything, everything, everything, because none of it mattered any more.

*

I heard the tinkle of water being poured from a jug.

'Here you go, lovey. You're white as a sheet,' Cath said pushing the glass towards me. 'That elderflower champagne – not as innocent as it looks!'

I felt drained and disorientated. I looked at the concerned faces trained on mine and wondered how long had I zoned out for this time? A few seconds? A minute? I could hear a rasping, vibrating sound and looking down, saw that it was my own hand trembling uncontrollably in my lap. I stilled it with my other hand and when I felt able to do so, picked up the tumbler and took a sip of water. Gradually the chat resumed, haltingly at first and then more naturally, the conversation turning to local walks, the plethora of stately homes in the vicinity, which ones were open to the public and when.

I nodded along and smiled, all the while avoiding Nick's eye. I knew if I caught it, I would read only disapproval there. It was another few minutes before it occurred to me to glance towards the far end of the table where, the last time I'd looked, Ethan had been deep in conversation with Ray.

Both chairs were vacant now. I swivelled my head towards the living room, expecting to see the two of them poring over the jukebox together or leafing through a pile of old biker magazines, but when I heard the ear-splitting stutter of a motorbike engine coming from the other side of the kitchen window I leaped up in dismay, knocking a glass of rioja straight into Melissa's leather-clad lap.

11

'Well, that was embarrassing,' said Nick, as we got into bed. It was the first time he had spoken to me, other than in monosyllables, since we had left Min and Ray's.

'I'm sorry but Ray was out of order,' I hissed, even though there was no one else in the house to hear me. 'I don't *care* if he's tee-total. I don't *care* if he biked from Land's End to John O'Groats when he was Ethan's age; you don't let a teenager drive a death machine like that and then leave them in a strange pub and piss off home.'

'Ethan rode *pillion*. It was the local pub and it was half past fucking *nine*, for God's sake. I don't think you realize how fucked-up your attitude looks to normal people.'

'Well, it's not half past nine *now*, is it? It's way past closing time, so where's my son?'

I snatched up my phone and checked again, but Ethan had not responded to my texts.

'It's probably a lock-in. In which case, good luck to him. He's more in with the locals than we are after months of trying. I wonder why.'

'Sorry...? Are you blaming me? You think I'm not making

an effort? Because I'm totally making an effort. I've *even* said we'd go to the Gaineses' Auction of Promises, which I can't say I'm looking forward to. It's not like they're going to be our new best mates, is it?'

'I don't know, but Min and Ray might have been if you hadn't just thrown their hospitality back in their faces. Honestly, Karen, you're a fucking genius at pressing self-destruct, aren't you? Some lovely, good-hearted people invite you round, introduce you to their really classy, really interesting friends, who could be very useful to your career...'

'My *career*...' I scoffed.

'To your *career*,' he repeated, 'and what do you do? You flirt with Melissa's husband...'

'I flirt...? *I* flirt...?'

'You blabber on about reproduction...'

'They asked about my work!'

'Knock back so much of Cath's hooch you turn into a zombie...'

'It wasn't the alcohol, Nick, I barely had a glass. I was having a...'

'Don't say panic attack,' he clenched his jaw fiercely. 'They are *not* panic attacks, Karen. People who've been in war zones have panic attacks. They are a documented side-effect of medication which, by the way, you ought to be off by now.'

I took a breath and closed my eyes.

'I didn't know where to put myself,' he muttered bitterly. 'Have you any *idea* how much leather costs to clean?'

'Oh, that fucking dress!'

But Nick had turned his back on me and his body, shrouded in duvet, looked hostile and unassailable as a long-barrow guarding its secrets.

I moved a bit nearer, but didn't yet dare reach out. He was right, I had lost the plot; ranted embarrassingly; made fools of us both.

'I'm sorry,' I murmured into the darkness, touching his back, tentatively. He didn't even flinch, just lay inert – which was somehow more troubling still, so I snuggled up under the bedclothes and spooned him.

'I'm sorry, I'm sorry, I'm sorry.'

Kiss, kiss, kiss.

His skin was warm, and smelled of sweat and spice. He was right about the self-destruct button. I did have a knack for pressing it. I was going to press it now. It was already too late to go back. To give him his due, he resisted for a while, and quite right too. I deserved to abase myself, after the way I had behaved. I deserved to be humiliated after the way I had humiliated him. And I felt better afterwards. I had let him do... what he needed to do, and I, well, enjoyed it is perhaps not the right term, but I had got where I needed to go. And the shame and compunction he seemed to feel afterwards, whilst unnecessary as far as I was concerned, at least seemed to restore our equilibrium. At any rate, the next morning he seemed in fine fettle; I could hear him in the bathroom, humming under his breath as his piss cascaded into the toilet, then clattering about in the kitchen before bringing this time, not just the usual tray of tea, but toast and jam and the best news I could have had, which I was nevertheless careful to receive with an air of casual indifference.

'Ethan's home, you'll be pleased to hear.'

'Yeah?'

'Either that or a fucking yeti's trodden muck through the house and left its trainers on the stairs...'

His tone was amused and indulgent.

'What a bum,' I said.

'Do you think I should go round and apologise?' I settled back down against the pillows and took a sip of tea.

'To Ray and Min? Nah. You'd be making too much of it. It'd only be awkward.'

'Did I come across really badly?'

'Look, Karen, they're not stupid. I think by now most people have caught on that you're not...'

'... The full shilling,' I said, tilting my head and dropping my mouth open in a mad Quasimodo stare.

'... That you're in *recovery*,' said Nick, reproachfully. 'Except maybe the Gaineses. But they're upper class so...'

I nudged him.

'Naughty.'

'So are you going to crack on with your pots today?' he said, taking a bite of toast and showering the duvet with crumbs.

'*Crack* on,' I winced, 'is that a sick joke?'

'Oh. No, no it's not.'

'I suppose I could, couldn't I? Only, I did say I'd get Ethan some jeans... No, bugger it, I'm going to work.'

'You don't seem very keen. Last night when you were talking to Melissa you were all "Lust for Life" about it. Like it had you in its grip. Or was that just for show?'

'No it wasn't,' I said hotly, 'I'm just a bit... nervous, I suppose. I've only just got my mojo back, so the thought of making something that ambitious is a bit daunting. I never really meant to tell anyone.'

'Not even me?' His tone was casual, but I could tell he was hurt.

'Well, I would've, I just didn't think you'd be interested.'

He turned towards me, and after licking the butter off his fingers, gathered my hands in his.

'How could you *think* that?' he said, looking at me reproachfully from beneath his beautiful eyebrows so that I could barely remember what it was I had thought. 'Do you think I'd have built you a studio if I wasn't *interested*? Do you think I'd have brought us down here? I did it for you. So that you could be *you* again; so you wouldn't have to feel like everyone was... so that no one need know and you could make a fresh start. Nothing's more important to me than your wellbeing, and just to know you're working again... that you've got stuff you want to make...' He pursed his lips and shook his head, apparently at a loss for words.

'But do *you* like it?' I said, squeezing his hands in return.

'Our life here? Not working as much? The people? The quiet?'

'*God*, yeah,' he said, 'it's liberating. I feel so much more...'

Somewhere beside the bed, his phone beeped. He struggled to keep hold of my hands, to stay with his train of thought.

'... So much more myself, so much more *human*,' he finished, but already his left hand was fishing for the outside world.

He looked at the phone and sighed, putting it face down on the bed.

'Don't mind me,' I said.

'Nah,' he shook his head, 'it can wait...'

He lay beside me for a few seconds before emitting a basso profundo fart beneath the bedclothes.

'I tell you what can't though...' He mugged at me and threw back the duvet.

'Go on, get out!' I laughed, wafting my hand. He probably thought I didn't notice him take his phone off the bed as he left.

But I would not listen at the door of the bathroom on my way to the studio. I would not calculate at what point in the day I might sneak a look at his messages without his noticing, because I was no longer that person. I no longer needed to be. Did I pull on my clothes a little more quickly than I might otherwise have done, so as to be passing the bathroom door sooner rather than later? Did I slow down and cock my ear when I passed it? I honestly don't think so. I was more preoccupied with getting to the studio. Of having *left* by the time he came back – impressing him not only with my work ethic, but also with my independence, my empowerment. I liked the idea that he would breeze back into the bedroom yacking away and stop in mid-sentence when he found me gone.

I knew even before I'd rolled back the studio door that I must have left the kiln on. The heat in the room was intense. I closed my eyes at my own stupidity. How often had I double-checked the timer, determined not to ruin this first batch of prototype pots? And still I'd messed up. That meant they had been firing for – I cast my mind back to when I had last been in here – three *days*, which was some kind of record – strange that the override hadn't kicked in.

I didn't notice the smell at first – I was too focused on the baked linseedy aroma of scorched pottery – but by the time I was halfway to the kiln there was no ignoring it. It was a rank stench, sweetish and rotten. I lurched for the windows, fumbling to open each one in turn, before sticking my head out and gulping fresh air. Turning back to the room the smell came at me again, humming, singing, so thick I could taste it. Only death could smell this bad. It must be a rodent, I told myself, nothing bigger could have got in. No need to freak out. Just be a grown-up – locate it, get rid of it. I peered beneath my workbench and thought perhaps I could see something in the shadows. Taking the raku tongs off their hook, I got down on all fours and was sweeping them back and forth with wilder and wilder strokes, when my back collided with my wheel and it was on top of me – its blue-black wing across my face, its claw snagging my T-shirt, its body flipping through one hundred and eighty degrees and tumbling tiny maggots into my lap. I flailed my arms to fend it off and it thudded to the floor, face down, leaving a squirm of putrid viscera across my thigh. I scrambled to my feet and ran on jelly legs, casting a dread glance over my shoulder in case the vile thing should have resurrected itself to give chase.

Nick put down his coffee cup and thrust back his chair.

'Hey, hey, hey. What's this?'

I buried my face in the rough towelling of his dressing gown and shook and cried.

'What...? Tell me! Karen!'

I moaned and gestured feebly in the direction of the back door.

'There's a thing, a bird, a *crow*, in the studio. It's disgusting. It went on me... look!'

I held my hands out to him, expecting the maggots and feathers and entrails to be there, still, like stigmata, but my hands only looked a little grubby.

Nick met my gaze with cartoon compassion.

'Oh, sweetheart. Poor you. Don't worry I'll just throw on some jeans and then I'll come and get rid of it for you. It's more scared of you than you are of it, remember...'

'No, you don't understand,' I shook my head, 'it's *dead*; at least I think it is. It must have been on my wheel... I bumped into it and it fell on me...'

'A dead bird *fell on you*?'

Big eyes; sympathetic, pitying, amused.

'Yes, it was horrible, Nick! One minute it wasn't there and the next it was all over me, on my hands, on my clothes...'

My body convulsed again at the memory and Nick drew me close.

'Shhh, shhh, shhh.'

'Nick...' I murmured, my voice muffled against his chest. He patted my back consolingly.

'*Nick!*' I pulled abruptly away, as the thought solidified in my head, 'Someone *did* this. They must have. It couldn't have got there by itself.'

'It's fine,' he said, 'everything's fine.' He encircled me in his arms again, patting, patting.

'It's not fine,' I mumbled into his chest, 'the place was baking hot – my kiln was going full blast. My pots will be ruined. I set it to go off, Nick, I know I did.'

The patting stopped for a second and he drew a deep, martyred breath.

'Of course,' he said – pat, pat, pat – 'of course you did.'

'You don't have to work you know, if you're not ready.'

We were sitting opposite each other at the kitchen table. I was towing my Earl Grey teabag around my cup by its label.

'I *am* ready.'

'Just because I made you a studio, you don't need to feel obliged.'

'Nick, I really, *really* want to work.'

'I don't care if you *never* use it. We can convert it into a self-catering chalet. Rent it out through Airb—'

'Do you think I'm making stuff up to avoid going in there? You do, don't you? You think I'm that warped.'

He had been as good as his word. He had taken a bucket of hot water and a mop and gone striding down the garden in my Marigold gloves. If I thought *that* was bad, he'd said, rolling his eyes, I should have seen the state of Gabe's guinea pig when they got back from a fortnight's holiday and realized the neighbours had forgotten to feed it. I smiled wanly at Nick's idea of consolation.

'Hey, come on, it's over now,' he said, drawing me to him. 'I know it gave you a fright, but these things happen.'

'Do they?' I said, doubtfully. 'All by themselves...?'

'Oh, come on. You seriously think somebody's sneaked in and *put a dead blackbird on your...*'

'It was a crow, not a blackbird, Nick. It was absolutely massi...' my voice trailed off.

'Karen, sweetheart...' He'd adopted that tone now; the one he used to use on the ward when I'd get things back to front – gentle and patronising, with just a hint of impatience. 'I know you're upset, I appreciate it, I do, but you're getting this – literally – all out of proportion. It was a *blackbird*. It hopped in when you weren't looking and you shut the door on it without realising. No one is *doing* this. No one is out to get you.' He clasped my shoulders, stooped and smiled in my face. 'I'm afraid you're just not that important.'

12

I watched Ethan make his way back from the buffet car, a paper cup in each hand and a packet of crisps clenched between his teeth. He sidled into the seat opposite, handed me my tea and pulled a cellophane-wrapped muffin from his pocket.

'Thought you might be hungry.'

I wasn't, but I opened it and took a bite anyway. The least I could do was keep up the pretence that we were off on a spree – Ethan to replenish his wardrobe with an uncharacteristically lavish float from Nick, me to meet up with Jude for an afternoon of pampering. In fact, we both knew that Ethan was my chaperone and Jude my counsellor, enlisted by Nick to probe my state of mind and feed back her impressions later in a phone call. 'Is it just me, or is she losing it again?'

Ethan devoured his crisps greedily, like the child he once was, and then wiping his hands on a paper napkin, reached for his phone. He caught my eye and turning it guiltily face down on the table, searched very conspicuously for something to say.

'Lucky it's not raining…'

I smiled and nodded. Seconds dragged by.

'When did you last see Jude, then?'

'Month or so ago. We had a housewarming.'

'Oh… nice…'

There was a pause. I took a dog-eared paperback out of my bag and opened it pointedly, smiling to myself when he reached once more for his phone. I read half a chapter without taking in a word and then stared aimlessly out of the window, watching the telegraph wires rise and fall over the fields and housing estates, the goods yards and retail parks. When I looked up again, Ethan had nodded off; head slumped against the window, a bead of drool gathering at the corner of his lip. He had always had the knack, I mused, seeing his forehead bump gently against the glass; had always been an easy baby, contented, smiling. We'd been able to take him anywhere – at least until his father had become squeamish about my breast-feeding in public. And later, a childminder being, according to Nick, beyond our budget, I had simply hoiked the toddler Ethan onto my hip and carried him down to the basement to keep me company while I potted. Turned out Ethan and clay were a match made in heaven. I had only to dump a wodge in a washing-up bowl on the floor and while I worked mine up to throwing consistency on the bench, he wrestled his around the lino until he looked like he'd crawled out of a swamp. Then I'd put him in his bouncy chair with a bottle and the hypnotic thrum of the wheel would send him off to sleep.

That had been the start, I supposed, looking back. Me and Ethan, Ethan and me; joined at the hip from infancy, Nick somehow cut adrift. Did that make it all my fault?

The train entered a tunnel and jolted him awake.

'Your tea's gone cold,' I said, smiling at him, 'do you want me to get you another?'

He looked at me for a moment, as if trying to recollect who I was, then shook his head pleasantly.

''S'all right,' he said.

A fine rain was falling as the train pulled into Paddington, and the platform was teeming with not especially good-tempered people. I had lost the habit of negotiating crowds – that instinct that enables you to swim in them like fish. Ethan still had it. He had to keep hanging back for me, his exasperation thinly disguised with a cocked head and a patient smile. A man swore at me under his breath and a porter driving a wagon along the platform blared his horn as I stepped momentarily into his path. I jumped and clasped my hand to my breast and then I started laughing and couldn't stop. I still had a stupid grin on my face as we moved through the ticket barrier and out across the concourse.

'Are you OK with the tube?' Ethan asked and I frowned at him comically. What other mode of transport would a Londoner take? All the same, as we made for the entrance,

I found myself turning my old Oyster card over and over in my pocket, as if it might let me down. What if I were turned back at the border? What if they recognized me for the interloper I now was? But the gates slipped back, just as they did for everyone else.

I had never noticed before how beautiful the Tube was. In the brief phase during my early twenties when I had commuted to a poorly paid administrative job with a theatrical outfitter in Covent Garden, I had moved through its windy corridors with the same air of world-weary indifference as my fellow travellers. Only now did I see it in all its Brutalist splendour. The soaring arched ceilings and the majestic sweep of the escalator, the Soviet-style brick tiles and the clinical white down-lights, the digital adverts for tooth-whitening gel and executive recruitment services. And the *people*. I couldn't take my eyes off the people: metropolitan sophisticates staring vacantly ahead, gawping tourists annoying everyone by standing on the left, gangs of giggly teenage girls with armfuls of carrier bags. All of them pleased me – their proximity, their remoteness.

'Are you feeling OK?' Ethan asked, as we shuffled along the platform.

'Fine,' I said, 'why?'

'You just look...'

'Happy,' I said. 'I'm happy.'

The train arrived with a gusty moan of its brakes and we surged forward and crammed in as if it were a children's party game.

Reaching awkwardly across my fellow passengers to claim my few precious inches of hanging rail, I jerked and shimmied like a puppet as the train rattled along. It heaved perilously over the points and I stumbled, but Ethan took my arm to steady me. I thought I might burst with pride then, even though no one in the carriage seemed to notice. This is my son, I wanted to tell them. This tall, self-assured young man may be on his way to Topman now, but he has come via Phnom Penh, Chiang Mai and Myanmar, so a little respect, please.

In the ticket hall at Oxford Circus, Ethan slowed down to work out which exit we needed, but I took his arm and led him decisively to the correct one.

'You've done this before.'

'Just a few hundred times.'

'God, you're so...'

'Knowledgeable?'

'Old.'

It was true. I had been coming here most of my life. I had seen retail empires rise and fall. C&A, BHS, Freeman, Hardy & Willis. Even after I got together with Nick, and he used to try and drag me to the more exclusive environs of Kensington and Chelsea, I would sneak back here, given the choice. I found the high-end shops intimidating and the few items of designer clothing I had bought to please him always made me feel, when I was wearing them, as if I had raided the dressing-up box. Nick never said anything and neither did his friends, but I always felt, entering a room on his arm, as though the ghost of his first wife came with us – poised, elegant, effortlessly stylish. There was always that moment of frozen politeness on people's faces, as they tried to disguise their surprise and disappointment that Nick had exchanged that for *this*.

No, I was a chain-store girl at heart. That's why I gravitated back here. I liked the buzz, the sleaze, the sense of anonymity. I knew all the back streets and short cuts, could get from John Lewis to Soho in ten minutes flat.

As we emerged from the Tube, a ray of sun, hot as an electric fire, hit the sodden pavements and made them steam. I took Ethan's arm and steered him past Muji and River Island towards the Levis shop.

'Woah,' he said.

'I thought you wanted jeans.'

'Yeah, not from here, though. They're crazy expensive.'

'Dad's paying,' I pointed out.

'Even so...'

Everything was too dear all of a sudden – even a multi-pack of boxer shorts at nine ninety-nine. As we left Primark with one flimsy carrier bag, containing less than thirty pounds' worth of clothing, it occurred to me that he was probably squirreling the money away to pay back the Aussie girl. I felt a little indignant on Nick's behalf, then realized it was really on my own behalf, before finally acknowledging to myself that whatever the motivation for his new-found thrift, it was none of my business. Nevertheless, once I'd had that thought, it took a supreme effort of will to keep up my stream of friendly prattle all the way to Soho, especially as I could tell he was only half listening. I suppose I was conscious that this might be the last afternoon we would be spending together for a while, and I wanted to make it count. I felt slightly manic, truth be told, the energy of the city buoying me up, but never quite rescuing me from an undertow of melancholy, which, were I to yield to it, I knew might drag me under.

'Are you hungry?' I said on a whim, as we passed a trendy new eatery calling itself The Soho Refectory.

'I doubt we'll get a table,' Ethan shrugged, but we did. A hipster waiter showed us to a booth, took our drinks order and then disappeared for twenty minutes to chat to his friends.

We pored over the menu, discussing how rare was rare, and whether blue cheese dressing would be nice or not, and then Ethan ordered the Wagyu burger with the lot, and mindful of the full body massage to come, I went for a salad. While we waited for the food, I watched Ethan study the other diners – a couple of tourists Instagramming their latte art, a handful of geeky creatives on their iPads and a table of young women, so preternaturally beautiful that they could only have been models, picking at a shared bowl of fries.

'What?' he said, defensively, when he saw that he'd been rumbled.

'Nothing,' I said, with a smirk. It would have been unusual, I suppose, for a heterosexual nineteen-year-old *not* to ogle beautiful women, but it felt like a minor triumph nevertheless – one in the eye for her in Queensland.

'You know you could always stay on in London for the weekend,' I suggested casually, as the waiter served our food. 'It might be fun. I bet some of your mates'd be glad to see you. What about that girl, Sophie, you used to hang out with. Didn't *she* take a gap year…?'

Ethan shook his head, his mouth full of burger.

'Noh boghered reahy…'

'Because I know Jude'd be only too pleased to…'

He forced down his mouthful half chewed.

'No thanks,' he insisted, mustard still clinging to his lip, 'I'd rather come back with you.'

I tilted my head in surprise. 'Well, that's nice.'

'Because I'm not going to see you for a while once I go, so…'

Always the sucker punch.

'You'll be back at Christmas…'

He screwed his face up, doubtfully.

'We'll pay…' I wheedled, aware, even as I said it, that I wasn't helping my cause.

He closed his eyes in exasperation.

'No, no. You're right,' I said, 'it's an adventure. It should be open-ended. It's great. I wish *I'd* done it.'

All the same, it spoiled the day. We walked from Soho to Covent Garden and I kept up my banter – 'See that fancy cinema? That used to be a right fleapit. Dad and I had our first date there. And that place – the Italian Patisserie – the one they've franchised. That's where I told him I was pregnant with you!'

Ethan gave a 'too much information' wince, but I heard myself prattle on all the same, trying to re-imagine it as the romantic watershed moment I had longed for, instead of the damp squib it had turned out to be.

'He guessed something was up when I ordered the second chocolate éclair!' I smiled. 'God, you wouldn't believe how hungry you get in early pregnancy. Not that I made a habit of eating unrefined sugar, of course. It was wholefood all the way after that – that's why you're so smart – but this was a celebration of sorts... well, it turned into one... once I'd told him...'

Not quite.

'I thought you were taking care of it!' Nick had said, pushing his teacup away, running his hands through his fringe the way he did when he was worried.

'Yeah... I... it's supposed to be ninety five per cent reliable, but hey.' I gave him a cheery grin, false jollity covering up for nerves, guilt, crushing disappointment that he hadn't been as thrilled as I was. 'It was only a matter of time. It's not like we didn't discuss names... do you still like Ethan for a boy?'

'Jesus, Karen...'

I should have heeded the warning then. In his mind this was entrapment. I was a fling, a bit on the side, consolation for a marriage that kept him too much on his toes – a trophy wife so brightly burnished he felt tarnished in comparison. I was never supposed to be her love rival, just an also-ran. But a baby is a baby and Nick's sense of chivalry – his sense of himself as a righteous man, wouldn't allow him to slip me the price of an abortion. I don't know what he thought would happen – perhaps he imagined he could lead a double life, have two families on the go, two wives, two sons: the glittering public version and the secret gimcrack one. But before I was into my seventh month she found out and chucked him out.

Jude was waiting on the steps of the spa – her punctuality an indication of how seriously she was taking her responsibilities. Usually she rocked up at least fifteen minutes late, arms laden with designer carrier bags.

'Ethan!' she cried, assailing him like an overfamiliar auntie, all lipstick and condescension, 'long time, no see.' She almost managed to bully him into coming to the café with us for a full debriefing, but he extricated himself with his usual awkward charm and I watched him disappear into the crowds, his footsteps getting quicker, his gait jauntier the further away he got from us.

'Got your cossie?' Jude asked, cheerfully. She linked my arm and led me through the reception area, where beautiful women in starched white uniforms wafted about on clouds of frankincense as though it were the antechamber to heaven itself.

'We didn't need to come here, you know,' I told her as I put on my white waffle robe in the changing rooms. 'I'd have been just as happy with a natter at your place.'

'Wait till you get your massage. Then you'll see…'

'It's very generous of you.'

'Actually it was quite selfish. I've always wanted an excuse to come here and Dave couldn't argue when I said I was bringing you.'

'Ah, the Loonytunes Freedom Pass. Well, glad I'm good for something.'

She put her head on one side and gave me an admonishing smile.

We entered a tiled atrium, which housed three glass booths – a sauna, a steam room and an ice chamber.

'Ooh, posh,' I said. 'What shall we do first? Steam room?'

'Whatever floats madam's boat.'

We hung up our robes, opened the Perspex door and peered into the hot, eucalyptus-scented fog. I could just about discern the silhouettes of two women on the other side of the room, but couldn't quite make out the echoey murmur of their conversation and was soon so engrossed in my own with Jude that we might as well have been alone.

'How's Dave?' I asked.

'Oh, you know.'

'Well, no, I don't. That's why I'm asking.'

'He's driving me nuts. He's worried about his mum, but he won't do anything about finding a home for her because he thinks if he leaves it long enough, his sister'll just cave in and have her to live with them.'

'And will she?'

'Will she hell. She can't stand her. And I'm damned if she's coming to living with us. It's bad enough having one child in the house, let alone two. Anyway, never mind Dave and his fucked-up family. How are things in Ambridge?'

I cast my eyes heavenwards.

'Seriously, though. Have you made any progress with that bed and breakfast couple? What were they called again...?'

'Min and Ray. Yes. Well, sort of. They had us round the other night. Introduced us to another nice couple who run a gallery. They might sell my work if I ever get round to making any...'

'Karen, that's fantastic! Just what you need to get you back to norm...' she checked herself, '... back in the *saddle*. You're all set now. That lovely new studio, a local gallery, friends, potentially...'

'Well...' I pulled a doubtful face and knowing me well, Jude folded her arms across her chest and waited for the full story.

'I'm not sure I made the most of it, to tell you the truth...'

'How do you mean?'

'Well, I fell out with Ray – the B&B guy, 'cause he sneaked off halfway through dinner and took Ethan to the pub on the back of his motorbike...'

Jude rolled her eyes; I wasn't sure whether at what Ray had done or how I'd reacted.

'And I spilled wine on the gallery woman's dress…'

'Could happen to anyone.'

'It was leather…'

'Ah.'

'And I think I might have made a bit of a fool of myself flirting with her husband.'

Jude turned to me, her face a cartoon of delighted surprise. 'Atta girl!' she said.

'He's Italian,' I boasted, 'name of Luca. Invited me out mushroom foraging. Nick got a bit antsy about it – don't look like that, I'm not actually going!'

'You should,' Jude said, 'you definitely should. Even if you don't fancy the guy, it wouldn't do any harm for Nick to think you do. Give him a taste of his own medicine, after what he put you through.'

I laughed but inwardly I winced. She meant well, Jude, but did she really think there was equivalence there; that some silly flirtation with a local lothario would balance the scales? Make things fair and square between Nick and me? Because that was… I couldn't put it out of my mind after that.

Long after we'd left the perfumed fug of the steam room, long after we'd stepped into and quickly out of the icy shower, long after we'd helped ourselves to fresh robes and padded upstairs to the treatment rooms, the phrase still chimed in my head: 'What he put you through… What he put you through…'

My masseur was a Filipino called Jorge. He seemed a gentle soul, but he didn't talk, except to introduce himself and ask me if I preferred music or silence. I chose silence. He placed a jasmine-infused towel over my bottom, and after uttering what sounded like a prayer in a language I had never heard before, he began to knead me with firm authoritative strokes. His hands were smooth and strong, his touch utterly non-sexual and the relief of it almost undid me. As his palms moved from neck to shoulder, shoulder to back, back to thigh, I stared through the face-shaped hole in the massage-table and the past came up to claim me.

*

I'd made quite the effort. A knife-pleated ankle-length skirt dressed down (because I was going to a gig) with a T-shirt that said 'PSYCHEDELIC' in a groovy Seventies typeface. I'd ignored Ethan's meaningfully raised eyebrows when he clocked my outfit, and refrained from reminding him, as he loaded Tekken onto his PlayStation, that he had a Government and Politics A level re-sit in two days' time. The evening ahead felt stressful enough already.

I was at the bus stop when the first text came.

'*Running late. Bear with... X*'

'*How late?*' I texted back. No kiss, because I was annoyed. This was Nick's gig – I didn't even like Fleet Foxes – and we were going with *his* friends, Justin and Bridget, whose superabundant charisma and flamboyancy always returned me to the tongue-tied, mousy imposter I had felt like in my first year at art college. It didn't help that they'd been Nick's ex's friends first and that, despite their supreme tact in never mentioning her when we were out as a foursome, her presence still cast its long shadow. I never came away from an evening in their company without the impression that their smiles had been false, their laughter hollow – that the whole thing had been the most enormous effort.

And yet I'd been unable to bring myself to opt out, to leave Nick to pursue this friendship solo. I needed to be there to assert my status. *I* was his wife now. Besides, it had seemed much less intimidating two months ago, when I'd signed up for it. I suppose I'd imagined that by the time it came around I'd have magically transformed myself into the kind of person who enjoys swaying to impeccably harmonized indie folk alongside people who look like they've stepped out of a Jean-Luc Goddard movie. I should have known better. If I hadn't managed to become that person in eighteen years, why should it have happened in the last nine weeks?

By the time Nick's second text came – '*Half an hour max*' – I was feeling slightly panicky. We were meeting at the venue and I had the tickets. Even when Nick was there to keep the conversation flowing, I found Bridget and Justin hard work. Half an hour on my own with them would feel like purgatory. I was queuing to get off the bus when the final text arrived.

'*Best leave my ticket on the door.*'

As I joined the hoard of hipsters massing on the pavement, waiting for the lights to change, I gave myself the pep talk. They're just people. Knock back the first drink and then keep the questions coming. Doesn't matter how inane. What was their daughter called again? Scout? Shiloh? You can do this. But then the lights changed, the crowds surged across the road and I caught sight of them standing on the steps, Justin in his Rupert Bear suit and pointy shoes, Bridget in a leopard print coat, her hair cut in a funky, asymmetric bob.

'Guys,' I said, thrusting their tickets at them before they'd even worked out who I was, 'I'm really sorry... I know this sounds crazy but I've just had a call from Ethan. He's locked himself out and the neighbours can't find the set of keys that we normally leave with them and he needs to get his stuff because he's booked on a train from Euston in an hour's time and if he misses that one he'll have to upgrade...' On and on I went, until they were the ones telling me I must rush, and to think nothing of it and if I got back in time for the second half that would be fantastic, but if not they'd see me soon and then I plunged back into the mêlée, my cheeks burning, my own voice repeating on a loop in my head, 'Guys, I'm really sorry... Guys, I'm really sorry...' Who *said* that?

My bus home had just lumbered round the corner, when I remembered I still had Nick's ticket. I made a cancelling gesture at the driver to indicate that I had changed my mind. As peeved as I was that my husband had dropped me in it, I knew he'd be gutted to miss the gig. Not just gutted – angry. We'd paid fifty quid apiece, apart from anything else. I took out my phone and tapped Google Maps. It should be easy enough to walk to Nick's office from here, once I got my bearings.

The interior was in darkness when I got there, except for the sleek blue strip lights around the reception desk and the pale glare of the security guard's TV. The receptionist was long gone. I jiggled about on the pavement, waving foolishly until I caught Samuel's attention and he buzzed me in. I was all set to explain the whys and wherefores, but to my surprise he recognized me and with an absent-minded smile and one eye on *Top Gear*, waved me through. I hadn't planned on handing the ticket over to Nick in person but already my righteous indignation was ebbing away. The weighty imperative of a work deadline seemed a more convincing excuse, somehow, with a fifteen-storey office block looming over my head; the smoked glass and lavish flower arrangements, leather sofas and corporate art, part reproach, part aphrodisiac; reminders all of my husband's diligence, of his status, of how good he looked in a suit. I would hand over the ticket myself, with a good grace; hell, the way I was starting to feel, I might yet go with him… I pressed the button to summon the lift.

As I waited for it to descend a second light came on, indicating that another one was on its way down from higher up the building. So Nick wasn't alone in putting in the hours. I felt ashamed of myself by now. How could

I have failed to acknowledge the pressures he was under; they were *all* under?

When I got out at the second floor, the lights were off and Nick's office was empty. I glanced up and down the corridor, confused. Could he be in the boardroom? Hot-desking somewhere? A thought occurred to me then. That other lift; I must have just missed him… the doors would be opening now in reception. He'd be saying goodnight to Samuel, touching his lanyard to the target…

I hurried to the end of the corridor, where a floor-to-ceiling plate glass window gave onto the street. I saw the electronic door swing open and watched Nick emerge, followed by a colleague. A woman. Hair in a ponytail, pencil skirt, heels. Not his type. I raised my hand to bang on the window, but something stopped me. As they moved away from the ambient light of the office frontage, their demeanour changed. They moved closer together, there was an ease, an intimacy in the way they fell into step beside one another. My forehead was throbbing now from being pressed so hard against the glass. They were almost at the corner of the street. They were slowing… stopping. They were about to go their separate ways. He put a hand on her shoulder, she inclined her head; he kissed her mouth.

I thought I was doing OK. I walked home from the bus stop doing a passable imitation of a person. My limbs moved, I registered immovable objects – litter bins, bollards, and negotiated my way around them. I even muttered 'thanks' when a man walking in the opposite direction stepped off the narrow pavement into the gutter to make way for me.

But when I got to our front door and tried to put my key in the lock, it was as though I'd had a stroke. I had to clutch my right hand in my left and guide the tip of the key, which still skittered across the slot as though it had a life of its own. At the third attempt, I managed it.

'Hello?' Ethan's voice sounded alarmed and slightly indignant.

'Only me,' I called, my voice high and fake, like a bit-part actress who only had one thing to do and nevertheless blew it.

'I thought you said you'd be late…?'

'Yeah, not feeling great. I'm just gonna…' With a huge effort of will, I hauled myself to the top of the stairs, so I should be out of sight of the lounge door, if he opened it. He didn't.

I didn't know what to do when I got in the bedroom. I felt as though I was outside my body. The script required me to throw myself onto the bed and sob into the pillow, but it was a hackneyed script, which reduced my situation to the cliché it was and I couldn't do it. It felt both too histrionic and not histrionic enough. The thing I had expected to happen from the moment I got together with Nick had finally happened and I was shocked at how shocked I was. Too shocked to act. Too shocked to move. I needed to shatter.

*

'Finished!'

Jorge's voice in my ear was so gentle that I was almost more aware of his breath, stirring my hairline. I looked up from the massage table, and blinked at him, dumbly, a tissue paper halo still sticking to my face, where it had been thrust through the hole.

'I'll leave you to get dressed. Drink plenty of water.'

I nodded and lowered my face back over the portal, almost as if expecting my past to be down there still, but all I saw was the herringbone sisal flooring, liberally spotted with massage oil, or possibly tears.

13

'Well,' said Jude, putting a peppermint tea down in front of me, 'no need to ask if that did the trick!'

I nodded gratefully and she pulled up a wicker chair and sat down beside me.

'How was yours?' I remembered to ask.

'Yeah, not bad. Could have done with a bit more oomph, but...'

We sipped our herbal teas and gazed around us at the clientele. A Chelsea hen party here, a gaggle of Botoxed baby boomers there, everywhere the aura of entitlement, the scent of money. I looked at my watch and Jude gave me a reproachful look.

'Said I'd meet Ethan at five,' I said.

'I wish you'd stay.'

'I would've,' I said, 'but he wants to go back tonight and he's not going to be around for that much longer.'

The words stuck in my throat.

'He seems really well,' Jude said after a pause.

'D'you think? I'm a bit worried about him.'

'That's your default position, though, isn't it? Where Ethan's concerned.'

I bridled at this. Jude, who didn't have any kids of her own, always knew best about other people's.

'I don't think so,' I said, testily. 'He's going halfway round the globe to be with this girl he's not even bothered about!'

'How do you know he's not bothered?'

'I can just tell. He feels obliged, because he owes her money. And she's told him she can get him a job when he gets there, but...'

'Maybe that's OK.'

'How can it be OK? She's manipulating him.'

'Maybe he's manipulating *her*...'

'Well, that's no better. I just think, what if it all goes to shit and he's miles from anywhere with no money to get home?'

'He'll work it out.'

'Jude, he's nineteen!'

'Exactly!'

She had been so kind to me – dropped everything, stumped up for the best massage I had ever had, so how come I wanted to slap her? Maybe they were right about me. Maybe I was possessed by demons.

All the same, when we hugged goodbye at the entrance to Covent Garden tube, I found myself holding back tears.

'Hey!' she said, pulling back and looking into my face. She tidied a wisp of hair behind my ear.

'You're doing great,' she said, 'you're doing fine.'

*

'You're doing great, Karen,' my psych said, her eyes round and earnest.

Really? I wondered, was this what 'great' looked like? Sitting on the edge of my seat, a nerve twitching in my cheek, my eyes glazing over with the effort of trying to focus.

'You've made a lot of progress and shown great resilience, bearing in mind how unwell you were when you first came to us.'

Nick's eyebrows shot up. I suppose, considering the state I'd been in when they'd admitted me, 'unwell' was a bit of an understatement. The psych turned to him and smiled tolerantly.

'As I say, considering how symptomatic Karen was when she joined us, for us to be contemplating discharge as early as this…'

'It's been five months,' Nick interrupted.

'… Which, as I say, represents remarkable progress,' the psych insisted.

Right on cue and as if to amplify her point, a kerfuffle broke out somewhere in the corridor – another patient presumably.

'So,' the psych turned to me, once the brouhaha had died down, '*I feel that the next stage for you, Karen, should be one of re-engagement.*'

'Re-engagement?' I must have looked alarmed.

'Yes, sorry – what I mean is, we're comfortable, if it's

what you want – and I can't stress how important your own agency is in this – for you to go home now. We can devolve your care to the outpatient clinic most local to you, which in this case will be...'

She glanced at the computer screen, '... Muswell Hill.' She looked me in the eye and smiled. 'They have a really excellent self-help group which I think you'll find very supportive.'

'Will you er...?' Nick swivelled his chair towards the psych and murmured, sotto voce, '... be stepping down the anti-depressants? Because she's not really herself when she's on them and I gather dependency can become a bit of an...'

'Yes, I do understand your concern,' the psych interrupted him, her professional smile not quite disguising her irritation, 'And Karen's being "herself"' (did I imagine it or did she give Nick a sharp look as she said this?) 'has, as you know, been very much the guiding principal of our entire care package, since admission...'

'Yes, I'm not saying go cold turkey just...'

'Karen,' the psych turned pointedly to me, 'how are you getting on with the Fluoxetine?'

'Yeah, it's OK. I mean, I wouldn't want to be on it for ever or anything but it keeps things at a manageable level day to day. I don't feel like killing anyone.'

They both did a simultaneous double-take, for, I imagined, rather different reasons and then, seeing that I was being humorous – and humour indicating a level of social *engagement* that suggested my drug regimen was in fact doing the job – laughed heartily and with some relief.

*

'Kaz... Karen...?' I gave a little involuntary shiver at the touch of Jude's hand as she rearranged my hair and refocused on her concerned face.

'Yeah,' I said doubtfully, 'thanks...'

She braced my shoulders but I didn't trust myself to meet her eye again, so I turned abruptly and hurried away towards the tube.

I got a seat, unusually, and found myself sitting opposite a mother and daughter who had obviously been on a spree together. They were a golden pair – not ostentatiously striking, but with an understated not-quite beauty that made it hard, once you noticed it, to look away. They didn't talk to each other, just stared straight ahead, in an attitude of repose, as though they had done all their chatting and were quite comfortable in their bubble. As the train rattled out of Covent Garden station, the mother pulled back the top of the daughter's carrier bag with one finger, glanced inside it and met her daughter's eye with a look of complicity. I felt for a second that if I could have glimpsed the contents of that expensive-looking paper carrier it would have yielded the secrets of the universe. In there was everything I lacked: self-assurance, wit, style, allure. Everything Nick's ex had had in spades. The mother noticed me staring and I gave an apologetic half smile and raised my gaze to the triangle of dark glass between their shoulders. There I was, reflected in the carriage window, hair limp from the steam room, my face amorphous and blotchy, hanging between these two sirens like a poltergeist. It was a relief when a couple of shift workers in hi-viz donkey jackets got on at Regent's Park and stood between us.

Catching sight of Ethan from a distance on the concourse at Paddington, I could see that he was no longer a Londoner. With his tanned skin and bleached hair, he was a citizen of the world – a bum. A handsome bum, a privileged bum, but a bum nonetheless. All the other people were tethered to their lives, scanning the departure board, eager to get home, while Ethan was floating free, headphones in, a vacant expression on his face, as if this place were as good as any other. How I envied him. Our train came up on the departure board so I shouted and waved frantically to get his attention and then gestured towards the platform. He rolled his eyes as if he'd been wondering where I'd got to and we converged on the barrier.

The train was crowded, most of the seats were reserved and everyone was doing that British thing of waiting with exaggerated patience for the slow-coaches to stow their luggage when what they really wanted to do was shoulder-charge them out of the way and bag a seat. I noticed a man and woman take up neighbouring reservations at a sociable four-seater across the aisle. Ethan and I had only been able to find single seats, one behind the other. I leaned forward and whispered to him that they might not mind swapping with us as they obviously weren't travelling together, but he just shrugged as though he didn't really care.

I settled into my seat and stared blankly out of the window, watching the platform, empty now except for a few scavenging pigeons. A woman came barrelling through the carriage with a lot of carrier bags and accused someone nearby of occupying her seat. By the time the mix-up had been resolved and both parties accommodated, the train was moving and London was slipping away from me in a blur of council flats and flyovers and advertising hoardings. I pressed my head against the glass and watched the reflection of Ethan's thumbs in the darkened window, flying like pistons over the keyboard of his phone. Before I knew it, I wasn't just watching, I was reading.

'Are you kidding me?' – thumb, thumb, thumb, thumb – *'fucking gagging for it'* (tongue hanging out emoji).

I sank back into my seat, sick to the stomach both at what I had read and in shame that I had read it. Well, I had brought it on myself. No wonder he couldn't get there soon enough. Who wouldn't travel ten thousand miles to escape an overbearing mother? At least I wouldn't be able to read his texts from there.

I closed my eyes and leaned my head on the window. A tear squeezed its way from beneath my eyelid. Pathetic.

By the time I'd sighted my first cow, standing lugubriously beside a pylon in a field, all the therapeutic effects of my day trip seemed to have evaporated and a great despondency had settled in their place. The sights that were supposed to be balm to the soul – rolling hills, big skies, hedgerows, sheep – flicked past my gaze with such regularity that I began to think the scenery was on a loop, like the backdrop in an old black and white movie. That tractor I had seen before, I'd swear it; those walkers with their dog; that flock of crows massing in a tree. Crows. I closed my eyes, felt briefly the flurry of feather on cheek, smelled the sour-sweet stench of eviscera. I shuddered. Paranoia. These were the symptoms. Thinking oneself conspired against, imagining one's life controlled by hidden forces. I should have to buck up – keep my wild imaginings at bay, or I'd end up back at the funny farm...

I started typing a text to Nick. '*Wonderful day, thanks for organizing. Train on time*'... I stopped; deleted it. Too needy. He'd said he would be there to meet us and he would be. In the small things, he was unfailingly reliable.

The Range Rover hunkered in the Arrivals car park like a Sherman tank. Nick was studying *The Times* crossword, impervious to the unfriendly gesticulations of a woman in a Nissan Micra whom he had blocked in. He looked up when Ethan opened the rear door.

'Good time had by all?' he asked.

I climbed into the front passenger seat and he leaned across and gave me a peck on the cheek.

'Yes,' I said, 'lovely.'

'Get some good gear, Ethe?' Nick asked him.

I glanced doubtfully over my shoulder, at Ethan's one flimsy carrier bag.

'Uhuh,' he replied.

It was damp as we drove back through the valley. Bruised-looking clouds hung low over our hill.

'Has it been wet all day?' I asked Nick.

He looked out of the window as though he had only just noticed.

'Yeah, I guess,' he said. 'Good for the garden, though.'

There was something in his tone, a coolness.

'Jude OK?'

'Yeah, not bad,' I said. I considered telling him about the domestic wrangles between her and Dave, but it seemed inconsequential now.

What was this aloofness? Had I done something wrong? Or just cramped his style by coming back? I closed my eyes and tried to banish the images that came to mind of phantom infidelities. I was meant to be over all that.

He looked across and gave me a pensive smile.

Dusk was falling. We were almost home. Nick was signalling right, ready to take the turn into our lane

'Hey, Dad,' Ethan piped up from the back, 'can you let me out here?'

'Why, where are you going?' I asked, in surprise.

'I think I left my denim jacket in the pub,' he said, glancing over his shoulder as a passing car honked its disapproval. 'Just gonna check if it's been handed in.'

'Isn't it a bit late for…?' But he had already slammed the door. I watched, perplexed, as he set off alone along the dark footpath.

'There you go,' said Nick, his tone faintly reproachful. But I wasn't sure whether he meant 'there you go, you've made your kid into a boozing ne'er do well,' or 'there you go, despite your neurotic imaginings your son has turned out perfectly normal.'

Nick made a grinding gear change and coasted down into the hamlet.

'Oh yeah,' he said, as we passed Prospect Cottage. 'I nearly forgot. There was a bit of a drama this morning. An ambulance came.'

'Jean!'

Nick turned his head sharply.

'How did you know?'

How *did* I know?

'What happened?' I asked. I saw Gordon's raised hand, the glint of fury in his eye.

'She had a fall,' Nick said. 'Nasty black eye but no bones broken, thank goodness. She's back home now.'

I bit my lip.

'I know,' Nick said. 'Awful, isn't it?'

'I feel terrible.'

'Why should *you* feel bad?'

'Well, I've been meaning to call round and see her, but I've just… I don't know. Place gives me the creeps. I always think it might be him who answers the door and…'

Nick shot me a disapproving frown.

'You're putting some dodgy spin on this, and I don't know where you've got it from,' he said grimly, then after a beat he murmured, 'Well, I do…'

He glided into our pull-in and switched off the ignition. We both sat in silence, listening to the ticking of the engine as it cooled down.

'What's that supposed to mean?' I asked sullenly. 'Oh, I get it. It's like the bird in my studio. You think I'm making shit up again, don't you?'

'Not making it up, no, just…'

'… Fantasising. Hallucinating. Losing the plot.'

He turned to me then and laid a consoling hand on my thigh.

'None of those, no. I just think…'

He looked into my eyes, and in the half light of the car his expression was sweet and regretful.

'Doesn't matter…' he said removing his hand and making to open the driver's door.

'Nick!' I clamped my hand on his to stop him.

Suddenly we were kissing. He clambered on top of me and reclined my seat with one deft movement of his hand. I heard myself gasp, then groan, and then we kissed some more while Nick ground his pent cock against the sturdy double seam of my denim crotch like a randy schoolboy. Just when I thought I might die of wanting to be fucked, he reached down and fumbled first with my button, then my zip, rearing back briefly to brace his knees against the seat, before yanking my trousers down as far as my knees. I unzipped him in turn, and shuffled his jeans over his hairy thighs, then he dropped onto me, and, thrusting blindly, found his way in.

There was something so illicit, so thrillingly *amateurish* about this set-up. If it hadn't been for my gaping wetness and Nick's staying power, we might have been a pair of teenage virgins at a drive-in. I was getting to the point when I no longer cared *where* we were, or what I looked like, or how sore I was going to be afterwards; had just felt, in fact, the embryonic quiver of my first orgasm, when a flicker of movement outside caught my attention. Turning my head I saw a blur through the windscreen, which, by the time I had identified it as a person, was already disappearing into the darkness.

Nick was still rutting away on top of me, oblivious.

'Nick,' I said urgently.

He groaned and shuddered and collapsed on me like a corpse.

'Nick!' I pulled his hair sharply and he recoiled, staring at me like an angry baby.

'I just saw someone…'

'Big deal.'

'Nick, you don't think he was... what if he was watching us?'

'What do you want me to do, call the cops?' Nick said. '"Officer, we were just doing a bit of dogging in the lane and some pervert had the cheek to walk past."'

'There's no need to make it sound so sordid.'

'It *was* sordid,' said Nick, cheerfully. 'We should do it in the car more often.'

'Stop it,' I said, cracking a smile in spite of myself, 'this is *serious*. Someone saw us. Someone was watching.'

'Baby, lighten up. Birds do it, bees do it. This is the countryside. We're man and fucking wife. If some pervert wants to get off on it, good luck to him. Now I don't know about you but I need a drink. Are we going inside or what?'

14

Nick had tidied up. Not that the cottage ever really got messy in the way our house in London used to, with sports bags and skateboards and shoes all over the place. But as I walked in, I felt as though I were seeing it through the flattering fish-eye lens of an estate agent's camera. The trail of clutter that I tended to leave in my wake – junk mail catalogues and odd earrings and headphones and keys – had been tidied away. He had restacked the log pile and lit a fire in the stove. The coup de grâce was a huge bouquet of flowers on the dining table. He had put them in water, but they were still in their cellophane, in case, I supposed, I overlooked the fact that they had not been picked, but purchased at great expense, from a florist.

'Gosh, they're lovely,' I said going over to take a sniff, although they were the kind of flowers – roses and lilies and variegated carnations, hot-housed out of season – that did not have much scent.

'Aren't they?' he said, with the same coolness of tone I had noticed earlier in the car.

'Are they not from you, then?'

'I'm afraid not.'

'No need to be afraid,' I said, 'I just thought…'

'… I might have made a spontaneous romantic gesture?'

'Well, no, only – I was upset, wasn't I? About… that *thing* in my studio.'

'Oh, the bird, yeah. So you were.'

What was going on? I didn't like this. I was somehow being invited to feel complicit in a gift of flowers that was as much a mystery to me as it was to him.

'Doesn't it say who they're from?'

'You tell me.' He shrugged as though it were a matter of inconsequence, although when I went over and found the little gift card in its envelope, I could tell it had already been opened.

'*From an admirer*,' I read aloud. 'That's a bit creepy.'

'Is it?' said Nick elliptically.

He uncorked a bottle of red wine and switched on the telly, flicking through the channels until he found the news. It was as though our adolescent slap and tickle had never happened. I cast him a wary glance.

'Well, *I* think it's creepy,' I said. 'Who round here would be admiring *me*?'

He poured himself a glass of wine.

'You really can't guess?' he said, sipping it, and staring at the screen.

I found myself blushing furiously. On the one hand, I was a bit disturbed, especially after the other weird stuff that had been happening lately. On the other, Nick seemed – jealous was too strong a word, *piqued,* perhaps – and this was new. He looked at me, eyebrows raised in amused reproach as if it were obvious who the sender was – as if I were just being coy.

'Well, whoever they're from I don't want them,' I said, grabbing them from the vase, marching them to the front door and flinging them out into the darkness.

'Methinks the lady doth protest too much,' said Nick inscrutably. He poured a glass of wine, pushed it across the coffee table toward me and turned up the volume on the news.

I woke early. Light was streaming through the blind and a single bird was chirruping loudly at intervals of exactly seven seconds. Once I had started to count them, I couldn't stop. I crept out of bed, glancing over my shoulder to make sure I hadn't disturbed Nick. He gave a great shuddering sigh before subsiding into sleep again. I pulled a sweatshirt on over my pyjamas and went downstairs.

The porch light was still on. Ethan's boots, usually to be found lying haphazardly near the doormat, were conspicuous by their absence. The 'missing' jean jacket was nowhere to be seen. He hadn't come home from the pub. My mind set off on its usual rat-run of worry. I imagined him lying in a field comatose from drugs; disfigured in a car wreck, sitting in Casualty waiting for a pint glass to be removed from his cranium. And then I remembered the '*gagging for it*' text I had seen on the train, and the thought occurred that it might not, after all, have been addressed to the Australian girl, but to someone local. I tried to feel relieved.

I hadn't gone far down the garden when I found the bouquet of flowers lying on the grass where I had thrown it last night, its cellophane wrapping spangled with dew. I was heading down the path to put it in the dustbin when my conscience pricked me. It seemed such a waste. The velvety cream petals of the lilies were still pristine, the rosebuds tightly furled. The flowers didn't know or care who sent them and in the optimistic morning light they seemed to have lost their menace. There must be someone who would appreciate them, surely? I considered for a moment, then, peeling the envelope off the cellophane, I threw that alone in the bin and set off down the lane for Prospect Cottage.

I hesitated at the gate. Day had not yet penetrated the overgrown garden. Shrubs huddled like boulders in the crepuscular light and a faint breeze stirred the Leylandii. Steeling myself, I hurried up the crazy-paving path, pushed open the porch door and leaned my bouquet against an étagère crammed with ugly old-fashioned houseplants. A whiff of soil and rot and PVC caught in my throat. The outer door had swung to behind me and hearing a sound from inside the house, I scrambled to make good my escape, barging against the étagère in my haste and knocking a spider plant in a flimsy plastic pot upside down onto the floor. I panicked, knowing I should stop, clear up the mess, behave like a grown-up, but the dread of being caught in the act by Gordon was too much for me. I kicked the plant out of sight with my foot and yanked the door hard, but it juddered on its hinges and bounced back open, and I found myself running, heart pounding, down the path, as guilty and exhilarated and terrified as when I'd played Knock Down Ginger as a child.

Back on the lane I collected myself and tried to adopt the demeanour of a middle-aged woman returning from a well-meaning errand, but I felt like a criminal. Already the re-gifting of the bouquet seemed a terrible idea – cowardly, mean-spirited and strange. I should not be sneaking round at the crack of dawn, but calling at a decent hour, ideally bearing home-made scones, having brushed up my bedside manner. I would do better later, I promised myself, but for now the studio beckoned.

I had almost reached our house when the Gaineses' two golden Labradors came bounding round the bend. I put a spurt on, reluctant to be buttonholed by whichever of their owners was on dog-walking duty, but my haste only seemed to excite the dogs and soon one was sniffing my hand while the other cocked its leg on our gatepost. I was manoeuvring my way between their furry haunches when I heard Douglas's voice behind me.

'Not the ideal calling card,' he said. 'Sorry about that.'

Like me, he was still in his pyjamas, though his were tucked into wellingtons and topped with a Barbour jacket. Unlike me he seemed to feel no compunction.

'Bad girl, Frieda!' he admonished the dog affectionately. 'Lucky it wasn't number twos. Although I'm equipped for that,' he said cheerfully, pulling a small plastic bag out of his pocket and waving it at me.

He must have noticed my moue of distaste.

'Ah yes, TMI, as the girls say. Apologies.'

I kept my hand on the gate, determined to at least convey the impression of forward motion.

'By the way, Karen, as long as we're chatting...'

'Yes?'

'... Imogen'd have my guts for garters if I didn't mention the Auction of Promises.'

'In the diary,' I said, cheerfully. 'We'll be there.' Both dogs had by now pushed past me and were sniffing around our front garden.

'Ah yes, very good,' Douglas said, 'but I'm also on the scrounge for lots.'

'Lots of what?'

'Oh, haha. Yes, very funny. *Lots*. To auction. It's in aid of two very good causes, the chur—'

'Oh yes, I know, Imogen told me.'

I cast a despairing glance over my shoulder, wondering, in light of Douglas's supremely relaxed attitude, if I would ever make good my escape.

'Splendid. So... I just wondered, with your being a local craftswoman and so forth...'

'Oh, you want a *pot*? Ah, that's not... I'm not really...'

'Now, now, no need to be modest. Doesn't have to be a

Ming vase,' he said. 'Can be as humble as an eggcup. You'd be surprised what people'll bid for a one-off. Year before last I paid a silly amount of cash for a personalised bedside lamp for Honour's birthday. Little toadstool house with a resident pixie. Cost me a small fortune, because of course once Grace caught sight of it, I had to commission another for her. Local woman – you might know her actually. Thriving little business…'

I looked up at him, booming away at top volume, pyjamas rippling around his thighs in the breeze and I couldn't help smiling.

'… And the beauty of it is, you can fit it in as and when. It's a promise, but it's up to you how long you take to make good on it. People are very patient, very trusting, because of course it's not really about the lots at all, it's about the cause.'

'Well, I suppose if the timescale's fairly generous…' I conceded, thinking that at this rate I would waste more time talking to him than it might take to throw a pot for his wretched auction.

'*Marvellous!*' he said, flashing me a grateful smile. 'I'll pop you on the list. Frieda! Diego! Leave poor Karen alone, she doesn't want your piss all over her lavender.'

I watched him trudge off down the lane with the dogs and wondered whether life was as uncomplicated for him as it seemed. Plenty of money, a smart and pretty wife, a Grade Two-listed home and a sense of entitlement the size of the county. Perhaps he'd have liked a son and heir; then again, he was probably an equal opportunities Nob. His daughters would no doubt end up doing Masters degrees in earth science or running environmentally friendly energy companies and good luck to them. But did he wake in the early hours of the morning tormented with existential fears? Did congenital defects lurk in the gene pool that made him dread grandparenthood? Did he secretly feel unworthy of the luminous Imogen, and track her movements on his mobile phone? I was projecting now, my psych would have said, and she'd have been right. That was what therapy was for – to give you the insight to recognize your triggers – to stand at one remove and say to yourself, 'Ah yes!' The unhealthy impulse to put a tracking device on one's partner, whilst perhaps *occasioned* by a breach of trust, might actually stem from deep-rooted insecurities going all the way back to childhood...

*

'So, you're a ceramicist?' my psych had asked.

'A potter,' I'd replied, sulkily.

She'd uncrossed her legs, clicked the end of her biro and written something down.

'But clay is your medium. You feel comfortable around it?'

I shrugged and she'd produced from a drawer a little wooden board, a slab of pale hobby clay and a few wooden tools – no serrated edges, I noticed.

'Suppose I were to say,' she said, blinking at me earnestly

from behind her stylish tortoiseshell spectacles, 'show me, in clay, why you think you're here...'

I sat for a moment, arms folded, not sure if she was joking.

Then, glancing up at her carefully managed expression – curiosity disguised as professional detachment – I thought I might amuse myself. I took half the clay and made it into an oval, then rolled it between my palms until it became first a fat sausage, then a long thin snake, its head and tail whipping back and forth in time with my hand movements. She sat up attentively and reached for her notepad, ready, no doubt, to jot down the words 'phallic' and 'repressed memory?'.

I smiled to myself, took a smaller piece of clay, fashioned it into a flat base and coiled the clay snake upwards around its edge until I'd made a rudimentary vessel.

She looked at me for a long moment.

'And what does that mean to you?'

'It's a pot,' I said, innocently.

I thought I'd won, but it seemed this answer was as useful to her as any other. She wrote a lot of things down, at any rate. I got tired of second-guessing her in the end.

It turned out to have been a good instinct of hers, the clay. The miniature board and cheap, air-dryable modelling material returned me to the mind-set of a nursery child – a free and unselfconscious state. I ended up quite enjoying myself. I spent one whole session dividing the ball of clay into a collection of smaller balls, each of which I halved and re-rolled until by the end of the session, I had a couple of hundred tiny balls, about the size of the sugar pearls used to decorate cakes. She wrote a lot of stuff down about that. Another time I amused myself making a doll-sized rocking cradle, about as big as my thumb and she asked me where the baby was.

I shrugged.

'Are you the baby? Is that why it's missing?'

I pulled a sceptical face.

She checked her notes.

'You were an only child, weren't you?'

I nodded, warily.

'So no siblings?' she said, as if I might have inadvertently forgotten one.

The silence stretched on.

'Was there an *absent* baby in your family?' she said gently. 'A twin that didn't survive? A stillbirth?'

When I spoke, it was with a break in my voice that I hadn't anticipated.

'My dad had a kid with someone else.'

Scribble, scribble, scribble.

'A brother or a sister?'

'Sister.'

Scribble.

'And when did you find this out?'

I shook my head.

'You don't know? Or it's painful to remember?'

'I must have been ten or so.'

'And did you meet her... this half-sister?'

'One time, by accident in the playground. My dad said she was my cousin but I heard her call him Daddy.'

She stopped, pen poised and looked into my face, clicking the pen on and off, on and off.

*

Douglas had disappeared from view now. Only one of the dogs, Diego or Frida, I wasn't sure which, could still be seen, sniffing in the nettles by the side of the road, as though it had caught the scent of a fox.

15

As I rolled back the studio door, I told myself the nervous flutter in my stomach was one of anticipation for the potting I planned to do, rather than one of dread that some new voodoo tribute might await me. The hapless bird had, after all, been trapped and slow-cooked thanks to my oversight, not to some phantom stalker's malevolence. I had worked hard to overlay my recollection of the event with Nick's more plausible one, and had, for the most part succeeded, except when a sudden vivid flashback brought to mind the gape of the bird's hollow eye socket or the rake of its inch-long talon against my skin. Then I would find my pulse racing all over again.

The first thing I did – to freshen things up rather than to release any bad bird juju – was to open all the windows, although it was disconcerting when a sprightly breeze sprang up, rattling the polythene around my clay and riffling the pages of my notebook until it skittered off the workbench onto the floor.

I'd expected my precious pots to be in pieces when I opened the kiln, but I hadn't bargained for the hundreds of splintered shards I discovered, nor for the layer of clay dust that their shattering had left on its every plane and crevice. I could have cried, especially as it could only have been my mistake; it must have been. What random stalker would know how to adjust the temperature and switch off the override? They wouldn't. And even though I'd been working this same kiln for over a decade, could have programmed it in my sleep, I couldn't deny that my concentration lately had been on the patchy side.

It felt cathartic, sweeping the detritus out of the kiln, chipping away at the hardened splashes of glaze, poking into every hard-to-reach corner with my cloth. It reminded me of spring-cleaning Trenchard Street when the boys were young. I'd known I couldn't compete with Nick's ex in looks and charisma, so I'd put myself at his service instead – and not just in the bedroom. Naïve of me really to think that keeping on top of the housework would be any substitute for whatever dirty tricks *she'd* had in her repertoire, but for a while I'd given it a go – letting home-made cassoulet catch on the hob while I vac-ed round and plumped up cushions and lit scented candles in time for his homecoming.

I suppose if I'd known then that he hadn't really chosen me – that when he'd left his wife in my seventh month of pregnancy, he hadn't jumped, but had been pushed – I might not have bothered. But I was still pursuing the dream at that point. Nick might not any longer have the swanky house in Fulham or the glitzy social calendar but he had the love nest in Hackney, and it was my job to keep it cosy and beautiful and open for business. In Nick's version he had woken up one morning to the blinding revelation that I was his one true love and he was destined to be with me. He would always stand by his precious firstborn Gabe, would see right by *both* his children if he had to work two jobs to do it, but he couldn't live a lie any longer and he was damned if he'd sacrifice his own happiness to a loveless sham of a marriage. Had I really believed him or had I just wanted to?

Well, if nothing else, I had honed my skills as a cleaner, and whereas with domestic cleaning, you had nothing to show for it as it all began again the next day, here I was cleaning to a purpose. I needed a clean kiln in which to fire my pots; not just a handful or even a series, but battalions – pots enough to face down the scorn of a hundred critics. Pots enough to march forward into posterity. Pots enough to cease being pots and become topography.

I don't know how much time had passed before I had three new pieces hardening off on the shelf, all I knew was that I was enjoying myself. The wind had died down, the sun was creeping up over the treetops and if I didn't get a move on, the heat of the work surface would cook the next batch of clay before I could get it to the wheel. I was pounding it back to a throwing consistency, wiping the sweat off my temples with the inside of my elbow, when a figure appeared in the doorway.

It occurred to me, fleetingly, that I shouldn't have left my door open to all-comers in light of recent events, but by the time I had turned to acknowledge him, he was already in the room, standing foursquare between me and my only route of escape. When I saw that it was only Luca I breathed a sigh of relief. Then I remembered the flowers.

'Forgive me for interrupting,' he joined his palms in a prayer of supplication, 'I wouldn't have disturb you but your husband say I'm OK.'

'Then I'm sure you must be.'

He blinked at me perplexedly. I suppose I must have looked a sight – flushed with exertion and wild-eyed, still in my pyjamas and up to my elbows in slip. He picked up my notebook off the floor.

'Oh yes, *thank* you...' I said, holding my hand out.

'Always so interesting to see the artist's process...' He returned it to me reluctantly.

'Right...'

'Which is why I'm here, in fact.'

'I'm sorry?'

'Oh, not to intrude in that way. I wouldn't dream to be so impertinent... no. To ask whether you might be prepared to participate...?'

'Participate?' I said, frowning a little impatiently. First Douglas with his eggcups and now this.

I saw the consternation on his face and felt a pang of guilt.

'Sorry,' I said, 'I'm just a bit busy... go on. Participate in what?'

'So, I don't know if you are aware that every year Melissa and I organize an art trail for the commune...'

'The *commune*?'

'The area. The locale.'

'Oh, I see. Yes, you mentioned it the other night, but I think I said then…'

'It's very popular and it brings many visitors to the area. We produce a little catalogue with photographs of our artists' work and their biographies, and their studio location on a map and…'

'The thing is, Luca,' I said, the moment I could get a word in, 'it's too soon for me. This is literally only the second time I've managed to get in the studio and as you can see…'

I flung my arm in the direction of the almost empty shelves and a large gobbet of slip flew off my wet fingers and landed on Luca's navy polka dot scarf. I gasped in dismay and had taken a step towards him to examine the stain before I realized this might not be the brightest of moves, in view of his possible crush on me. He glanced down, and then at me, and took both my hands in his.

'Can't leave you alone for a minute, can I?' came a voice from the doorway.

I stepped back from Luca in guilty haste and Luca turned to Nick, with the round eyes of a toddler caught raiding the biscuit tin.

'I just got slip on Luca's scarf,' I said.

'I'm sure Luca will forgive you,' said Nick drily. I blushed and Luca withdrew to a safe distance and somehow we all danced around each other in a very awkward, very civilised way until Luca managed to invent a place he urgently needed to be and left, giving Nick an ill-judged pat on the shoulder and me a mortified glance on his way out.

'Lucky I didn't leave it any longer...' said Nick when we were alone.

'Don't be daft,' I said lightly, 'he was just being nice.'

'Yeah, looked like he was gearing up to be a whole lot nicer...'

I tilted my head admonishingly, but couldn't prevent my cheeks from reddening.

'Well,' I said, 'so much for getting some work done.'

'There's your "admirer", anyway...'

'You think...?'

'Oh, sure. He's got it bad. You can see it in his puppy dog eyes.'

'Nick!'

I eyed him warily as he strolled around the room, thwacking the supporting beam with his palm, stroking the work surface, casting a critical and ultimately approving eye over the quality of the workmanship he had commissioned. He walked over to the kiln and stood in front of it, arms folded.

'My second batch of pots got wrecked,' I told him ruefully.

He pulled me close and stroked my hair and for a moment, I surrendered, breathing the scent of him through his T-shirt. I wanted him then, and he wanted me, I could tell, and even though I suspected his amorousness was piqued more by Luca's interest in me than my own intrinsic charms, when he nuzzled my neck I was tempted to succumb. We hadn't yet 'christened' the studio. But then I remembered my clay – the striations and splits that would, if I didn't get some moisture on them fast, soon render the whole batch unworkable and with a great effort of will, I took him by the wrists and with a chaste kiss to his cheek, gently eased myself out of his embrace.

'Sorry but I really ought to…'

I gestured towards the bench and he looked surprised and not a little put out.

'Oh, OK then,' he said, a little brusquely, 'I'll let you get on.'

I made three more good pots that morning. I was beginning to get a feel for it so that I knew instinctively how to make each one the same, but different. Sensing the thickness of the clay, the moment to flare it out and the moment to draw it back in again. The finishing too had become a sort of ritual – the growing on of the neck, the slicing of the rim with the clay wire and the sponging of the rim into a lip. The smoothing of the surface, so that no crack or bump or infinitesimal graininess remained.

Moving the latest pot across to the shelves to join its companions, I saw that my idea was good. In just those nine pots I could see continuity but also variation. At a glance they looked more or less identical, but closer inspection revealed subtle differences, which, once extrapolated over sixty pots, let alone the hundred or more I planned to throw, might very well, depending how I arranged them, replicate the undulations of a landscape. I went over to the window and stood on tiptoe, trying to catch a glimpse of the distant hills, for comparison. But as elevated as my studio was and as lovely the view, it was too small a slice of valley for my purposes. I needed panorama. I needed to get up high.

'Anyone fancy a walk?' I breezed into the kitchen, buzzing with energy, barely registering that Ethan was back, or that he and Nick were sitting companionably at the kitchen table munching bacon sandwiches.

'A *walk*?' Nick gave a puzzled laugh. 'I thought you were working, Kaz. I'm not being funny, but don't you think you ought to stay focused? We can always go for a stroll this evening.'

'This *is* work,' I said. 'And I don't mean a stroll. I mean a *climb*.'

I waved my phone at him.

'Can I print photos from this on your printer?'

Nick shook his head as if befuddled.

'Yes. I think so, but what's that got to do with…?'

'I'm going to take some reference shots. I'll print them out and stick them up on the wall – make a sort of montage. So I can see the bigger picture, literally, while I'm throwing the pots.'

'Sounds great,' said Nick doubtfully. 'But I can't come with you. I'm pitching for a job at half past three.'

'How about you, Ethan?' I said. 'Walk off your hangover, maybe?'

Ethan wrinkled his nose apologetically.

'Did your jacket turn up by the way?' I added.

'My jacket…?' He looked momentarily nonplussed.

'You thought you'd left your denim…'

'Oh, right, yeah, no. No one had handed it in.'

He didn't meet my eye.

'Right, well, I'll just grab a bit of toast and I'll be off,' I said.

'What about breakfast?' Nick seemed quite crestfallen. 'I was just going to bring you a bacon sarnie…'

'It's all right,' I said, helping myself off his plate, 'I'll have yours!'

I took a cheeky bite, flicking a stray bit of ketchup into my mouth with my little finger.

'I'm not sure you should be going on your own,' Nick fretted, 'after what happened last time…'

'What happened last time was *you* freaked out for no good reason,' I pointed out, through a mouthful of bacon, relieved that he had not been there to witness my spectacular meltdown on top of the hill.

'I'll be fine, Nick. I'll stick to the path, I'll be less than an hour; I'll take my phone.'

'You won't get a signal.'

'OK, OK,' I said, laughing, 'well if you're that keen for me to be chaperoned…' I raised my eyebrows and Nick looked apprehensive, '… I'll call for Cath. She knows the lie of the land.'

Touché, I thought to myself.

16

I hurried down the lane with a spring in my step, but slowed as I passed Prospect Cottage, remembering my bungled flower delivery earlier that morning. Glancing up towards the bedroom window, I thought I saw the top of my bouquet, just visible between the half-drawn curtains. I felt a flush of relief – that my second-hand tribute had at least been taken in; that Gordon had bothered to put the flowers in a vase – but I felt foolish, too, for having fled so fearfully. I really did need to grow up, I told myself, resolving to knock at the door on my way back and ask after the patient. Maybe Gordon would invite me in and I could satisfy myself that he was no Bluebeard; just an old curmudgeon who'd fallen out with his daughter. Such things happened, I reminded myself. Families were complicated – of that I was well aware – and thinking of the uneasy détente between Nick and Ethan, it was probably best not to rush to judgement – there but for the grace of God... I took a deep breath and strode on. Here was progress. Here was perspective. My psych would be proud of me. The clouds were beginning to part...

I galloped two at a time up the steps to Cath's place and rapped smartly on the door. Despite its being after one, the house still seemed deep in slumber. Cath's ginger tom, winding itself round my legs in expectation of food, seemed more confident of a response than I was. I had knocked and hallooed a few times and was on the point of giving up when a startled-looking face finally appeared at the downstairs window. She looked a wreck, her spiky white hair whorled into crop circles; her eyes like two gashes in a side of ham. It was obvious she had spent the night boozing or crying or both. I smiled, gestured, shrugged – unsure quite what message I was trying to convey, but when her face disappeared I took it for dismissal and had got halfway down the steps again before I heard the door open and her voice call hoarsely, 'You'll not bugger off now you've woke me!'

'I was just heading off for a walk and I wondered if you wanted to...?'

She ordered me inside with a jerk of her head.

The place smelled like a shebeen. Sagging cushions and a rumpled blanket suggested she had spent the night on the sofa. Next to it on the coffee table stood an empty wine bottle, a large cut-glass ashtray brimming with fag ends and a wallet of colour photographs, a number of which were scattered across the floor. Making to follow her to the kitchen, I almost stepped on one and, picking it up, glimpsed a younger, slimmer, rather more handsome Cath standing with her arm around a smiley young woman in a red beanie, whose face, it took me a moment to realize, owed its indistinct babyishness to an absence of eyebrows and lashes. Even without those features Cath's companion was lovely; dark eyes full of humour, chin tilted defiantly as if daring the camera to pity her. Cath's demeanour, too, was staunchly cheerful; poignantly so, given what must have lain ahead for both of them. If love were enough to face down death, you would have given them good odds, seeing this photograph; but knowing that it had *not* been enough, knowing even a little of what followed, made my witnessing it feel all the more intrusive. I stuffed it guiltily back into the wallet and followed Cath through to the kitchen.

I found her scattering coffee grounds over the work surface as she attempted, with trembling hands and through a tobacco haze, to spoon it into the cafetière. The kitchen was in an even worse state of disarray than the living room had been. The sink was piled high with dirty dishes, empty bottles crowded the base of an erupting flip-top bin and a dish of rancid cat food was attracting a host of flies.

'You know we don't have to do this,' I said, with a doubtful smile. 'You can go back to bed and I'll call in on my way ba—'

'You'll do no such thing,' she interrupted fiercely, 'you'll have a coffee with me and then we're going on that walk, if it bloody well kills me.'

At Cath's suggestion, we took the westerly route up to the hill to avoid the dog-walkers whose cars tended to clog up the lane at weekends. Turning left at the track that ran beside the Gaineses' walled garden, we negotiated a dilapidated stile and then began an arduous twenty-minute climb through the woods. For a while the only noises were our puffing and panting, the crunch of our feet over last year's hazel shells and an occasional bout of phlegmy coughing from Cath. Despite the imminence of autumn, the canopy was still dense. Now and then, a shaft of light filtered through, highlighting an eruption of gorgeous purple fungus or a curiously shaped tree stump, and I remarked on them just to make conversation. As the woods became denser, however, such picturesque distractions were fewer, and the narrowing path and subfusc light seemed to confer an intimacy for which neither of us was quite prepared; our silence, broken only by the occasional snap of a twig underfoot, began to weigh heavy. Several times I opened my mouth to speak and then thought better of it.

'She died four years ago yesterday,' Cath said at last.

'I'm so sorry.'

We trudged on for a bit.

'I don't suppose you want…? If it helps, you could tell me about her…'

So she did. They'd met on a walking holiday in Andalucía, to which Cath had forced herself to sign up after the break-up of a long-standing and destructive relationship.

'It was either that or sit in my wee flat in London and drink myself to death,' she said. I raised a meaningful eyebrow and she gave me a wry smile and continued. She'd been drawn to Annie straight away, she told me – her sunny disposition, her inventively foul mouth – but she had not looked on her 'like that', both because Cath was too bruised from her recent heartbreak and because Annie was coupled up. However, long-story-short, by the end of the holiday, the cracks in Annie's relationship were beginning to show, Cath was utterly smitten and although not much more went on in Spain than meaningful looks, within a few months of returning, Annie's ex was, well, Annie's ex and she and Cath had moved in together.

'When you know, you know,' she said and I could only agree.

We walked on for a while in silence, our footfall prompting urgent rustlings in the undergrowth as various unseen creatures dived for cover.

'So *you* knew, did you, with Nick…?' Cath said.

I nodded ruefully.

'It was like an illness,' I said, 'I didn't recognize myself.'

I told her how we'd met, the cheesy chat-up, the cocktail, the kiss.

'He rang every alarm bell going,' I remembered with a grin.

'And you ran towards the burning building,' smiled Cath.

'Yup.'

'Worth it though…?'

'Oh yes,' I said, emphatically, 'we had Ethan for one thing…'

'Of course, of course,' Cath acknowledged, 'and a lovely young man he seems too.'

Silence fell again, except for the crunch of our boots on the forest floor.

When we started speaking again, it was both of us at once.

'It must have been awful for…'

'Is he right for you, do you…?'

Nervous laughter.

'Nick? Right for *me?*' I pursed my lips and considered. 'I don't know that I ever really looked at it like that. I was too busy asking myself if I was right for him.'

Cath gave me a puzzled look.

'Oh, come on. You only have to look at us,' I chastised her. 'Anyone can see I'm punching above my weight with Nick; when we first met, even more so. God, he was handsome. Still is, of course. But *then*! I mean, phwoar!'

'So it's physical?' Cath said and I had to smile at her directness.

'Not *just* physical, no,' I replied. 'I suppose…'

It made me squirm a little, trying to identify what it was.

'It's like… I don't know… like, there's a hole in me that only he can fill… oh God, that sounds rude…' Cath gave a little frown of frustration. I was stalling and she knew it.

'It's like… if I'm with *him*, then I must be OK. He's got all the credentials. You know, he's smart and funny, he always knows what to do and what to say. And I *never* do. He's a good dad…'

My voice trailed off as I wondered to myself if this last claim were true. He had certainly been a good dad to Gabe, but judged on the last few months, his relationship with Ethan had not, I supposed, been an unmitigated success; then again, nor had his relationship with me.

'Well, I'm happy you're happy...' Cath nodded slowly and deliberately, '... except...'

'What?'

She gave me a searching look.

'You don't seem that happy.'

I felt my face crumple.

'Sorry,' she said, before I could speak, 'sorry... I shouldn't have said that. Blame it on the skinful I had last night. Blame it on Annie.'

'It's OK,' I said, trying to mask my distress with brisk-ness, 'you're right. I'm not. *Wasn't* anyway. We've had our troubles, Nick and I. He let me down... had an affair. Such a cliché.'

She raised her eyebrows inquisitively and I was about to go further when it occurred to me that this would be disloyal. 'But he paid the price. Still is, really...'

'How so?'

'Oh well, all this...' I waved my hand vaguely towards the trees, '... isn't Nick. He's no country bumpkin, but I think he thought it'd be good for me – the peace and quiet and the space and so forth. So he found us the cottage and made it all lovely and built me my studio, which I absolutely adore and he's busting a gut to make me happy and you know, it does, it *does* make me happy, but it's early days and I still have my moments…'

'And what moments are those?' Cath said gently. Suddenly I couldn't speak.

I stopped and bit my lip. Tears filmed my eyes.

'I have… gaps,' I said, 'absences. Times when I just zone out, or get muddled. You know, like the other night at Min and Ray's…?'

'Call *that* zoning out?' Cath shook her head humorously. 'You're talking to the woman who just lost two days of her life to a bottle of Scotch!'

I smiled and looked a bit sheepish.

'Sorry,' she said, 'I didn't mean to trivialize what you went through… God, Annie used to hate me doing that. Why don't you tell me? Tell me how it started. Tell me all about it.'

I shrugged, then began, haltingly at first.

'I don't know. I can barely remember the first time now. It was so… not me. But it was prompted by the…' I tailed off, not wanting to sound histrionic, '… well, the *trauma*, I suppose you'd have to call it. When I found out Nick had been seeing… When things came to a head between us, it was all very sudden… I didn't handle it well. I had a meltdown – went wild, got very destructive and then, well, it was kind of a blank after that… '

Cath nodded ruefully. I had never really been this honest with myself before, let alone with anyone else. Not even with the psych. I had felt too ashamed.

'I suppose…' I added haltingly, wondering if it were true

even as I said it, 'I suppose maybe I knew deep down that something would go wrong between us. The next thing I was in hospital, feeling as though I'd lost everything. They wouldn't let Nick visit at first...'

Again, the beady look from Cath.

'... Just because, you know, they needed to stabilize me, plus someone had to be at home for Ethan... poor kid didn't know *what* was going on.'

Cath raised a sceptical eyebrow.

'And of course Nick didn't want to bring him until I was more recognizably his mother, because if he'd seen me how I was at first, well... it wasn't good. But then because nobody came, I sort of got the wrong end of the stick and thought I was being punished and I just kind of checked out. Just sat and rocked and didn't eat anything. And I didn't even know I was doing it. That's what I mean by blanking out. I mean... pathetic. So then they put me on these horse tranquilizers – you know, really heavy-duty antidepressants, and it was like being at the bottom of a fish tank. The days just blurred together and the food tasted of nothing and I was in la-la land. It was quite nice in a way because nothing felt real or connected, but I knew, I think, a little bit of me knew deep down that I had to be careful or I might not come back, which I didn't care about for my sake, but I was worried about...

'... Ethan,' Cath murmured, 'of course. Of course you were, hen.'

She bit her lip, as if such territory might not be unfamiliar to her and I felt a pang of shame that on this most painful of anniversaries, I was hogging the limelight.

'Anyway,' I gave a cheerful shrug, 'it's been much better lately. I hardly ever do it now, blank out, I mean. And as I say, Nick's pulling out all the stops now, so...'

'You're off them now, are you?' Cath said sternly. 'The happy pills...?'

'God yes!' I said, laughing. 'And so much better for it. Unrecognizable, really. Everybody says so. Just being here, where it's quiet; where things are so much more relaxed – it's done me the world of...'

My voice tailed off and our eyes met, hers full of kindly scepticism; mine hopeful, even a little desperate.

'Well, that's good to hear,' she said. 'Let's get you up that hill so you can take your photies!' and she folded my hand into the crook of her arm and, patting it consolingly, led me onward along the path.

We hadn't been walking long before the woods began to thin and the path veered up a nettle-covered bank and out into sunlight. We clambered over another stile and by the time we had picked our way, with much slithering, swearing and arm-clutching, across the cattle-trodden bog that lay beyond it, our conversation had reverted to a cheerful but evasive prattle. The path divided now, one branch climbing steeply up the ridge, the other, little more than a goat track, dropping down to skirt its flank. I paused for a moment to allow Cath to catch up with me.

'OK, Sherpa Tensing, ready for the north face?' I said.

Her eyes followed mine to the top of the crag and she clutched her chest comically. I felt a pang of disappointment and then one of guilt for as much as she was making light of it, I knew there was no way she could climb a slope like that in her present state of health. Striking out onto the lower path, I muttered something about the views being just as good from there, but she overtook me and blocked my path, arms akimbo.

'Oh no, you don't,' she said, 'you'll not wimp out on my account. Get yourself up that hill and take your snaps. I'll meet you at the cattle trough by the lane. You can't get off the hill without passing it, so we'll not miss each other.'

'Are you sure?'

'Are you sure?' she repeated, mocking my mealy-mouthed Sassenach politeness, so that I swiped her arm and laughed and headed up the slope without a conscience, as she no doubt intended I should. Stopping once to catch my breath, I turned and watched her wend her way along the lower track, shoulders hunched, eyes cast down. She might as well have been wearing chainmail.

I struggled to the top of the ridge, grabbing at tussocks of grass to haul myself over the escarpment onto a wide and scrubby heath. The landscape up here was more rugged than the polite pastureland that surrounded our hamlet. No hedges, roads or rivers carved it up. No distant estuary drew the eye. I was on a hill besieged by other hills, their slopes clad not in picturesque deciduous woodland, but in close-ranked spruce and pine. Here and there, abandoned clay pits had bitten chunks out of the landscape, leaving scars of sand and scree. I circled slowly on the spot, taking it all in, feeling exhilaration mount in me, realising that I could throw pots for evermore and still not do justice to this scene, but knowing too that I would have to try. I fumbled with my camera-phone, setting it to video mode and accidentally recorded several short films of my own feet before finally getting the hang of it and taking a slow three-hundred-and-sixty-degree panning shot of the horizon. I followed that up with photographs: forty or fifty regular frames from different angles, and then a couple of panoramas. By the time I was done, my wrist was aching, my head spinning and the battery on my phone was in the red zone, but I had got what I came for.

I headed down again and it wasn't long before I was back on familiar territory – the town in the distance, the church and the pub across the valley, hikers, picnickers and dog-walkers milling about on my hill as though it were Hampstead Heath. I could see Cath now, reclined on the lower slope near the cattle trough as she had promised. She was petting a large dog, wrestling its russet head playfully from side to side and looking up to converse with its owner, a skinny boy who reminded me of Ethan, who stood chatting to her with an air of awkward reluctance. She turned and gestured up the hill. I waved to her and she waved back and the boy looked in my direction and it *was* Ethan. I broke into a jog. The path narrowed and I stood to one side to allow a posse of elderly hikers to pass me and by the time I looked back again, Cath was alone.

17

'Was that…?' I asked, panting up to Cath.

'Your wee man?' she hauled herself unsteadily to her feet and turned to greet me. 'It was, aye. Didn't hang about, did he? I didn't know you'd got yourselves a dog.'

'We haven't,' I said, 'I don't know who that one belongs to.'

It occurred to me then that perhaps actually I *did*. I recalled the wetness of dog slobber on my hand, and a redhead looking enquiringly into my face, expecting an answer to a question I hadn't heard because my thoughts were elsewhere…

'Are you OK, love?' Cath put her hand on my arm and I looked into her poor tired eyes and remembered, uncomfortably, that while I was recalling what had turned out to be an imaginary heartache, she was enduring a real one.

'I'm fine,' I said, 'I'm sorry. I was just trying to think where I'd seen that dog before…'

'Gorgeous pooch,' said Cath, fondly, 'and your Ethan's very nice too of course. Lovely manners.'

I grasped her arm to steady myself as we slithered down the steeply rutted bank.

'He's stopping with you for a bit then, is he?' Cath said as we hobbled over the cattle grid and headed down the lane.

I shrugged.

'Not for long. He's saving up his airfare and then he's going to be heading Down Under. Some girl in…' My voice cracked before I could finish the sentence.

'Hey, lovey!'

'I'm sorry,' I said, flapping my hand stupidly in front of my eyes, 'ridiculous! He's nineteen. I should be pleased he's striking out and seeing the world, shouldn't I?'

Cath shrugged.

'I've never had a kid so I'll not tell you how you're meant to feel.'

'I'm being daft,' I said, 'I know I am. I just can't help thinking he wouldn't be doing this – dropping out, running away, whatever – if it wasn't for all the grief I've put him through this past year.'

'*You've* put him through?' said Cath sharply.

'Honestly, Cath,' I said, biting my lip, 'if you'd seen the look on his face the first time he visited me in that place…'

'Lovey, I think you're taking far too much on yourself. You had a breakdown because Nick betrayed you. It seems to me that the blame lies fairly and squarely with him.'

'I completely overreacted,' I interrupted sharply. 'People have affairs all the time. Christ, Nick and *I* had an affair. He was married when I met him and I knew it. It's not like I'm blameless. But his ex didn't end up climbing the walls in a psych unit, did she? She took him to the cleaners and exited stage left. *Their* son came out of it all relatively unscathed. No, it's my fault Ethan's leaving, not Nick's. If I'd acted like a grown-up, he need never have known.'

'You're being way too hard on yourself.'

'And then, just when it looked like things might be getting back to normal, Nick sells...' I corrected myself, '*we* sell the house out from under Ethan and instead of coming back to London in the holiday, where all his mates are, he gets to live in the back of beyond where he doesn't know a soul.'

'He must know *someone*,' Cath pointed out, 'if he's walking a dog.'

'Maybe,' I said vaguely. 'Anyway, the thing is...'

I stopped and hugged my elbows, throwing my face skywards in an effort to keep my composure. Cath laid her hand on my shoulder and waited. I took a great shuddering breath.

'... The *thing* is, I feel like Ethan's running away. From me... from *us*!'

'Don't we all run away at his age?' Cath said gently. 'I know I did. Govan in the Eighties was no place to come out as a lesbian, I can tell you!'

She gave me a wry smile.

'Did you ever go back?'

'I did, aye. 'Fessed up to my folks. 'Course they'd known all along. They were fine about it. Loved Annie like a daughter by the end...'

Cath's tears came then and I gathered her to me and patted her gently on the back and we stood there for a while, a pair of battle-scarred middle-aged women propped together in an awkward embrace, all but oblivious to the curious glances of passers-by.

At last Cath regained her composure and ferreting a crumpled paper tissue from the pocket of her jeans dabbed her soggy cheeks and blew her nose. Then, shoving the tissue back where it had come from, she linked my arm and we trudged down the lane in companionable silence, until saying our goodbyes at the foot of Cath's steps, we were drowned out by the manic barking of a dog coming from the other side of the hedge, silenced abruptly by a man's gruff curse. It was then that I noticed an acrid smell of burning rubber.

'Is he still there?' I whispered anxiously to Cath. 'The barn guy? I thought he'd be long gone.'

'No such luck,' Cath replied. I wished she would lower her voice. The thought of his overhearing made me uneasy.

'I've been on to the council umpteen times and they've said he's on their radar, but they've done nothing about it. I got so fed up in the end I went to have a word with him myself.'

'Gosh, was that a good idea...?' I whispered, peering through the trees. I couldn't see much – the side of the barn, all gaping holes and rusted iron, a smouldering bonfire and a stack of old oilcans.

'Ach, I'm not scared. He's wired, but there's nothing of him. I could lamp him if I'd a mind to.'

I couldn't help smiling at this.

'Is this him too?' I asked, indicating a ditch full of rubbish with my foot.

Cath nodded wryly.

'Reckons he's an environmental campaigner.'

'Yeah,' I said, 'Really looks like it...'

'Ach, he's off his heed,' Cath said dismissively. 'Self-inflicted'd be my guess. God knows what he's on...'

'You think he's a druggie?'

Cath shrugged.

'You only have to look at him to see he's not getting his five a day. Cheekbones you could shave parmesan on.'

'Oh dear,' I said. I thought of the Peeping Tom who had spied on Nick and I in the car. Hadn't he looked emaciated? Wild-eyed? No, I had barely caught a glimpse of him.

'Oh well,' I said, my voice unconvincingly cheerful, 'he'll move on soon enough, I expect, once the weather comes in. I mean – poor bugger – who'd want to be stuck in a draughty old barn all winter?'

'Oh, he's snug as a bug,' Cath demurred. 'The barn's just camouflage. He's got his van parked up in there.'

'His *van*...?' What had started as a vague feeling of unease began to coalesce into dread.

'Anyway hen, I'll love you and leave you,' Cath said, with stoic cheerfulness. She squeezed my hand.

'And thanks. It's done me the power of good to get out today. It's always a terrible time of year for me.'

'No, thank *you*,' I said, squeezing her hand in return. 'It's been good, really good.'

Did I mean good? It had felt cathartic, certainly, and had brought the two of us closer than ever, but I'd come away disconcerted and confused. Uncomfortable interpretations of the past now crowded my thoughts.

'Bye then.'

'Bye.'

I watched as Cath hauled herself up the bottom few steps. I couldn't bear to think of her returning to all that mess and squalor; the fug of stale smoke and the dirty kitchen. I wavered for a moment, thinking to follow her, roll my sleeves up, get stuck in, but I was already pushing my luck with Nick. After the fuss he'd made last time, I decided I had better go home.

'Hiya,' I breezed in through the front door, my voice a full octave higher than I'd intended. 'Sorry I've been a while. Turned out it was the anniversary of Cath's girlfriend's… oh!'

The sitting room was deserted. Nick's computer stood open on the dining table, its screen-saver flinging a neon parabola back and forth against a midnight blue background. Next to it his mobile sat atop a pile of papers, its various apps flagged with red dots where people had tried to contact him. The house wasn't empty – I could sense that even before I detected the low murmur of conversation coming from the kitchen. I heard a peel of feminine laughter, caught the faintest trace of perfume on the air. The wave of jealousy was visceral.

'Oh! Imogen, hi,' I said, trying to sound casual; friendly. She and Nick stopped talking and swivelled their heads towards me, their expressions happy and slow-witted, drunk on one another's company.

'Hello, Karen,' Imogen said, 'I hope you don't mind me sweet-talking your hubby. It's all in a good cause, I promise.'

'Be my guest,' I said, stretching the corners of my mouth into a smile. I took a mug from the back of the cupboard and pretended to dust it with a tea-towel whilst appraising myself more fully of the situation. Imogen was examining her immaculate fingernails, pale blonde hair only half concealing a becoming blush, her mouth pursed primly in an attitude of amused compunction. Nick sat back in his chair, arms folded defensively across his chest, as if to say, I'm drinking tea with a neighbour who happens to be female, so sue me. He was so busy acting the part of someone with absolutely nothing to reproach himself for, he didn't realize he was giving the game away. I could see now that they had only been flirting, but that was small consolation. I walked over and helped myself a little brusquely to the teapot that stood between them on the table and, sitting down, had no choice once it was poured, but to sip the tepid grey brew.

'Imogen's looking for volunteers,' Nick explained.

'Really,' I said.

'Oh, don't worry, *you're* in the clear,' Imogen reassured me. 'It's muscle I'm after.'

Nick waggled his eyebrows at me suggestively – a calculated double bluff.

'We've borrowed Jerry Chetwynd's marquee for the Auction of Promises,' Imogen said.

'The Earl of Amberleigh, to you,' put in Nick. I tried to look suitably impressed.

'We used it last time,' Imogen continued. 'It's great because it saves the cost of hiring one, so – more money for our good causes. But the downside is we have to put it up ourselves, which is where the muscle comes in... I've signed up Nick, Douglas and Ray, so far, but we could do with at least one more pair of hands, so if you know of anyone...'

The front door twanged on its hinges.

'Ethan...? Sweetheart...?'

I heard the sound of his boots flump one after the other on the floor and braced myself to make excuses for a taciturn, hung-over son, but when he popped his head around the kitchen door he was grinning broadly.

''Ello 'ello 'ello,' he said.

He entered the room on a waft of pungent odours: wood smoke and old sweat and a strange chlorine-ish scent that seemed out of place. He was filthy and dishevelled, but he had an air of exhilaration about him, as though he had just returned, victorious, from an iron man challenge.

'You know Imogen? From the big – from just up the lane?' I inclined my head towards her, and nodded encouragement.

Imogen half stood in her seat and held out her hand but

instead of shaking it, Ethan held his palm aloft and replied with a portentous Indian chief style, 'How!'

Imogen changed tack and gave a hesitant wave in response, which Ethan seemed to find hilarious.

I glanced anxiously at Nick, whose lips were pursed in displeasure.

'You look like you've been dragged through a hedge,' I said lightly. 'Do you want to give me that T-shirt and I'll put it in the—'

'Ah no, you're all right, Mum. Mummy. Mummikins!' he said, and then, as if he hadn't until this moment quite registered the full import of my role in his life, he clapped his arm around me and gave me a smooching cartoon kiss on the cheek.

'You're the best,' he said. 'She's the best!' he told Nick and Imogen.

I tried to behave as though this touching display of devotion was entirely normal, but I wasn't fooling anyone, least of all myself.

'Well, isn't that lovely?' said Imogen, tactfully. 'I was just telling your mum actually, Ethan, that I could use a bit of help tomorrow.'

'Oh, *were* you, *actually*?' said Ethan in an excruciating imitation of her cut-glass accent.

'Ethan,' I murmured quietly. I noticed Nick's jaw hardening with disapproval.

'I *could* use some help, yes,' Imogen said, her tone cooler, but still pleasant.

'Whaassup?' Ethan slurred. 'Your Roller need a wash?'

'I wish,' she said with a tight-lipped smile. 'No, we need another pair of hands to help with the marquee on Thursday.'

''Fuck's a marquee?' Ethan giggled.

I glanced nervously at Nick, who was staring deliberately away from his son, his fist clenched on the table.

'It's a sort of bigger than average tent we're borrowing for our Auction of Promises at the weekend,' Imogen explained. 'Takes quite a bit of putting up.'

'Don't you have servants for that sort of thing?'

'Ethan!' I remonstrated.

'Haha,' said Imogen. 'No. It's a community thing. Most people join in for the fun of it, but no problem if you're not available. Come to the auction anyway and bring your pals. There'll be a band and a barbecue. It's always tremendous fun.'

'Oh, jolly good show,' said Ethan, with a camp flap of his hand. 'I'll round up some pals and we'll come on over.'

Now Nick leaped out of his chair and lunged at his son. He manhandled him across the room in a scuffle of chair legs and grunting and pinned him against the wall, the boy's T-shirt gathered between his fists.

Imogen scrambled to her feet. 'Oh gosh, well. I... think I should probably be...'

I was barely aware of the door closing behind her. I was too busy tugging Nick's hand away from Ethan's jaw, which was mashed against the kitchen wall, while his whole body slumped in an attitude, not so much of passive, but of *insolent* resistance.

'... So you can fuck off back to whatever hole you've crawled out of and don't even think of coming back here till you've cleaned up your fucking act, apologized to our neighbours and stopped being a fucking little...' He stared into Ethan's eyes and Ethan stared back, stony with contempt, '... fuck-up!'

Nick seemed to remember himself then, giving Ethan's chin a final token shove and stalking out of the room.

Ethan gave a strange, contemptuous laugh, which quavered, halfway through, into a sob. A skein of snot drained out of his nostril and onto the floor, as if a tap had been turned on.

'Darling, please...'

I took a step towards him and put out my hand but he recoiled, throwing me a wounded glance, before slamming out of the back door.

I ran round the other way to collect his boots from the living room and yanked the front door open.

'Ethan!' I called, my voice hoarse with tears. 'Here, at least take your...'

But he continued walking away from me down the path, the only sign he'd heard me at all his raised middle finger.

Nick was clearing the tea things away from the table when I returned.

'I thought we could have chilli for dinner,' he said, his

manner casual, his tone placatory. 'There's some mince in the freezer and it'd save going shopping.'

You're a reptile, I thought.

'I'm not hungry,' I said. My head was still reeling at what had just happened.

'Oh, come on,' he wheedled, 'you will be later. You love my chilli, you know you do.'

He took a step towards me and made to catch hold of my hand. I jerked it away.

'How could you *do* that?' I hissed, my throat constricting with rage. 'How could you physically abuse our son? And humiliate him? You know he's left now, don't you? Probably for good.'

There was a beat in which Nick registered and then even seemed to savour my anger. I held my breath.

'*Him* humiliated?' he whispered furiously, his face so close to mine that I could almost taste the tannin on his breath. 'What about *me*? I've never felt so ashamed. And as for that poor woman...'

'Yeah, 'cause that's what this is really about, isn't it? *Imogen*. Lady of the Manor. No one must upset her highness, must they? You care more about what she thinks than you do about your own son. Then again, she's your type, isn't she? Blonde, clever, *posh*.'

'For God's sake, Karen, let it go...' He was looming over me now, I could see spittle glistening on his top lip; see the tiny hairs sprouting on his perfectly sculpted jaw. In that moment I hated him.

'It's nothing to *do* with Imogen,' he went on. 'She's happily married and so am...'

Our eyes met and his voice trailed off.

'So are we...' he finished, flatly. 'Or we would be if you weren't so fucking keen on holding a grudge. One mistake, I made, one. *One*. And Christ, have I paid dear for it. You in hospital, everybody hating me, my *son* hating me, your pots smashed to smithereens, the fucking neighbours... the gossip...'

'The gossip?' I repeated incredulously, '*The gossip*? Is that all you cared about? What people said? Jesus Nick, the stakes were a bit higher for some of us. Or didn't you notice?'

He stepped back from me then and cast a despairing glance at the ceiling, as if this were exactly the sort of irrational stuff he had come to expect from me.

'Oh Karen,' he said, shaking his head sorrowfully. 'You really can't see it, can you?'

'See what?'

'How it looks from planet Earth.'

'I don't know what you mean.'

'It's your reputation I'm trying to protect, love, not mine...'

I shook my head as if to clear it of a mist.

'It's you who needs the fresh start. The clean slate. We've come here for *you*. That's why it's so...' He lifted his hands as if in supplication.

'So... *what*?' I said warily.

'So disappointing, when you shoot yourself in the foot like this.'

'Like what?' I shook my head, baffled.

'When people reach out to you. Kind people, good people. Like Imogen. Like Min and Ray – and all you do is throw their goodwill back in their faces.'

'That's not true – I'm trying to make friends with people here. I am...'

'Oh, really? Is that why you bawled Ray out in his own kitchen...?'

'I didn't mean to, I was worried. I said I was sorry...'

'And why you just treated Imogen like something you found on the sole of your shoe? Not to mention standing by simpering while your waster of a son humiliated her...'

I saw then what he was doing: turning everything inside out and upside down; making me the crazy person and him the arbiter of reason. It would have worked, too, if he hadn't invoked Ethan. But I wasn't so far gone that I couldn't see how messed up it was for a father to pin his son against the wall and choke him; or, when the son has left the house – perhaps for good – to start discussing what's for dinner like nothing has happened. And that's why I started to scream.

18

'... So we're splitting up. I'm sorry to spring it on you, and I'm really sorry I had to do it in this Godforsaken hole... but I couldn't have you back to our place because we'd all have been walking on eggshells.'

I could hardly believe what I was hearing but Jude stared at me levelly from across the table, her expression one of weary resignation. If her crying was done with, the signs of her heartbreak were still very much in evidence in the persistent blotchiness of her carefully made-up face, the inch of regrowth in her immaculately dyed hair and in her general air of defeat.

'Jude, I'm so sorry.'

She was right it was a Godforsaken hole – a sushi chain on the rain-lashed High Street in Reading. I had been half-way to London before Jude's phone had stopped going to voicemail and I was able to tell her I was on my way to her place for gin and sympathy. In my discombobulated state it had taken me a while to understand what she was telling me – sotto voce and half in code, because she was still at work and she didn't want everyone to know her business

– but eventually I'd understood that for once my rock and helpmate was, herself, in need of support.

Nick had endured my screaming for all of thirty seconds. He'd made a token effort to calm me down, but when I'd pushed him away, he had stalked off upstairs and I was left pacing back and forth, fists clenched, muttering to myself like a madwoman. For a moment I'd felt that itch of destruction again; actually caught myself scanning the room for something to smash. And then I remembered where such behaviour had led me last time and the effect it had had on Ethan – concern for whose welfare had been the very thing that had sparked this rage in the first place – and I stopped myself. I had a hasty and nerve-wracking hunt for my bag, worried for a moment that I had left it in the bedroom and would have to endure the ignominy of storming in and searching for it with Nick looking on, but then I found it, spewing tissues and receipts next to the sofa. Piling them on Nick's pristine mid-century coffee table as a token insubordinate gesture, I zipped up the bag and left.

Jude gave me a jokey 'Aw shucks' shrug, as if her bad news were just one of those things and the pathos of the gesture broke my heart. I put my hand across the table and covered hers, noticing as I did so, the pale indentation made by her absent wedding ring.

'Don't you bloody start!' she said, frowning fiercely into my brimming eyes. 'I'm looking to you for a bit of backbone.'

'I know, I know. I'm sorry,' I smiled, sniffed and pushed my tears back into the corners of my eyes with my fingertips. 'It's just… I don't know… if you and *Dave* can split up…'

'Are you *kidding* me? You wouldn't have stayed with Dave for two weeks, never mind twenty-five years. No one would. He's a fucking nightmare.'

She was right. I'd have been out within thirty seconds of Dave starting his wedding speech. The guests had all howled with laughter, me included, as he insulted everyone from his mother-in-law to the maid of honour – Jude's half-Indonesian line manager from work, whom he'd nicknamed 'Dusky Denise' – to Jude's Jewish relatives, to his own brother, recently diagnosed with ME, whom Dave congratulated on going into 'remission' for long enough to enjoy a three-course dinner and a free bar. He'd insulted Jude, too, of course – calling her a ball-breaker and a feminazi, and insisting that she had, nevertheless, begged him to marry her; wearing him down with repeated proposals, until he had eventually capitulated. He'd claimed it would be Jude carrying *him* over the threshold, not the other way round, but that – you know – a man had to do what a man had to do, and the upside was she'd do anything in the sack, even… yeah, that.

It had been hilarious but also bizarrely touching because no one doubted, even as Dave slagged her off and Jude cut her eyes at him, that they were crazy about each other. Their first dance was to 'Truly Madly Deeply' by Savage Garden and for all that they began with a lot of mugging and silly exaggerated waltz-moves; by the end of the track they were smooching with their eyes closed as if they were the only two people in the world.

To be fair, I'm not sure Dave had had it so much easier over the years. Jude could be spoiled and competitive and sometimes shallow. She had a wardrobe like a supermodel's, but never anything to wear. She'd book the swankiest of restaurants and roll her eyes if you under-tipped. She could bitch for England – I knew for a fact she had bitched about me – and although I'd probably deserved it, I still cringed at the betrayal. But when I'd had my breakdown she'd stepped up. She had visited me often, in Chalford House, bringing copies of *Grazia*, expensive toiletries and illicit cigarettes. And instead of talking in the hushed compassionate voice that other visitors adopted as soon as the lobby doors slid closed behind them, she used the same frank, gossipy tone as if we were lunching in Selfridges. We would speculate about the sex lives of the nurses and lay sportsmen's bets on the rehabilitation prospects of the other 'clients' and she would beg me to slip her half a Fluoxetine to help get her through another weekend with Dave. For the time she was with me, she made me feel as though it was me that was sane, and the world that was mad. She had been there for me, and I knew now, looking at her across the table, her face drawn, her eyes bloodshot, her manicure a fortnight overdue, that the time had come for me to return the favour.

'So you're absolutely at the end of the road then...' I said, tentatively. 'You don't think it's worth trying—'

'Don't you dare say "counselling".'

'Yeah, I suppose... Dave and counselling...' We both winced.

'He's so fucking *stubborn*,' she said bitterly. 'Stubborn and repressed. I *hate* that he must have been unhappy for months – years maybe, but he never told me. He just battened down the hatches and carried on making terrible jokes and letting me believe it was just a mid-life crisis.'

'So there's definitely no one else?'

'I wish there *was*,' she said, and then, remembering, bit her lip. 'Honestly Kaz, I know it was a huge deal for you that Nick was unfaithful, I get that, but at least the fallout brought him to his senses...'

I thought of the cosy scene I had witnessed earlier in the day – Nick flirting for England, Imogen lapping it up. He had not struck me as a changed man.

'... But if there's no one else,' Jude continued, 'if Dave's not gay and he hasn't found religion and he doesn't want an open relationship or kinky sex or even a trial separation, well there's no hiding place, is there? It's not about what he does want. It's about what he doesn't want. And that's me!' She pressed her fingertips against her mouth and I thrust the condiments tray out of the way and grasped her other hand tightly.

'Come on,' I said, 'let's get out of here. We need a drink.'

'All right, ladies?' A man in a black nylon sports jacket, who had been propping up the bar in The Chequerboard pub, turned and leered at us as we walked in.

'I told you we should have found a wine bar,' I muttered to Jude. The man leaned across the bar.

'Can we have some service here please, Michael?' he called into the gloom, seeming to relish his status as the pub's sole regular.

'What'll it be, girls?'

'We'll get our own, thanks' said Jude.

'There's no strings attached, if that's what you're thinking,' he said, his eyes nevertheless lingering appreciatively on Jude's legs.

'*Strings?*' Jude gawped.

'Leave it, Jude,' I murmured.

Jude turned to the barman, a lad of no more than eighteen with a wispy goatee and a lot of freckles, who was by now awaiting our order.

'Sorry,' she said, with a polite smile, 'could you remind me what year this is?'

He looked slightly taken aback.

'Er... Two thousand and nineteen?'

Jude shook her head, as if to rid herself of a hallucination. Mr Smooth, who had by now grasped that his largesse was unwelcome, even if he still hadn't worked out why, gave his newspaper a contemptuous rattle and retreated behind it.

Jude turned to me.

'Gin and tonic...?'

I'd left the Renault parked up in the town, hardly thinking in my eagerness to escape, of a return journey at all, let alone

one the same evening. I wouldn't be calling Nick for a lift that was for sure. Still there were always taxis…

'Make them doubles,' I said.

We installed ourselves at a table on a carpeted platform behind an ugly balustrade and after clinking glasses and sipping our drinks, stared dolefully at the frosted glass window pane, etched in mirror-writing with the phrase STIRIPS & SENIW.

'So, you're staying at Anita's?' I said.

'Yeah. She's away with work quite a lot, and it's handy for the Northern Line.'

'I'm surprised Dave let *you* move out, when it was him who…'

'I wanted to. I couldn't stand the atmosphere. He was being so fucking nicey nice all the time. Like we didn't know each other. Like we were never even married…' She pressed a finger to the bridge of her nose and drew in a great shuddering breath. 'Sorry. I'm fine. *I'm fine.*'

'It's OK *not* to be fine,' I said. 'This is huge. I shouldn't think you'll be fine for ages. What is it they say? A month for every year you've been married. Something like that.'

'Cheers,' she said, with a bleak smile.

'No, I mean…'

'I know what you mean.'

'So are you… seeing anyone?'

'Seeing anyone? Already? Are you nuts?'

'No, I meant… therapy.' I mouthed the word as though it were inherently shameful.

'Ha! 'Course I am. I can't make *him* go but I'm damned if I'm getting divorced without making a massive fucking hole in the joint bank account.'

'And is it… helping?' I raised my eyebrows hopefully.

'It's going a long way to explain why Dave might have wanted to leave me, if that counts. Turns out I'm quite fucked up.'

'Oh, Jude, don't say that! You're a wonderful person. You're kind and generous and funny and smart and loyal. You shouldn't blame yourself because you and Dave have decided—'

'Dave's decided.'

'Because the two of you have… grown apart.'

Jude looked at me gravely while we both weighed the cliché and then burst into slightly hysterical laughter. At last, when we'd calmed down I turned towards the bar.

''S'cuse me, Michael,' I called. 'Can we get some shots over here?'

'So now it's your turn,' Jude said, when I had finished enumerating all the ways in which she would be better off without Dave in her life and we had toasted each of them with tequila.

'My turn to what?' I said warily.

'To tell me why you're here.'

'Why I'm…?' I must have looked alarmed.

'I'm not talking metaphysics, I'm asking why on earth you jumped on a train at teatime on a weekday, when you didn't even know I was splitting up with Dave. I know I'm nice, but...'

I looked at her. Why had I? It all seemed very hazy now. Compared to the cold hard reality of a pending divorce, my row with Nick seemed suddenly petty, my rage an overreaction.

'Oh, I dunno,' I said sheepishly. 'Nick and I had a fight. I walked out on the spur of the moment. Just to teach him a lesson really... it all seems a bit silly now.'

'What happened?'

'Honestly, Jude, compared to what you're dealing with, it's not even worth—'

'*I'll* be the judge of that,' she said. She settled back in her seat and looked at me expectantly.

'OK, well, I'd been out for a walk, with this new friend Cath – you remember, the—'

'Lesbian.'

'God, you're as bad as Dave... oops, sorry.'

She cast me a baleful glance.

'Yeah, so anyway I've been out with Cath and I get back to find Nick in the kitchen, cosying up to Imogen Gaines, you know, the posh woman whose chutney I...?'

'How could I forget?'

'Anyway, I walk in and they're looking guilty as fuck. She's totally coming on to him and he's like the cat that got the cream.'

'What's she even doing there?'

'Oh, she needs some big strong *chaps* to help put up this marquee for the Auction of Promises.'

I saw Jude suppress a smile.

'I know, anyway Nick's lapping it up. He's fancied her ever since we all did a pub quiz together.'

'Says you.'

'No really, she's just his type. You know what a snob he is and Imogen and Douglas have got this massive house. I don't know if they actually *are* gentry, but they certainly carry on like Lord and Lady Muck. Well, Douglas is all right, I suppose. I quite like him actually, if you leave his politics on one side, but *she's* fake as anything. She acts like she's this dizzy Aliceband wearing debutante, but she's actually hard as nails. I got this question wrong about Van Gogh at the pub quiz and she was all like, Oh well, *I've* got a degree in art history, so…'

'God!'

'I know!'

'Couldn't you just… not go?'

'Not go where?'

'To this auction thingy…?'

'Oh no, it's not that. Everyone's going. Anyway, I've pledged a pot for it which won't do me any harm, careerwise, because this other couple we met have an art gallery in town and he's interested in my new project, you know the conceptual thing?'

'Well, that's *great*, Karen! All these new friends, your career taking off again. Sounds like you've really turned a corner. Try and keep things in perspective; Nick can't help but flirt, it's in his DNA, but I think he's learned his lesson, don't you reckon?'

'I don't know,' I said. 'He's doing all the right things, but I don't know how he really feels. It's like we're *acting* being married.'

'How's the sex? You *are* having…?'

'Yes, of course,' I snapped, 'it's fine. It's good. Well, you know, good in a slightly fucked-up way, but that's how I like it.'

I wondered as I said this if it were still the case, if indeed it had *ever* been the case. Perhaps I'd just accepted the way Nick treated me in bed as the price I had to pay for being with a god. But what if Nick *wasn't* a god?

'Well, take my advice, keep it up,' Jude said, ruefully. 'Turns out all that bullshit our mothers told us about keeping your man happy is true. I wish to God I'd shut my eyes and thought of England a bit more often.'

'Oh, as if Dave left you because he wasn't getting any,' I said scornfully, and then raising my eyes to hers, regretted it.

'Don't take your marriage for granted is all I'm saying,' Jude said. 'Nick's been a bad boy, but he's learned his lesson. Look how keen he is to keep you. Gorgeous new home – no expense-spared ceramics studio…'

It was true, I supposed. I remembered the pride with which he had shown me around the cottage when I'd first arrived. The way he had tilted his head, like a dog wanting patting; his disappointment when I had found some tiny defect in the way he'd kitted out my studio. But had he done it because he loved me and couldn't live without me? Or because this was what a perfect life should look like? When

217

I thought of the two of us in our 'home', I didn't picture us on the sofa, my feet in his lap, nor eating bacon sarnies at the kitchen table; I saw us in the bathroom, that first night – a blurred reflection in a tarnished mirror. Siamese twins conjoined at the head – unable to function together or apart.

I doubted any of this would make much sense to Jude, however, so I just said, 'I wish he was a bit keener on keeping his son...'

'What do you mean?'

'Well, it's never been easy between them... but since Ethe turned up out of the blue, Nick's seemed on edge. Like Ethan's in the way. Like he's waiting for him to leave.'

'Karen, that's normal. London's full of boomerang kids, and anyway I thought you said Ethe was going to Australia.'

'Yeah...' I said doubtfully. 'He's supposed to be saving up for the flight.'

'Has he got a job?'

'Not that I know of... although...' I felt suddenly hopeful. 'I did see him walking someone's dog this afternoon.'

It had never occurred to me that he might be dog-walking for *money*. I felt absurdly heartened by the thought.

'It's going to take a lot of dog-walking to get him to Queensland,' Jude pointed out, 'and in the meantime, it's a small space. Nick's working from home, Ethan's hanging round like a spare part...'

'Except he isn't. He's hardly ever in. Just comes home to raid the fridge and borrow mon—'

'There you go,' Jude said. 'He's taking the piss. No wonder Nick's fed up.'

'Yeah, there's fed up and there's downright abusive. You should have seen them this afternoon. Nick had a right go at him. Had him by the throat. In front of Imogen, too. Well, *because* of Imogen, actually...'

'Oh?'

'Yeah, I'd just sat down with them and Imogen's being all sugar and spice and then Ethan walks in. He's been out all night again, and he's in a funny mood – sort of spaced-out and silly.'

'High.'

'Maybe,' I conceded reluctantly. 'Anyway, then Madam starts in on *him*. Like what a big strong boy he is – really queasy stuff...'

Jude mimed sticking a finger down her throat.

'Exactly, and she's trying to get him to help put up this marquee with Nick and Douglas and everyone, which he was perfectly fine with, but he just makes this one little crack like, haven't you got servants to do that? And Nick goes fucking ballistic!'

'Oh dear...'

'I know. One minute we're sat round having this bit of banter, and the next, Nick's pinned him to the wall, reading him the riot act.'

'Oh my God, what did you do?'

'Tried to stop him, of course. Imogen's made herself scarce by now, and I'm shouting at Nick and trying to drag him off but he doesn't let go till Ethan's turning white. And then when Ethan storms out – in his *bare feet* by the way, doesn't even stop to put his shoes on – Nick's not the least bit bothered. Just shrugs it off. Asks me what I want for dinner. I mean, what's that about?'

'I don't know...' Jude met my gaze and bit her lip '... tough love, maybe?'

I stared at her, uncomprehending.

'Only... you did say Ethan was off his face...'

'God, Jude!' I said, my indignation concealing a stab of unease. I remembered what Cath had said about the man in the barn, recalled the odd chemical smell I'd detected on Ethan. 'Are you saying my kid's got a drug habit?'

'Of course not,' she backtracked hastily. 'But they all dip in and out now, don't they? It's a big thing, drugs in the countryside. County lines they call it. Maybe Nick thought he was saving Ethan from himself. Look, I don't know, Kaz, I wasn't there. All I know is, Nick loves the bones of you. He's no saint. He's got a filthy temper and an ego the size of the planet. If he were my husband, I wouldn't trust him as far as I could throw him, but you know what...?'

I shook my head, barely trusting myself to speak.

'... If I had a marriage like yours that's endured for twenty years, that's produced a son like Ethan, that's been tested to breaking point and survived; where you can still stand the sight of each other; still sleep in the same room, still get off on the sex...'

Jude looked at me, her expression grim with pragmatism and loneliness.

'... I'd hang on to it, because from where I'm standing, it looks like paradise!'

19

I slept on the train. When I woke it was to the slamming of doors. I leaped up in a panic and without checking where we were, grabbed my bag and hurried to the door, only just managing to get off before the guard waved the train off again. Luckily it was the right station. It was only as I followed the eight or ten local passengers out onto the forecourt that I realized how drunk I still was. Not staggering, falling-down drunk, but the kind of drunk where imitating sobriety becomes the overwhelming challenge; where every little movement from unzipping one's handbag to smoothing a fly-away strand of hair seems as exacting as brain surgery. Certainly I knew better than to get behind the wheel of the Renault, which, as the last couple of commuters reclaimed their vehicles, soon looked lost and lonely in the long-stay car park.

I found the taxi rank and tried to look like the respectable fare I would have been, had I not had the last couple of shots. I watched the flurry of activity as the few remaining passengers were met by relatives and swept away in hatchbacks and four-wheel drives. I waited a few minutes and then walked to the corner and looked up and down the high street. Apart from a flashing neon sign advertising payday loans, and the bluish glow of refrigeration coming from the organic butcher's, the town was dark. There would be no taxi. I reached into my coat pocket for my phone, but despite Jude's special pleading, I found I couldn't bring myself to ring Nick. I was still too angry and hurt. I knew just how it would go – he would swoop down on me in the Range Rover and fling open the passenger door, hatchet-faced. Then he'd be aloof and condescending on the way home as if I were the one who had something to apologise for. It would get sorted in the bedroom, but I couldn't face that either. Not this time, not tonight. I was a grown-up and I could get myself home. It was a distance of barely two miles, only the last little stretch without pavement. It would be a chance to walk off the booze.

It was the blue hour. Dusk had not yet quite turned to night, but in the Victorian terraces that lined the road out of town, the curtains were mostly drawn. I could hear canned laughter from a TV sitcom and the distant barking of a dog. On a steeply sloping drive, someone revved a motorbike, shrouding me in exhaust fumes and I crossed on a diagonal to the other side of the road. Soon house gave way to cottage, cottage to barn and barn, finally to open countryside. The land fell away to pasture on my right and climbed behind dense hedgerows on my left and except for the occasional swoosh of a passing car, I was alone.

A harvest moon was rising, silhouetting the trees on the opposite side of the valley and giving a strange radioactive glow to the cream-coloured cows that dotted the fields below me. 'Beautiful,' I murmured out loud in an effort, I suppose, to convince myself that the walk might be a pleasure rather than the ordeal it was beginning to seem. I stopped and reached for my phone, thinking to choose an appropriately jaunty soundtrack. I jammed the headphones in my ears and was soon striding out in time to the soft reggae of Jimmy Cliff, feeling if not quite cheery then empowered. I had, after all, drawn a line in the sand: let Nick know that despite my recent frailties, his behaviour had consequences and shown him I was no longer prepared to be a pushover. There had been no messages all afternoon, but that was classic Nick. Never show weakness, never capitulate. He would, I knew, be furious with me for walking out and have resolved to punish me with silence. By now, though, I reckoned he would be getting twitchy, might already be wondering if I were coming back at all. Let him sweat.

I had been walking for about five minutes, when instinct told me I was no longer alone on the path. This in itself was hardly sinister. Plenty of people – well, all right, a few – made the journey from the town to our village just to enjoy the charms of The Fleece. I picked up my pace a fraction – more to put a decorous distance between us than because I felt scared. Another hundred yards on and I'd decided that it was just the echo of my own footfall bouncing off the steep sides of the valley. Fifty more and he was definitely there, slowing when I slowed, speeding up when I did. Now I was rattled. I switched off the music, and surreptitiously tugged the headphones from my ears. *Clack, clack, clack, clack.* Whoever it was ought to know better. If he was there… was he there? Soon I was resenting the intrusion of my breathing, of my own heartbeat for getting in the way of all the listening I needed to do. All it took was the creak of a bush in the field below me for my pulse rate to soar and my pace to quicken. I stole a glance over my shoulder. Did someone shrink back into the hedgerow? A few yards ahead, the road curved into a canopy of trees, the branches arching overhead like the ribs of a whale. How had I forgotten this was here? This cave, this unlit catacomb? If I speeded up, could I be out the other side before my pursuer entered? Probably not. What had possessed me to think walking was a good idea? I turned on the torch app and its pale beam faltered. I cursed myself and Jimmy Cliff. I had a choice to make now – torch or phone call, phone call or torch. There was not enough battery for both.

Calling… calling… still calling… pick up, pick *up*…

'Nick Mulvaney here, can't get to the phone right now…'

My heart was going like a pile-driver. Decision time. I could follow the path through the tunnel of trees or I could peel off and go across country. I could see the lights of the hamlet down in the dip. It looked close, but it would be a good twenty-minute scramble, through bog and nettle patch. Still, glancing behind me, seeing a tell-tale movement in the darkness, a cross-country assault course seemed preferable to ploughing on into the cave of trees, pursued by this figment, this wraith, this *crow-man*. I had one leg slung over the wall and was poised to drop down into the field when the phone vibrated in my hand.

'Nick!' I almost sobbed. 'Can you come and get me? I'm on the main road out of town, about half a mile from our turn-off. You know just before it goes into that…?'

The phone cut out.

I stared at it, stunned, trying to remember whether I had given him enough information to find me. Whether I had or not, I must stay put now; make myself a sitting duck. Well bollocks to that. I swivelled my legs back over the wall, strolled casually out into the middle of the road, arms folded, and cast a shrewd appraising glance down the road.

There was no one there. There never had been. What had looked, at a glance, like a sinister figure shrinking back into the darkness was now nothing more than a nest of brambles stirred by a brisk autumn breeze, the footsteps I'd heard after all just the echo of my own. I felt foolish and cowardly and annoyed with myself. I could already see the headlights of the Range Rover carving their way up the lane in the distance, its headlights vanishing and reappearing as if on a lifeboat navigating choppy water. I could hear the expensive purr of its three-litre engine; discern each brief hiatus as Nick moved up the gears, gathering speed until he reached the junction. Then a silence, so long I thought he had dropped clean off the planet, almost long enough to make me believe in my bogey man again, before his tyres squealed onto the main road and his xenon headlamps turned the arch of trees from a gloomy cavern into a green cathedral. I stepped out and waved my arms as if landing a jumbo jet.

'What the fuck did you think you were doing?'

I turned to find the buckle of my seatbelt, telling myself to stay calm, to not let him rile me.

'I was mad with you,' my words tumbled out in a garbled stream, 'rightly say I'd so... I mean rightly *so*, I'd say, after what you did to Ethan. You've got Jude to thunk that I came back at all. She sheems to be under the impression we've got something worth savaging.'

He leaned towards me and sniffed.

'Have you been drinking?'

I gave a loud hiccup and laughed in surprise. Now the danger had passed I realized I was still quite squiffy.

'Jesus, Karen! How much have you had?'

'Not that mush,' I said.

'You walked from the station in that condition? You might as well have stuck a sign saying "rape me" on your back and have done with it.'

'Oh, don't be riduc – ulous!'

Nick turned up a rutted track, reversing back out straight into the path of an oncoming car.

'Fuck off!' he muttered under his breath as the driver flashed his lights, then accelerated homewards, the silence between us stretching out until it seemed impossible to breach.

'Jude and Dave are getting divorced,' I blurted, unable to bear it any longer.

Nick didn't react. I stole a curious sideways glance at him.

'I know,' he said after a long moment and I gawped at him.

We had turned into our lane by now. Nick was hurtling recklessly over potholes and around bends, making me feel queasier than ever.

'How come?' I said, closing my eyes briefly and gripping the front of my seat.

'Dave told me when they were down.'

'But that was ages ago...'

Nick shrugged.

'Why didn't you tell me? Jesus. He hadn't even said anything to Jude then...'

We were on the home stretch now.

'Because *you'd* have kept it under your hat, wouldn't you?' Nick took his eyes off the road momentarily to give me a scornful glance and in that instant, something loomed out of the dark, pale and sudden as a hologram.

'Nick! *Stop!*' I shrieked and he stamped on the brake so that we were both flung back against our headrests.

'What the fuck?'

'It's OK. It's OK,' I said, 'You didn't hit her. It's Jean. What on earth is she—?'

Nick applied the hand brake and I scrambled out of the car and ran around to where the old woman stood like a rabbit in the headlights, white hair stuck out at all angles, clothing in disarray.

'Jean!' I said, taking her arm gently. 'You gave us a terrible fright. What are you doing out here?'

She jerked her elbow away touchily and I realized she didn't know me. I had fretted over her, empathized with her, watched her house for signs and portents, but for all my supposed concern, I realized, I had never bothered to befriend her.

'Hello, Jean,' Nick appearing suavely on her other flank, 'bit late for a stroll, don't you think?' She cowered as he tried to take her arm, huddling towards me as if for protection.

'Now then love,' he said, more firmly this time, but she batted his arm away, whimpering.

'Nick, you're frightening her.'

'This is ridiculous,' Nick muttered grimly, 'I'll go and get Gordon.'

I stroked Jean's arm to reassure her and she turned her face towards me so that the moonlight illuminated a fan-shaped purple stain on her cheekbone – the remnants, I realized, of the black eye she had sustained on the day I went to London. For a split-second I saw again the same subliminal tableau I had conjured that day – a man's hand raised in violence, a woman's body crumpled on the floor, only this time the man was Nick and the woman was me and I didn't know whether I was looking at Jean and Gordon's past or my own future; whether this was a warning or a curse. And then the image was gone and Jean's claw-like hand was clutching at me in distress and Nick and Gordon were heading down the path towards us, chuckling grimly like a couple of poachers about to bag a deer.

'It's OK, love, we've got this,' Nick said, replacing me at Jean's right elbow, while Gordon, hatchet-faced, took her left. I bowed my head and hurried homeward, not looking back, only stopping to catch my breath when I could no longer hear the sound of her keening.

20

I had my key in the lock of our front door before I noticed through its mullioned window the indistinct shape of a figure sitting on the couch. Joy and relief flooded through me.

'Hello, *stranger*...' I said, the emotion in my voice betraying my attempt at levity. He turned round in surprise and the disappointment winded me; it wasn't Ethan, as I'd thought, but Gabe. I should have known from the hair; Gabe's was much lighter and cropped closer to his scalp.

'Oh!' I said, trying not to sound dismayed. 'Nick didn't tell me you were coming...'

Gabe muted the television and sprang up to greet me with an awkward air kiss-cum hug.

'You're OK, then?' he asked, backing off again. 'Nick said you needed rescuing.'

'I'm fine, thanks,' I said, a little touchily. 'Just, my phone was dying and it's pitch-black on that road without a torch. When did *you* arrive?' It sounded like an accusation.

'This afternoon. I thought it was about time I checked out the Country Seat and Dad said the er... room... was free.' He looked a little shame-faced. I could imagine all too well what Nick had said. Abel, come down quick, Cain's done a bunk.

'Well, it's lovely to see you,' I said briskly. 'Nice for you and your dad to spend some time together, too.'

He nodded eagerly and there was an awkward silence. I realized I must cut an odd figure, breathless and dishevelled from my encounter with Jean. I was conscious too that he would have smelled alcohol on my breath.

'Well, I... I might just pop up and have a shower,' I said. Gabe gave me a puzzled look.

'Where's my dad...?'

'O-h-h. Yeah, there was a bit of a... this elderly neighbour of ours, Jean. She gets a bit confused now and then. Anyway, she was out on the lane just now, wandering about on her own, so he's just helping her husband... round her up.'

I closed my eyes briefly at the memory and opened them again to find Gabe giving me a bemused smile.

'She's too strong for me,' I said, 'I gave it a go, but...'

Why was I explaining myself? How did he always manage to make me feel like a lesser mortal? A freak?

'Nick'll be back any minute. You just...' I waved vaguely, '... make yourself at home.'

He looked perfectly at home already, I thought, watching him reach for the TV remote again; more at home than I was.

The heat of the shower felt like love. The water cascaded down on me, relaxing my tense muscles, sloughing off the dead skin cells and the pollution; evaporating the last fuzzy traces of tipsiness. I closed my eyes and luxuriated for a few minutes in the feeling of warmth and wellbeing, steering my mind deliberately away from Jude's predicament and Jean's – my own, come to that – and focussing instead on the physical pleasure of the water drumming on my head, the scent of the shampoo and the feeling of vitality and rejuvenation.

I put on some clean jeans and my favourite sea green jumper. Coming back downstairs, I could hear Nick and Gabe bantering like old mates. Nick was sitting forward in the leather armchair, ankles crossed, scruffy old deck shoes sliding off his calloused heels, beer bottle dangled lazily between two fingers.

'... Bloke's a fucking animal. He's spent more time on the bench than on the pitch, but defensively they're screwed without him...'

He turned at the squeak of my damp feet on the last few stairs and his eyes flicked over my body as if taking an inventory. Finding everything to be in order, he gave me a faintly vulpine smile and said, 'Hello, you.'

'Hi.'

'Hungry?'

'I could eat,' I conceded, although I was hardly in the mood.

'Boil a kettle for the rice, will you, mate,' Nick murmured to his son, 'and grab some knives and forks.'

I watched Gabe spring out of his seat and lope over to

the kitchen. He was so like his father; not in his colouring or even his stature, but in the way he carried himself. He had a grace, a confidence so compelling that even his deficits – the overly long Byzantine nose, the eyelashes so fair as to be almost invisible – seemed like assets. No wonder they had named him after an angel.

'So...?' I said looking at Nick.

Nick smiled perplexedly as if he didn't know what I was getting at.

'... How was Jean?'

He pulled up the sleeve of his sweater to display a livid scratch on his forearm.

'Pretty fierce, actually. I don't know how the old boy copes with her.'

I knelt beside him, pouting sympathetically and ran the pad of my thumb over the scratch, pressing just a little harder than I should have when I got to the middle. He didn't flinch.

'Did you go in the house?'

Nick pulled his sleeve back down.

'Of course.'

'Is it...?'

What? What was I asking? Is it a dungeon? Is she chained to the bed? Forced to wee in a bucket?

'It's spotless.'

'You're kidding.'

'No wonder the poor old sod's a bit uptight. Must be a full-time job. He's not getting any help from social services either. Different generation though; they've got a lot of pride. I'd like to think I'd be like that if you went gaga...' he grinned roguishly, 'but who knows...'

I shuddered.

'Poor baby,' he said, 'the cold's got into your bones. Shall I light the wood burner?'

'Do you want the curry in a dish or what?' Gabe called from the kitchen.

'Nah,' Nick said, 'just bring the pan to the table. We're family, aren't we?'

Are we? I wanted to say. *Are* we family? Isn't there someone missing? I couldn't pretend any more. I couldn't dissemble. I leaned forward and said to Nick in an urgent undertone, 'Have you heard anything from him? From Ethan?'

He closed his eyes briefly in exasperation.

'Nope,' he said and then, not even as if he were changing the subject – as if to him there had *been* no subject, he turned his head and called, 'naan breads, mate. Bottom left oven...'

'Is he staying long?' I said, jerking my head towards the kitchen. I sounded about six years old. A sulky brat. Pitting the boys against each other in precisely the way I had promised myself I wouldn't.

'Till Tuesday, probably. He had leave owing and it was a case of use it or lose it.'

I think we were both aware of the unspoken comparison. *This* son's no slacker; *this* son's on a career path.

'Don't worry, though,' he added pleasantly, 'we'll be out of your way tomorrow. Little job to do for your favourite neighbour.'

I frowned, Jean still being uppermost in my mind.

'Which neighbour?'

'Imogen's marquee, remember?'

'You're actually going to show your face?' I asked incredulously. 'After what happened?'

'Ethan behaving like a dickhead, you mean?' Nick said, meeting my eye.

'Nick, you nearly bloody strangled him...'

Gabe was hovering beside the table by now, holding a pan in each hand. Nick leaped up to put a tablemat beneath each of them.

'Ethan can come and apologize any time he likes,' Nick muttered, sitting down again and pushing the rice towards Gabe. 'He knows where we live.'

Gabe spooned rice onto three plates and handed them out.

'Where we *live*?' I hissed, incredulously. 'He lives here too, Nick. It's his *home*, in case you hadn't noticed. The only one he's got.'

'Lamb bhuna?' offered Gabe uncertainly.

Getting no response, he shrugged and served that out, too. I sat down mechanically and picked up my fork.

'P'raps he ought to treat his home with a bit more respect then,' Nick fixed me with a defiant glare. 'Treat the *community* with a bit more respect.'

My fork clanged on the table.

Both men looked up in surprise.

'I'm not hungry,' I said, pushing my chair back abruptly as I stood. 'I'm going to bed.'

The bedroom was immaculate: the duvet smooth, the chair adorned only with Nick's clothes from yesterday, somehow even more stylish in their slight dishevelment than fresh from the hanger. The room smelled not just of his aftershave, but of the deep-down Nick scent that still stirred something in me despite everything. The blind was open and the moon had risen higher in the sky since my walk, illuminating the summit of the hill like a spotlight trained on an empty stage.

I got into bed. Hunger gnawed my gut and I tried not to think about my helping of lamb bhuna, probably even now being divvied up between Nick's and Gabe's plates. If it were me, left downstairs after such a scene, I'd have been too upset to eat. Nick, I knew, would just say 'waste not, want not' and tuck in.

I fell asleep quickly and had a nightmare. I could hear Ethan crying in the attic of our cottage. Nick had put him to bed in the cot he'd slept in as a baby. His fully grown arms and legs were splaying awkwardly through the bars, but his cries were the needy hiccupping sobs of an infant. He was dehydrated in the dream, his eyes sunken, his breathing rapid and shallow. He was going to die if he didn't get water. I tried to run down to the bathroom to fetch some, but the staircase kept turning into an escalator carrying me backwards. When I did finally make it to the bathroom sink, the tap was rusted up. Ethan's cries were becoming fainter and more pitiful now and I was frantic. I ran out of the cottage and found myself not on the lane, but on our old street in London. I ran up the path of our next-door neighbour's house shouting, 'Help me! Help me!' but as I got nearer, the house became overgrown and by the time I had thrashed my way through to the front door, it had turned into Prospect Cottage. Through the window, I could see Nick sitting at a table with Imogen. He was pouring water from a crystal jug into her open mouth. I pounded on the glass with my fists, but they ignored me. Nick just kept pouring the water so that it overflowed from her laughing mouth, onto her breasts and pooled around them both on the floor. I pounded on the glass until my fists ached, but Nick just kept pouring and Imogen kept laughing and the water kept pooling...

'Hey, hey. Baby. Relax. It's just a bad dream, OK?' It was Nick's voice; Nick's hand softly stroking my cheek.

'No, no,' I heard myself mumble, '*bringha waggah, godda geggah waggah...*'

The dream was slipping away from me; Ethan was slipping away. I blinked up through the semi-darkness, my heart rate gradually slowing, my powers of recognition returning.

'The *wagher*...' I mumbled forlornly.

'Yes, it's here, take a sip,' Nick pushed a glass into my hand, 'here, let me help you.'

'No, no, it wasn't for...' I muttered confusedly, but the dream was already hazy and remote. I could no longer tell what was real and what was a figment. It was easier to give way, to succumb. He was gazing down at me now with concern in his eyes, and yes, perhaps even love; kneading my shoulder, murmuring endearments.

Nick moved his hand gently down my upper arm and his touch became intentional; erotic. It was with a strange detachment that I registered his thumb massaging my inner elbow, his hand sliding down my forearm, clasping my palm and interlacing his fingers with mine. He squeezed my hand interrogatively and more out of curiosity than desire, I squeezed back. He turned me over then and hitched up my hips so he could work the pillow underneath them and I splayed my legs to make it easier for him. I heard the rattle of his buckle and the rasp of his zip, but I did not, to my surprise, have the usual Pavlovian response of wetness, of readiness. He took a handful of my hair, wrapped it around his fist and bracing against the pillow, used his free hand to twist my arm a little way up my back – not too far, just far enough.

Usually by now I would be breathless; thrilled to be overcome, to be taken. Usually by now I would be burying my face in the pillow to stifle the first groans, because the rule was that if I appeared to be enjoying it, he would stop. Usually by now, my hips would be writhing and he would have to tug on my hair to slow me down, to remind me that gratification was best deferred. But tonight, I felt nothing; no, not nothing, I felt indifference, inconvenience, *boredom*. He was getting into the rhythm now, his thrusts growing stronger, more emphatic. He had not yet adjusted for the angle of maximum penetration. Usually that was the point at which I got so turned on by his desire that my own satisfaction became an irrelevance. *I* became an irrelevance and that was the biggest turn on of all. I would raise my head, take one last gulping breath, like a long-distance swimmer and go down again, biting the pillow so as not to cry out. Not tonight though.

Tonight something strange was happening. My face was in the pillow, yet I could see the back of my own head. It was as though I had floated up to the ceiling – was in my body but also outside it. Looking down on the pair of us from on high, I noticed how strangely my hair sprouted from my crown and that my knuckles were getting bony with age. I saw how ridiculous Nick looked – buttocks going like the clappers, jaw set in a rictus of ferocious concentration. I had an overwhelming urge to laugh and forgetting that I was down there as well as up here, I *did* laugh – a big irreverent snort into the pillow. Luckily, Nick took it for a groan of ecstasy and when, despite my best efforts to subdue them, my shoulders continued to shake uncontrollably, he seemed to think I was coming.

21

I was woken by an incongruous noise – a city noise; the gasp of air brakes on a truck followed by five syncopated toots of a horn. For a moment I thought I was back in Trenchard Street.

'Nick,' I mumbled, rolling over and patting his side of the bed. It was empty, the duvet thrown back. I sat up groggily, my head still pounding from the hangover and remembering where I was, stared one-eyed around the room. Nick's jeans had gone from the chair and the bedroom door was ajar.

I could hear shouting coming from the lane now, more cheerful in tone, more 'can-do' than it would have been in London. Then came the electronic *woop woop* of the truck's reversing, the clatter of metal; more bellowing. Imogen and her bloody marquee! No wonder Nick was up and at it. No doubt Gabe had been pressed into service too; I pictured a gang of able-bodied males, all waiting eagerly for Her Ladyship to say jump so they could chorus, 'How high?' I squinted at my phone. Seven forty-five a.m. They had a nerve. I flopped back onto the pillow and closed my eyes again but it was too late, I was wide-awake.

Thinking I might as well make the most of the early start, I put on an old T-shirt and my dungarees and made my way down to the kitchen. The sink was still full of last night's dirty dishes. I was so hungry that even the slightly stale morning-after whiff of curry made my mouth water. I'd had nothing to eat, I realized, since the sushi I'd picked at yesterday with Jude. Nick and Gabe were long gone, the only evidence that they'd even passed through, two soggy teabags on the draining board. I put the kettle on and while it was boiling, opened the fridge and scooped cold rice into my mouth with my fingers. I'd have liked to help myself to a bowl of leftovers, but the thought of being in Nick's debt, even in this small way, stuck in my craw. Instead I took a bruised banana out of the fruit bowl and, once the kettle had boiled, made a cup of tea and took my makeshift breakfast down to the studio.

I opened the door with trepidation, half expecting to find pottery shards on the floor, some sinister message scrawled in the clay dust, but everything was normal – perhaps not quite as clean as I might have left it on an average day, but orderly enough. I thought of the unexpected turn events had taken since I'd walked out of the studio on a whim to take my photographs – the heart-to-heart I had had with Cath in the woods, the disconcerting discovery of the van parked up in the barn, the whole Nick and Imogen fiasco, Ethan's departure...

Ethan... I tried not to think about where my son might be now; what he might be up to. If I'd let it, my imagination would have run the gamut from crack dens to petty crime, but I chose to remember the dog-walking and trust in his essentially good character. When had worrying ever helped in the past? It hadn't. I perched on a stool at my work surface and, peeling the banana, surveyed my studio, now so crowded with finished pots that there was scarcely room to dry new ones. The pots were more numerous than I remembered, but also, somehow, more accomplished. They looked like the work of a craftswoman, an artist, someone who had put in the hours and knew what she was doing. I washed down my last bite of banana with a swig of tea and hopped down from my stool.

The block of clay I had re-wrapped cursorily yesterday, expecting to be gone no more than an hour, still lay on my work surface like road kill. I heaved it off the melamine – a leathery dead thing – and lowered it into the bucket of viscous brown slip which I used to revitalise old clay. I fetched my cutting wire, wiped over the work surface with a clean cloth and, when I judged the clay to have had enough to drink, hauled it out again and set about dividing it in three.

I was wedging the first piece; had it almost ready to throw, when it all kicked off next door: clanging, banging, the clatter of mallets and the whirr of electric tools. Every kind of repetitive, spine-jolting, head-jangling noise and all of it accompanied, not by calling, not even by shouting, but by bellowing.

'To you!'

'To me!'

'Left a bit… right a bit. Hold it there. Hold it… ho-o-old it…'

I marched over to close the window, but once there, I became distracted. It was too compelling an entertainment to ignore: the bluster, the camaraderie, the underlying masculine competitiveness; the sense that the very future of civilization depended on the successful completion of the task. I could hear Douglas issuing instructions in his clipped patrician tones, Nick being cheerfully insubordinate and Gabe trying to mediate between the two. There were other voices I didn't recognize, an older gruff-sounding local and his sweary sidekick and an eager-to-please posh boy whose nasal laugh was frequently and ingratiatingly deployed.

Listening to their banter, I was relieved Ethan *wasn't* there. I knew how it would have gone. Ethan would have done his best in the face of a barrage of little jibes and criticisms from Nick, designed to deflect responsibility for his son's imaginary shortcomings. If they were lucky, they might have made it through the morning; if not, if Ethan had made some more conspicuous gaffe – mishandled a tool say, or twisted a guy rope (which his father's ungenerous scrutiny would have made more likely), Nick might well have lost his temper and given Ethan a public dressing down. I had heard – or more precisely, not quite heard – such confrontations too many times over the years, hovering on landings and in doorways, eyes closed, fists clenched, trying to summon the nerve to intervene; to remind Nick that carping criticism was not necessarily the way to bring out the best in an insecure adolescent. I shut the window with a defiant bang and went over to my wheel. It was too late to be the parent I'd like to have been.

I just about managed to screen out the background noise after that. Only once did the ballyhoo break my concentration mid-throw. I was nine-tenths of the way there on what would (I had counted) have been my forty-third pot, all told, when a collective shout of consternation went up, followed by a pause, a creak and then the faint tinkling of glass.

There goes the Orangery, I thought, with some satisfaction, before slowing the wheel and gathering my clay back into a formless lump, ready to start again. But it could only have been a setback, because twenty minutes later I saw the pinnacle of the marquee swaying drunkenly back and forth above the hedge as its central support was hoist aloft. There was a brief babble of excitement, then a long and suspenseful pause, and finally, an almighty cheer. You would have thought they had raised the *Titanic*.

I was loading a couple of bone-dry pots from the rack into the kiln when I heard a tactful cough from behind me.

I ignored it and carried on with what I was doing.

'It's up!' Nick said, his tone somewhere between pride and prickliness.

'Great,' I replied, closing the door of the kiln and ostentatiously devoting all my attention to setting the timer.

'Brought you a little treat to celebrate.'

I turned round. Nick was propping up the doorway, hair dishevelled, sweat patches ringing his T-shirt, a plate in his hand and a winning grin on his face. Seeing him, my breath caught in my throat as it had that first time, as it did still, whenever I was ambushed like this by the sheer fact of his physical beauty, his ease.

'What is it?'

'A croissant.'

'Where've *you* got a croissant from?' I narrowed my eyes. Don't flirt, I said to myself. Don't succumb.

'They be from 'Er Ladyship,' he said, tugging his forelock comically. ''Er at big 'ouse. Workers' perks.'

Of course! A second-hand croissant. Leftovers. I carried on with my task, pointedly refusing to make allowances for his presence.

'No?' he wheedled. 'I can make you a coffee to go with it. We could sit on the steps and shoot the breeze.'

I turned back to my work.

'I'm busy, Nick,' I said.

I continued to ignore him, but still he loitered in the doorway.

'So, it starts in a couple of hours...' he said.

'I'm not coming,' I said.

His face fell.

'What do you mean? You can't *not* come.'

He grew petulant now, like a child used to having its own way.

'You'll be letting people down. They're expecting you. It's for charity.'

He pulled a booklet out of his back pocket and chucked it on my work surface. 'You're in the catalogue, for God's sake.'

Now I saw. None of this was about me – his visit, the second-hand croissant, the making-nice. It was all about him. If I didn't turn up to the Auction of Promises he would look bad. People would talk behind their hands; speculate. He had become the sort of person he used to ridicule. Perhaps he had been that person all along.

'I have no desire,' I said, 'to sit around with a bunch of people who think I'm crazy, drinking sherry and making small talk to raise money for the church fucking *roof*, while my son's sleeping in a doorway somewhere, thank you very—'

'Karen!' he barked, and I winced. 'Karen… love…'

He took a step towards me, his tone already more reasonable, but beneath the surface I could sense pent-up rage, carefully mastered – the scariest kind. He came over to where I was squatting beside the kiln and, taking my hands, pulled me upright, holding my wrists gently. I felt my pulse quicken. I think he did too.

'… Just please come along. Not for them, not for the church roof, not for appearance's sake. For *me*. Because I'm proud of you. Because the pot you've pledged is going to raise a lot of money and put you on the map. Because you're the best. Because I love you.'

An hour and a half later I was making my way downstairs, showered, coiffed, as made-up as I dared and sporting the strapless stripy jumpsuit I had bought in the Stella McCartney sale and fallen out of love with when Nick said it made me look like Andy Pandy. I could hear voices coming from the living room, not just Nick's and Gabe's, another voice too.

'Cath!' I said, and my surprise must have been almost as obvious as my pleasure. The three of them were sitting stiffly around Nick's coffee table chatting awkwardly like wedding guests.

'Well, hello!' said Cath, turning round and giving my outfit the once-over. I could feel myself blushing, not only with the mortification of Cath's very evident approval, but also with the fear that it might be misconstrued. To my surprise, however, Nick joined in with a wolf whistle of his own, half satirical, half genuine, as far as I could tell, and I blushed a shade darker.

'Bit of Dutch courage before we brave the Gaineses',' Nick said, waggling his open beer bottle at me.

'*I'm* on Earl Grey,' Cath pointed out, as if to deflect any criticism. I shrugged and smiled.

'Can I get you a drink, Karen?' Gabe made to get up.

'Oh, no. No thanks,' I said, still trying to work out how this unlikely pow-wow could have come about. Nick seemed to read my mind.

'I bumped into Cath earlier on and we agreed it might be a bit less daunting if we went to this shindig together; safety in numbers type of thing…'

I gave Nick a sceptical smile. The idea that a man who'd been touring the conference circuit for a decade might need his hand held at a country garden party was ridiculous, but that only left the theory that he had joined forces with Cath for her sake, or mine, or both – all three possibilities recasting him in a more favourable light than I had been prepared for.

'Have you seen this?' Cath waved the auction catalogue at me.

I gave a noncommittal shrug.

'Some of the lots are hilarious,' Gabe said. 'Listen to this: "an antiques valuation in your home, offered by Marlowe & Foulkes, specialists in antique jewellery, Fabergé, Tiffany glassware and Russian antiques".'

Nick looked around the living room with narrowed eyes, as if trying to recall where he'd left the gold-plated samovar and we laughed obligingly.

'Or if that doesn't appeal,' Cath picked up her own copy and flicked through the pages, 'how about a wine-tasting tutorial with Jacinta Berryman, food and drink correspondent for *The Country Gazette*.'

'Oh, we should definitely bid for that, darling,' Nick said to me, drolly. 'We totally need to be refining our palettes now we're in the county set.'

I stretched the corners of my mouth.

'To be fair though,' he added, 'there's some pretty decent stuff in here. I thought when they said "Auction of Promises", it'd be like the ones they used to have at Inkerman Street,' I stiffened slightly at the mention of Ethan's school, 'you know, "lot twenty-three, a baby-sitting session from the childminder from hell, lot twenty-five, a romantic dinner for two in the Salmonella Tandoori…"'

'There was *some* good stuff,' I chastised him gently. 'There was a Reiki massage one time, I remember, and a nice lino-block print. We got outbid on that one.'

'Thank God.'

Gabe, who had been flicking through his copy of the catalogue, looked up and shook his head in amusement.

'Dad, there's stuff in here you *literally* could not make up. Listen to this. "A circus skills workshop with Hengist Debonair." I mean, what the fuck…?'

'And if you do yourself a mischief on Hengist's unicycle,' Cath put in, bashing her own pamphlet triumphantly with the back of her hand, 'a two-hour healing with crystals session from Marion Baverstock should do the trick.'

Once our guffaws had died down, there was a pause and we all sighed and shook our heads, the smiles of amusement fading from our lips and a slight awkwardness descending again.

'Well… shall we?' said Nick, standing and crooking his arm with exaggerated courtesy for Cath to take it, which she graciously did. Gabe turned and offered the same gallantry to me, and feeling foolishly overdressed, and in spite of myself, not a little curious, I took his arm.

The gates to Walford House were thrown wide and adorned with balloons and bunting. A large cardboard sign, coloured in felt pen and propped by the laurel hedge read, 'AUCTION OF PROMISES OVERFLOW PARKING'. A hectic rainbow-coloured arrow pointed towards the neighbouring farmer's field, but the overflow parking facility must itself have over-flowed, because a number of cars had been left straddling ditches by the roadside.

'Nice gaff,' Gabe said, and I thought again how much like his dad he was. He was right. It was a very nice gaff – not the formidable English pile I had been expecting but a simple unpretentious house of mellow stone, with a gabled three-storey elevation on either side of an unadorned square porch. That its sandstone tiled roof sagged, that an elegant arched window on the third floor had been bricked up by some seventeenth-century tax-dodger and that one of its chimneys listed alarmingly, only added to its quirky charm, as did the late-blooming wisteria which rambled all over it.

There must already have been over a hundred people milling around on the lawn, not a familiar face among them. It was a much more mixed crowd than I'd been expecting. There were the usual suspects in flannels and Panama hats and at least two women in the same Boden dress, but there were also hipsters with sleeve tattoos, arty types in vintage clothing and flash-looking youths in Hollister. Cath nudged me and nodded towards a red-faced man in slacks and a navy blazer. 'I swear he was on *Question Time* last week,' she said, in a loud stage whisper. From inside the marquee came not the genteel sound of a string quartet, but the easy-going chug of a blues band. The two little Gaines girls appeared beside us, offering from trays of drinks.

'There's Pimm's or prosecco or beer in the gazebo,' they chanted in unison.

'How *lovely*,' I said, accepting a glass of Pimm's from the one who had put the evil eye on me for splashing her dress with chutney. She gave me a chilly smile and turned to Cath who plucked a glass impulsively off the tray and stared at me defiantly. Nick bowed to each child in turn with exaggerated politesse.

'Thank you, Grace, Honour,' (either he'd struck lucky or he could actually tell them apart) 'but I think the beer will be more up our street.'

He clapped a blokey hand on Gabe's shoulder. 'Their old man's a bit of a craft ale fanatic,' he explained.

'Ladies,' he turned to Cath and me, 'shall we reconvene in the marquee in five?'

I watched them stroll across the lawn, their route taking them directly past Imogen, who despite being deep in conversation with a buxom dowager in a twin-set, plucked at Nick's sleeve as he strode past. He didn't break his stride, still less bother to stop and introduce Gabe to his hostess, just cast an amused glance over his shoulder. It was the sort of interaction, complacent and intimate, which you'd expect between very close friends – or lovers. I was still smarting from the pain of having witnessed it when Min appeared beside me, cool and stylish in a cream cotton Nehru jacket and jeans.

'Hello, Karen,' she said, 'I was hoping you'd be here. Haven't seen you in ages. You look lovely by the way.'

I blushed and stroked the back of my neck, unusually exposed by an experimental up-do, which I was already coming to regret. Given my behaviour last time we had met, I was surprised Min should evince such warmth, but I was grateful too and tried to show it.

'And as for *you*,' Min said to Cath with mock reproach.

'Aye, yoga, I know, I know…' Cath said, holding her palms up defensively, 'I should never have let you sign me up.'

'You do *yoga*?' I said, regretting my tactlessness as soon as the words were out of my mouth.

'Well, as it turns out, I don't,' Cath said ruefully, 'but I do subsidise the yoga class Min goes to, which is a public service of a kind.' She gave a wheezy chuckle and I thought how very fond of her I'd grown.

'Sorry,' I said blushing, 'I didn't mean…'

'She's made it to two classes all term,' Min said, coming to my rescue, 'but before she starts,' she raised a warning finger at Cath, 'she was complimented by the teacher on her exceptional core strength.'

'That'll be the gardening,' I said.

'It'll be the reinforced lycra leggings,' Cath corrected me. 'If you want to know *why* I only made it to two classes, look no further than those diabolical things. They all but gave me a hernia. Great for staking fruit trees, though…'

Min and I laughed.

'How about you, Karen?' Min said. 'It's Hatha yoga, the gentle kind; a dozen middle-aged hippies in the village hall. Thursday mornings, nine-thirty…?'

I raised my eyebrows challengingly at Cath.

'Aye, go on then,' she relented, 'I will if you will. We'll get some of them hareem pants off the market. Sign us up for next term, Min.'

People were starting to move towards the marquee in greater numbers now, willowy well-spoken Charlottes and gangly blushing Rufuses, sandal-wearing Ziggies and blue-haired Skyes. Min took my arm and we filtered into the procession behind a gaggle of sweary young Irish grooms from the local racing stables.

'Is Ray not with you?' I asked, furrowing my brow. She jerked her head towards the marquee from where a husky, booze-soaked voice could be heard growling, 'I laid in bed so long that I damn near saw another day come back round.'

'No!' I stared in delighted disbelief at Min and then at Cath for corroboration. But of course, it wasn't such a stretch that Ray the petrol-head should also be Ray the bluesman. He wasn't bad either.

'Always one to make the most of a captive audience,' Min said wryly, with just a hint of pride. 'Well done for getting *your* menfolk to show up, by the way. Not an easy task when the football's on telly. Ethan looks well.'

'Ethan…?' I said, looking around me in hopeful bewilder-ment. She waved vaguely towards the terrace.

'Oh, that wasn't Ethan,' I said quickly, 'that was Gabe, Nick's other son.'

'Oh, I didn't know he had a... they're very alike, aren't they?'

Were they? I wondered. They didn't seem so to me. The head-shape perhaps and the broadness of the shoulders. It wasn't that you'd call Ethan less handsome – the opposite if anything; there was a fullness, a slightly female prettiness to Ethan's looks which neither father nor half-brother possessed, but where Nick and Gabe bestrode the landscape like lions, easy and unselfconscious, Ethan's gait was alert and defensive, as befitted one used to slinking in the wake of mightier creatures, scavenging their kills.

'I suppose,' I said doubtfully, 'but Ethan's not... around at the moment.'

'That's funny,' she said, looking at me curiously, 'because Ray said he bought him a pint up The Fleece the other night. Him and his young lady...'

22

The marquee was already packed. We were lucky to get the last few seats at a plastic table near the back. The atmosphere was a cross between a society wedding and a folk festival. Barefoot primary school children chased one another round the tables and elderly couples sat behind untouched drinks, tapping along tolerantly to the music with slightly wistful smiles on their faces. At the margins of the tent, shifty-looking teenagers clustered in their different tribal groups.

Ray Chaney and The Sprockets were coming to the end of their set. They finished to cheers and foot-stomping from the audience and Ray slid his kerchief backwards off his glowing head and mopped his neck with it, before stowing his guitar and making his way towards our table, where Min had a chair and a pint of Bishop's Mitre waiting. We all sat forward, eager to congratulate him on the band's performance but he waved away our praise. An announcement over the PA system brought the last stragglers in from the garden, including Nick and Gabe, who edged their way through the throng, each bearing a plastic garden chair above his head. They had no sooner manoeuvred their way over to us and sat down than Melissa and Luca arrived, homing in on us as if there were only one place to be. Ever the gentleman, Nick sprang up and offered his seat to Melissa, who accepted with more eyelash-fluttering than seemed strictly necessary. Luca turned down Gabe's offer of a seat, choosing instead to kneel on the grass beside me and prop his arm on the edge of my chair. I inched my thigh surreptitiously away from his elbow, which he took as an invitation to encroach a little more, darting me a grateful smile for my trouble.

Douglas Gaines bounded onto the stage, adjusted the height of the microphone on its stand, tapped it and then recoiled at its amplified stutter.

'Always wanted to do that… Well, what can I say? What a turnout. On behalf of Immie and myself, oh – and the girls of course – welcome to Walford House and to our third Auction of Promises, once again in aid of the church roof restoration fund and the Saint Aloysius Hospice.'

There was a flutter of applause.

'I take it you've all got one of these?' he waved an auction catalogue. 'Now I know when it comes to good causes, you've got very deep pockets. Our last auction two years ago raised a cool nine and a half thousand pounds,' (much whooping and foot stomping) 'and we only had half the number of pledges we've got today, so I'm confident we're going to beat our record very handsomely this afternoon.

Because we've got so much lovely stuff on offer, however, we're going to divide the proceedings into two sessions and take a refreshment break halfway through, so do please stick around because we're saving the best till last and we'd hate you to miss out.'

Luca jabbed his elbow meaningfully into my thigh and looked up at me with a manic grin. Already I was regretting my slight over-familiarity with him at Min and Ray's dinner party.

'But now, without further ado, let me hand over to our esteemed auctioneer, everyone's favourite landlord, your friend and mine, Kevin Lister from The Fleece. Kevin!'

'Ladeez'n'genlemen, can I just say what a pleasure it is to welcome you to this episode of *Homes Under the Hammer*? Sorry, what... it's not? Oh, I do beg your pardon...'

It was strange hearing the landlord do his shtick again – it took me back to the night of the pub quiz – a season and a lifetime ago. How wide-eyed and anxious and eager to please I had been. How keen to make a success of this strange unaccustomed new life; how daunted by my fellow team members – all of them here in this tent now – who weren't really daunting at all. Not even Imogen, the hostess with the mostest, with her social graces, her superior art history knowledge and her glossy blonde hair. I watched her for a minute, glancing this way and that, checking on the caterers, acknowledging friends and acquaintances, and, when she thought no one was looking, casting covetous glances in Nick's direction. She saw me watching her and, embarrassed to be caught in the act, gave me a cute little wave. I realized with a sort of curious detachment that I did not in fact want to kill her; that perhaps I even pitied her.

'So ladies and gents, boys and girls, straight, gay, bi, trans, cis,' the landlord fixed the audience with a satirically beady eye, as if challenging anyone to object to his newly acquired PC nomenclature, 'that's the one I can't figure out,' he confided, 'cis.' He mugged at the audience, who laughed uneasily and then with a well-timed comic shrug, he moved on. 'A-n-yhoo... whoever you are, however you *identify*, if you've got money in your pocket and love in your heart, you are welcome, *most* welcome to the jamboree of charitable giving that is the third Walford House Auction of Promises. Let's hear it for our hosts Douglas and Imogen Gaines, lovely, *lovely* people. Now without further ado...'

The first lots went in a flash. Twelve chocolate and vanilla cupcakes pledged by the two little Gaines girls rose quickly from ten pounds to twenty-five, to thirty, finally selling after a nail-biting face-off between two ardent cupcake fanciers, for forty-five pounds. A weekend's dog-sitting went for a stingy twenty-three, and a tarot-reading offered by a garrulous local eccentric was won by a dismayed Min for only eight pounds.

'The next lot is for all you nature lovers out there,' the landlord said. 'It's a once in a lifetime experience. The kind of treat that only a landscape as fertile and abundant as this one can offer. No, I'm not talking about a roll in the hay with the missus...' Groans from the floor. 'It is, and I kid you not,' he peered closely at the auction catalogue as if to verify the sheer magnanimity of the offer, 'a mushroom foraging session, in our beautiful woods here, led by local lothario, fine art connoisseur and all-round fun gi, fun *gi*, ladeez'n'genlemen, did you see what I did there? Luca D'Agostino. I am reliably informed by the donor that no fewer than five varieties of delicious edible mushrooms can be found hereabouts if you know where to look and Luca D'Agostino, my friends, knows where to look. What am I bid for this gastronomic one-off? This unique chance to go foraging – yes *foraging*, ladies – at the crack of dawn with a handsome Italian?'

Luca shook his head in amused despair, cupped a hand to his mouth and called, 'Hey, I'm a married man.'

'Spoilsport!' called Imogen Gaines and everyone laughed.

'So, let's start the bidding. Mushroom foraging for four at a time of your choosing. What am I bid?'

After the landlord's hype, the silence and shuffling that followed was painful to endure. Luca sat up high on his haunches next to me, his knee held in the crook of his arm, his other hand tapping an anxious rhythm on the seat of my chair. The silence stretched on. Out of the corner of my eye I saw him glance up at me hopefully, but I stared straight ahead, determined not to further embolden a married man with whom I already regretted having flirted, and who had taken so little encouragement to send me flowers. There was a nervous cough, someone tittered, Luca raked his hand once more through his hair and my resolve cracked.

'Ten pounds,' I called, raising my hand. Luca looked up at me in adoration and already I was kicking myself. From across the table, Nick gave me a weary eye roll.

'Fifteen,' came a voice, plummy and amused, from somewhere near the front. It was Imogen.

'OK, ladies,' the landlord rubbed his hands together, 'looks like we've got a fight on our hands.'

Luca looked unbearably smug now, but it was too late for regrets, I had been assigned my role in the drama and not to up my offer would be to show my opening bid for the empty gesture it was.

'Fifteen pounds fifty?' I called feebly and the audience groaned.

'*Twenty* pounds,' called Imogen Gaines and the audience cheered. There seemed no way back now. We were locked in combat, Imogen and I, and as much as I did *not* want to go mushroom foraging with Luca and Melissa, nor did the spoilt child in me want to lose out to Imogen Gaines.

'Twenty-five,' I called.

'Thirty!'

'Thirty-five!' I dared not look at Nick.

'Fifty pounds!'

'Sixty!'

Out of the corner of my eye, I could see Luca bunching

his fists like a football fan watching an attack on goal. I was steeling myself to up the ante, when a man's voice called out, 'One hundred pounds!'

A little frisson of amusement and perplexity rippled around the room. Heads turned, but not mine. I knew who it was – it was Nick.

I couldn't see Imogen from where I was sitting, but I could hear the smirk, the challenge in her voice when she said, 'One hundred and *fifty* pounds.'

The marquee was quiet. A rope creaked and outside the caterers could be heard chatting amongst themselves.

'So, for one hundred and fifty pounds, going once, going twice...'

'Two hundred pounds!' Nick called.

The landlord looked enquiringly towards Imogen, but must have received a shake of the head.

'*Sold* to the gentleman at the back for *two hundred pounds sterling*, thank you for your generosity, sir!'

There was a collective sigh of relief. People started chatting and drinking again.

'Congratulations,' I said to Luca. 'That's a lot of money you've raised.'

'Yes, it's very good,' he replied. 'I hope you will come on the trip also...?' He looked up at me with bloodhound eyes.

Lots came and lots went. Some raised even more than Luca's mushroom hunt. A spa break bought for one of the Boden ladies by her stockbroker husband made three hundred pounds, a weekend at Min and Ray's B&B a very respectable two hundred and seventy. Hengist Debonair's circus skills proved more popular than Marjory Baverstock's healing crystals. Cath's window boxes went for seventy quid apiece.

By the time the landlord announced that he'd faint if he didn't get a cucumber sandwich, it was already five forty-five and the total raised had exceeded the proceeds of the previous auction by five hundred pounds.

We poured out of the marquee onto the lawn as intoxicated with our generosity as if we had paid off the national debt of a small developing country. Douglas's voice crackled over the PA system informing us that the auction would resume in half an hour's time and that meanwhile we should top up our glasses and fill our boots as it looked like being a late one. A boogie-woogie number came tootling through the loudspeaker and people started to relax, mingle, eat and drink.

I felt light-headed and a little bit sick, a fact I chose to put down to the three glasses of Pimm's I'd drunk on an empty stomach, rather than to Min's casual mention of Ethan, which had flustered and perplexed me in ways I didn't really want to confront. I suppose I should have welcomed news of him. If he had gone to the pub, he must have had the price of a pint. The fact that he had exchanged pleasantries with Ray suggested at least a vestige of social responsibility and if he had a local 'lady friend', his plans to emigrate must at the very least be on hold. More importantly, it suggested that he probably wasn't shooting up smack in a bus shelter somewhere, an unacknowledged dread that had been nagging at me ever since his shopping 'spree' in London had left at least a hundred pounds of his father's largesse unaccounted for. Somehow, though, the thought that our son should be living in our community completely estranged from us – that our neighbours should be more au fait with his movements than we, his parents – seemed not just humiliating, but a badge of failure.

I stopped a teenage boy in a bow tie, carrying a tin tray of egg and cress sandwiches and took a fistful in a shroud of napkin.

'Sandwich, anyone?' I said, through a mouthful, but no one else seemed hungry. I was wondering what to do with the surplus when Imogen Gaines descended on me, one hand raised in the air. Realising in the nick of time that she intended not a recriminatory slap, but a celebratory high-five, I jettisoned my sandwiches and met her halfway.

'Yay to foraging!' she said. 'That was so fun. *Wasn't* that fun?'

'Yes… great,' I said, rubbing my smarting palm.

'And your super husband has invited me and Douglas to be your guests!'

'Terrific.'

'It's crazy really to have a whole living larder out there and not take advantage of it, isn't it?'

'Mad,' I said.

There was an awkward silence.

'I love your...' she gestured towards my jumpsuit with the back of her hand.

'Thanks.'

I suppose it might have looked a bit rude, my turning my back on her, but Ray looked like leaving the group and I needed to catch up with him.

'You're a dark horse!' I said, a little breathlessly, following him up the steps to the terrace. 'Great band you've got there. I had no idea.'

'Oh, yeah, thanks,' he said. He seemed wary of me, and who could blame him. 'Having fun?' he added.

'Fun might be a bit strong...' I had rolled my eyes, before I realized how mean-spirited my attitude must seem.

'Well... I was just going to top up my...' He jerked his head towards the beer tent and started edging away from me and I saw that I had blown any chance of friendship with him. I was the uptight snobbish Londoner, the helicopter parent, the crazy lady. Come back, I wanted to say. Never mind Ethan. Tell me about you, your marriage – how you and Min, with love to burn, can be childless, whilst Nick and I, with two strapping boys between us, have...

But he had gone and I was left stranded on the terrace. Below me on the lawn I could see Nick giving Gabe a matey slap on the shoulder, Imogen and Melissa enjoying a joke, Cath and Min helping themselves to scones. The sky was turning periwinkle blue. Cardigans and cigarettes were coming out. Gestures were becoming more expansive, laughter more raucous, strappy sandals lay abandoned on the grass.

'Karen!'

'Yoo hoo!'

'We're going back in!'

I snapped out of my reverie and looked down to see Min, Cath and Melissa on the lawn below me waving their arms like sirens.

23

My pot was the second to last item in the catalogue, sand-wiched between a weekend course in Discovering Ayurveda and a pre-owned dressage saddle. It would have been nice to have got it out of the way earlier so I could relax, but I could see what Douglas's thinking had been. Get everyone drunk, then load the back end of the auction with a combination of big-ticket items and white elephants. I wasn't sure into which of these two categories my donation fell, but as long as *somebody* bid for it I no longer cared. Even now, a dusty-looking bottle of red wine was going up in increments of fifty pounds and had just surpassed the amount I'd paid for my 2009 Renault Clio.

'Serious money's stuck around, anyway…' Nick whis-pered, nodding towards a table of scruffy-looking eccentrics who were braying ever more loudly as the evening went on.

'Just as well,' I murmured back, 'I can't see normal people affording this stuff.'

'Going once, going twice, sold to the gentleman in the fetching red braces, thank you, sir, and don't drink it all at once.'

The atmosphere inside the marquee had changed since the refreshment break. Very young children had been taken home to bed, and some of the older folk too had wearied of the proceedings. A younger crowd had dropped in, some on a whim, having picked up the spare catalogues that were lying around in The Fleece; others, I suspected, who just wanted to see how the other half lived. The noise level was higher, the landlord's patter more liberally scattered with double entendres, the vibe generally more lairy.

For me, the drink was starting to wear off. I was beginning to feel remarkably clear-eyed; detached almost. Between lots, I watched Cath chatting with Ray and Min, her accent growing stronger, her conversation more meandering with every slug of wine she took. I watched Gabe and Nick compete instinctively and unwittingly for the attention of Melissa, who, sitting between them, turned her face sunflower-like toward whoever shone the brightest. And every so often, when Luca's forlorn stares became too much for me, I stared back at him, and he affected a sudden fascination with the roof of the tent, or the auction catalogue, or his fingernails.

Caught up in the drama of a bidding war for a sourdough starter kit, I don't think any of us noticed the latest group of newcomers shoulder their way into the back of the tent. I heard one of the Gaineses' Labradors snarl and the other one bark, but Douglas shushed them and it was on to lot number forty-three, a bespoke hat donated by Anastasia Baines-Cass, whose creations, the landlord would have us know, had graced the cover of *Vogue*. One of the newcomers gave a satirical wolf-whistle and turning round half amused, half indignant, to see who was responsible, I caught my breath. There were five or six of them – louts, you would have to say. Not because of the way they looked – they were no scruffier than many of the other youths in attendance – a knitted beanie here, a lobe-stretcher there. No, it was their swagger, the deliberate air of menace they projected. As if they had come to take stock, to see what gave, to decide on a whim whether to let the event pass off without incident, or if they'd a mind to stir things up a bit. Two of them in particular were familiar to me and of these I didn't know whose presence dismayed me most. One looked a little different from the way he had the last time I'd seen him. His head, then fully shaven, now had a Travis Bickle-style Mohawk stripe down the middle. He was not wearing the aviator sunglasses he had worn when he had driven his van at us, but even if I hadn't recognized his air of jittery grievance, I should have known him by his neck tattoo. The other one was my son.

'What...?' Nick said, noticing the look on my face as I turned back to face the front of the room but there was no time to explain because suddenly all eyes were on me.

'There she is, give us a wave Karen,' the landlord was saying and I realized that he had been introducing my lot.

'And it can be anything they like, can it? A fruit bowl, a nice vase?'

I was trembling. My mouth seemed to slice sideways as I spoke, as if I'd been injected with Novocaine.

'Yes,' I stammered, 'whatever anybody wants.'

'There you go, ladies and gents, whatever you want, from our local ceramic artiste. Who wants to start the bidding?'

'A blow job,' shouted one of the newcomers.

Nick started out of his seat, but I tugged him back down.

'All right, that'll do,' the landlord said, his tone betraying just enough anxiety to undermine any authority he'd hoped to assert. 'This is a charity function. If you want to bid on this lady's pot, by all means do, otherwise you'd better make yourselves scarce.'

'We're after something a bit stronger than pot, mate.'

This witticism was met with sniggers from the newcomers, sucked teeth and partially turned heads among the wider room. Women gathered cardis and bags towards them; men sat up straighter in their chairs and tightened their fists round their glasses.

'Fifty pounds!' Cath's voice rang out, deep and Glaswegian and fearless.

For a moment there was silence, and then another voice – Luca's – called, 'Seventy.'

The landlord resumed his habitual pose, like a conductor on a podium and the room was wrested back to something like normality.

'One hundred pounds,' called Douglas Gaines.

'A hundred and twenty!'

'One fifty!'

'A hundred and seventy-five!'

All over the room, different voices pitched in. Barely any of them, I was sure, really wanting a bespoke fruit bowl, all of them keen to play their part in this symbolic reassertion of civilization over mob rule. The asking price had reached a ludicrous eight hundred and seventy pounds, before people gradually came to their senses and dropped out of the bidding, leaving the floor to the two genuine enthusiasts.

'Nine 'undred pound,' Luca said recklessly.

'Nine fifty!' said Cath.

'Nine 'undred seventy-five'

'A thousand pounds!' Cath banged the table decisively. For a moment there was silence. Luca seemed to have lost his nerve. He darted a doubtful glance at Melissa, who shrugged in reply but as he opened his mouth to raise the bid, a volley of ear-splitting barks drowned him out. The dog must have been with them all along – kept on a tight leash, I suppose, and trained to respond to the flicker of its master's eyebrow, in the way such creatures are by men who think it's clever to assert their power by the abuse of a dumb animal. It was off the leash now, all right, and launching itself toward the front of the marquee with a skitter of claws and a low-pitched snarling. A volley of ear-piercing barks briefly drowned out the cries of startled observers, who stood up and surged forward so we at the back could no longer see.

'Call your fucking dog off!' I heard Douglas shout.

I heard screams and stampeding feet, the ferocious snarling of the attack dog and the pathetic yelps of its victim.

Gabe took me by the arm and tried to lead me away, but I shouted, 'No!' and shrugged him off. I had seen Ethan plunge into the mêlée and I wasn't leaving as long as he was in harm's way.

I barged as far forward as the cluster of people and furniture would allow and craned my neck to see. Now everything seemed to slow down, the expressions on the faces of the two camps frozen and exaggerated – the atavistic leers of the gate-crashers; the shock and dismay of the guests. A punch was thrown; a glass deliberately smashed on a table's edge. There was a scuffle. I saw the landlord jab in panic at his mobile phone; Douglas and Ray circled the dogs, poised to intervene, then, someone, oh God... it was *Ethan*... pitching straight into the middle of it all.

He grabbed the dog by its hind legs and yanked them apart as if pulling a Christmas cracker, but the dog had its jaws clamped around the Labrador's flubbery neck and wouldn't let go. It was then that Ray made his move. I think he must have punched the dog on its muzzle because it uncoiled like a spring and rounded on my son with a snarling, slavering sound I shall never forget.

I couldn't remember afterwards how much I actually saw of that part, and how much I filled in the blanks, based on the injury Ethan sustained – a deep gash to the fleshy part of his right hand. It was horrible. Even at a glance and in the dark, I could see he'd need stitches, but *she* wouldn't let me anywhere near him – his girlfriend. She must have been there all along. I don't know how I'd missed her – I suppose it was because I was so focused on Van Man, but looking back, I think it was probably just a coincidence that they arrived together. Ethan was with *her*.

They were halfway down the Gaineses' drive when I caught up with them. She was wrapping her scarf round his hand to staunch the bleeding, which didn't look too hygienic. I told her as much, but she didn't want to know. She shouted at me; said there wasn't time to argue the toss because she needed to get him to A&E. I'm not saying her speech was slurry, but she'd obviously been drinking. I said I'd call an ambulance, but she said there wasn't time and we had a bit of a scuffle near her car, which I'm not proud of. It was just the thought of her speeding off three sheets to the wind, with my son in the passenger seat.

There were several versions doing the rounds in the days that followed. For some, Douglas had saved the day; for others, Ray had played the decisive role. One rumour claimed that a flick knife had been pulled; another said one of the Labradors had had a heart attack, a third said that one of the onlookers had. Depending on whom you believed, someone had performed the Heimlich manoeuvre on one of the dogs (half true), someone else had had hit one of the thugs over the head with a bottle and was now going to be prosecuted (almost certainly untrue). Even Nick and I couldn't agree – or perhaps I should say, of course we couldn't. For him, Ethan had been the villain; for me, the hero. But leaving aside the facts of the matter, Nick's predisposition to condemn his own son was the thing I couldn't forgive. Shouldn't a parent stand by their child through thick and thin? Wasn't that what we were there for?

It didn't matter either way in the end. Ethan knew nothing of my unconditional parental support. I don't think he said a single word to me throughout the whole hideous episode. He'd have been in shock, of course, and I was in a dreadful state myself, but even so our eyes met only once and that was in the passenger wing mirror as I stood in the middle of the lane watching her drive him away.

24

'Came to see how you are,' Cath said.

She was standing on the back doorstep, holding a lit roll-up furtively behind her back.

'I'm fine,' I said. 'Come in. Actually, I could do with one of those. I'll come out.'

'Just saw Nick head off in the car.' Cath nodded towards the lane as though his departure had been part of some rarely witnessed seasonal migration.

'He's dropping Gabe at the station. He was supposed to be staying till Tuesday, but I think he's had enough of the countryside. Too much excitement!'

We both smiled ruefully.

She handed me my roll-up and lit it for me. We smoked in silence for a minute or two. She looked at me and bit her lip.

'Any news of Ethan?'

I shook my head.

'Last I saw his girlfriend was taking him to A&E... at least I assume she's his girlfriend.'

I sounded huffy and aggrieved. I despised myself.

'He must be OK then,' Cath said, kindly. 'You'd have

heard if not. It was front-page news in the local rag, "Brawl as yobs invade charity fund-raiser…"'

'Comes to something when you have to read the news-paper to find out if your son's alive or dead,' I muttered.

'At least you know *someone's* looking out for him…'

She must have seen the look on my face.

'She's a nice girl by all accounts,' Cath added gently. 'Sally, her name is. Works in that estate agent's in Rivington. Does the odd shift at The Fleece…'

'I'm sure she's perfectly lovely,' I snapped sourly.

We stubbed out our cigarettes in the plant pot by the back door and went inside. I poured us both a coffee and we sat down. I looked into Cath's big, anxious face, its cheeks so scribbled with broken capillaries that red had become its predominant colour, and I felt a rush of remorse.

'I'm sorry I was rude,' I said, 'I just feel so…'

'No, lovey,' she patted the back of my hand, 'you've had a nasty shock. It's to be expected.'

'Is Ray all right?' it occurred to me, belatedly, to ask. 'Have you seen him?'

'I have, aye,' Cath said. 'Called in on my way up to you as it goes. He's fine. They gave him a tetanus booster to be on the safe side, but he didn't get bitten at all apparently. Amazing really. He was telling me the technique. You have to take the dog by surprise and then, the second it loses concentration…'

I continued to watch Cath's lips move and to nod vacantly from time to time, but I couldn't hear her voice any more.

I was thinking of Ethan shacked up in some local bedsit with Sally; the two of them spotting me from a distance in town and crossing the road to avoid me. I wouldn't blame them. At least Sally had stuck up for him – taken his part. Not like me. To think I'd stood there in my own kitchen and watched his father physically abuse him... *colluded* in it, you might almost say.

'... Anyway,' Cath went on, 'on the plus side, your friend and mine'll be out on his ear. Van Man. I doubt they'll have the evidence to charge him, but he'll definitely get his marching orders from the barn. You see, if the council had evicted him when I first made a complaint, none of this would have happened.'

'Hmm,' I said. A couple of weeks ago, this news would have had me falling to my knees in relief. The crazy guy; the stalker – dismemberer of crows, toppler of pot plants – was to be evicted, once and for all. But I hardly cared any more. All of my hauntings and stalkings, watchers on hills, the dark forces of long barrow and ley line, now seemed fanciful and overwrought. A spell cast by my own troubled mind.

Nick came back full of bluster and bonhomie and kissed me on the cheek as though nothing had happened.

'Hiya, Cath,' he said, 'how are *you*?'

'I'm all right, aye,' she said a little coolly.

'I bumped into Imogen in the lane,' Nick said, avoiding my eye. 'They just heard from the vet. Looks like Frieda's going to pull through.'

I caught my breath. The *dog* was going to pull through. Put out the bunting. Strike up the band. His son might lose full use of his hand, but the neighbour's Labrador was going to be OK. Cath saw the look on my face.

'Well, that's something,' she said.

'She and Douglas are very concerned that the auction shouldn't be eclipsed by all the bad publicity,' Nick went on. 'They're worried it'll put people off; that they'll think for some reason the results of the auction won't stand.'

'Who *cares* about the results of the auction?' I snapped. 'Who cares about the fucking church roof?'

'They want people to know,' Nick said in a low, even voice, as if he was talking to a child, 'that despite all the worry they've had, they'll be following up with the admin and the best thing everyone can do to support the family is to make good on their payments, if they haven't already, and enjoy the things they bought.'

'Well, I shall be making good on my payment, don't you fret,' Cath said with a breezy cheerfulness. 'I'm looking forward to owning an original Karen Mulvaney.'

I rolled my eyes. Her effort to lighten the mood was transparent, but it seemed unkind not to meet her halfway.

'You paid far too much for it,' I scolded her, 'I'm embarrassed.'

'I don't think Luca would agree...' Cath said.

'Ah yes, Luca!' said Nick, as though the mention of his name had jogged a memory. He took his mobile out of his pocket. 'I have a text here from Luca. He put on a terrible

Italian accent and read, "*I 'opa you all OK after traumatic events of a the weekend. If nota too soona for you guys, I propose mushroom hunt for theesa Thursday. Condeetion looksa good.*"' Nick made a goofy thumbs-up sign, satirising, we could only imagine, Luca's chosen method of signing off.

'Mushrooms! I mean, *honestly...*' I said.

'You don't need to come if you don't want to, darling. I don't think anyone'll think any the less of you under the circumstances. Although of course Luca will be disappointed.' This last with a meaningful smirk.

I hated him in that moment. I had had a lifetime of his flirting, had been all but destroyed by his affair; watched him revert to type within a year of supposedly turning over a new leaf yet he had the nerve to tease *me* over the unwanted attentions of an amorous Italian, whom I'd done precious little to encourage. It would no doubt suit him very well if I dropped out of the mushroom hunt and left him with his female fan club.

'Oh, don't you worry, I'm coming,' I said.

'Well, that's great,' he said, lightly planting a kiss on my cheek. 'Now if you ladies will excuse me, I think I'll go get a shower.'

'Well...' said Cath awkwardly, 'probably time I went.'

'Oh, please don't!' I said, 'I'm sorry. I didn't mean to...'

'No, it's not that,' she looked pained, 'I've got to ring someone back about a job.'

'How about you call in at the studio on your way out?' I suggested. 'You could tell me what kind of thing you've got in mind for your pot. I could do a few sketches.'

'You won't need any sketches,' she said quietly, 'I know exactly what I want.'

To a newcomer I suppose the state of my studio must have looked pretty bizarre – pretty obsessive – row upon row of more or less identical, but otherwise undistinguished, unglazed pots proliferating on every surface. Cath, being Cath, got it at once. She stood on a chair, surveyed the room through half-closed eyes and nodded her approval. They would make a stunning installation, she agreed, in the right kind of gallery space, with the right kind of lighting. She could see what I meant about a panorama – a rough-hewn, undulating whole. It would be moving, she said; it would be epic. She was full of practical advice about packaging and transportation and insurance. Hearing her enthuse, I found myself believing for the first time that it might actually happen. She got so carried away, it was as much as I could do to get her onto the subject of *her* pot, but eventually, and with an almost sheepish reticence, she showed me a photo on her phone of a lidded raku urn, fifteenth-century Japanese. About twelve inches high – a beautiful thing, decorated in whorls of rust and celestial gold-tinged blue. Much admired by Annie, apparently, on the last trip the two of them had made to the British Museum. Cath wanted as faithful a copy as I could make – colour, size, everything. Was that too big an ask? I didn't think so. I could see how I could attempt such a thing. It would be a pleasure actually; a privilege. Neither of us discussed the use to which it would ultimately be put. We didn't need to.

It was good, after she had left, to get my hand in again, to get back to that feeling of solitude and peace and purpose. The whirr of the wheel, the sensuous pliability of the clay, the requirement to focus, which prevented my mind from wandering to places it wasn't healthy for it to go.

I left it as late as I dared to return to the cottage, and if my stomach hadn't been clenching with hunger, I might not have returned at all. I could see Nick pottering in the kitchen. I slipped in through the open front door and was trying to sneak upstairs without his hearing me when his voice called out, 'Dinner in ten, love...'

'Not hungry,' I lied, my voice flat and resentful. He appeared in the kitchen doorway, a tea-towel draped over one shoulder.

'You're kidding,' he said, sounding not angry, but baffled; hurt.

He had no idea. He thought we would sit down to a romantic meal together, as if nothing had happened.

'Nick,' I said, spreading my hands feebly, 'can you not see that this...' I waved my hand at the cosy domestic scene – the simply set table, the napkins, the candles, '... under the circumstances, it's just not...'

'What?'

'... Appropriate.'

'*Appropriate?*' he laughed perplexedly. 'Karen, love, I don't know what you're talking about. How is it not appropriate to tidy up and cook a meal? I'm sorry but...'

I screwed up my fists then and, growling in frustration, raised my chin towards the ceiling.

'You just don't get it, do you? He's gone. You've fucked him over not once but twice. You're like... I don't know, some horrible Judas, denying that he's your son or something. And now he's gone. We've lost him.'

'Oh God. Not this. Not again.'

I gave a guttural groan of frustration, turned on my heel and stomped upstairs to the bedroom.

I lay there for a while in the gloom, with the curtains open, watching the sky turn from cornflower to navy blue, wishing I had had the foresight to at least grab an apple from the fruit bowl. I must have fallen asleep in the end, awakening when a slice of light from the landing fell across the bed.

'Sorry,' Nick's voice whispered, 'I didn't mean to wake you. Shall I sleep in the spare... in Ethan's room?'

I winced inwardly at his idea of tact, but otherwise played dead. Typical Nick, given an inconclusive response, chose the interpretation most favourable to himself. I heard him getting undressed in the dark, the clink of his belt, the slight grunt as he writhed his shirt over his head, sounds which, until recently would have piqued my desire, but which tonight left me cold; worse than cold – clenched tight with revulsion. I braced my body as he pulled back the duvet on his side of the bed, lest an involuntary shudder of distaste betray my wakefulness, but he got in and arranged himself in his metre or so of allotted space before lying there as stiff and cold as if it were his coffin.

25

The ragged pink streaks of dawn had barely begun to show themselves above the hawthorn hedge as we walked up the lane to the Gaineses'. Frost glittered on the lane and an owl hooted nearby. Once or twice, Nick turned to me, as if about to engage in conversation, then seemed to think better of it.

Walford House still seemed shrouded in night. A carriage lamp cast a feeble glow in the porch, but otherwise there was no sign of life. Nick pushed open one of the wrought-iron gates, wincing at its clamorous squeak.

'What do you reckon, shall we give them another five minutes?'

He glanced at his phone.

'They're late, Nick,' I objected, 'and it's freezing.'

He shrugged, turned up his collar and began the fifty-yard trudge over the gravel. As I watched him approach the house, he seemed to dwindle not just in size but in stature. He was a *little* man, I realized with a shock, and always had been – a snob; a vain philanderer. The jolt of recognition winded me. I grabbed at the iron strut of the gate to steady myself. I felt sick, but also exhilarated. By the time I looked up again Imogen had answered the door.

I heard the low murmur of conversation, punctuated by the faint tinkle of female laughter. They were halfway down the drive before I noticed Douglas wasn't with them.

'Sorry, Karen, have you been waiting ages?' Imogen broke into a little jog and laid a placatory hand on my arm. 'Bit of a hiccup on the domestic front. Douglas's mother was meant to come over and babysit, but she's been taken ill.'

'Oh dear.'

'Oh, I'm sure she'll be fine, she's got the constitution of an ox, but obviously we can't leave the girls...'

'Of course not,' I agreed, looking rather wistfully at her carelessly elegant get-up.

'I know. I look a fright, don't I?' she apologised and I realized I must have been staring. 'I just grabbed the first coat I could find from the cloakroom.'

With her blonde hair streaming over the cape of her navy blue Barbour jacket, skinny jeans tucked into green wellies and a wicker basket hooked over one arm, Imogen looked far from a fright, as she very well knew. She looked like a fresh-faced Red Riding Hood, all wide-eyed and virginal and ready to be eaten.

'Is that for the mushrooms?' I asked. 'I just brought this.'

I dragged a plastic carrier bag out of the pocket of my jacket

'Oh, plastic's no good,' she said, tilting her head regretfully, 'it makes the mushrooms sweat. But don't worry, we can share. Oh look, there's Luca and 'Lissa.'

She gave an excited little wave and hurried towards our guides, who had clearly been counting every second of the fifteen minutes they must by now have been waiting by the appointed stile. As soon as they saw us approaching, however, their air of mutual irritation switched to one of unfeasible jollity. A lot of air-kissing and hand-pumping went on. Luca assessed our footwear and clothing for suitability, Imogen and Melissa exclaimed at the coincidence of their identical wicker trugs, Nick stomped his feet, impatient to get going.

'Now just a few 'ousekeeping issues before we set off,' Luca said. 'You don't touch anything without you show me first. You don't taste any of the mushrooms until we get them back home and identify them and if you find a little colony, you don't take all. You leave some little ones to drop their spores, OK?'

He looked meaningfully at each of us in turn, his bespectacled face tilting in its wreaths of scarf like an owl in a tree trunk.

'But where is Douglas?' he asked, realising belatedly that we were a man short.

'He's had to cry off, I'm afraid,' Imogen explained. 'He sends his apologies...'

Luca shrugged resignedly. 'Ho-kaay then,' he said, 'let's get going.'

It felt like a school trip. Luca up ahead, calling bossily over his shoulder; Melissa and Imogen, the mean girls in the middle, secretly sizing each other up under cover of comradely chatter; Nick, the sixth-form prefect, chomping at the bit to catch up with them, but forced, for decorum's sake to slow down every few yards and wait for me, the class dullard.

We ploughed on deep into the woods, the scent of leaf mould and earth and dampness so dense you could almost taste it. Stopping to unhook myself from a vicious bramble, I fell a little behind the others and by the time I had slithered down a mossy bank to join them they were gathered around the gnarly root system of an ancient oak, poring over Luca's first find. He beckoned me over and I stared stupidly at the forest floor, unable to distinguish anything at first, but as my eyes acclimatised to the dappled half light, a colony of saucer-sized mushrooms seemed to sprout one by one into visibility.

'Aren't they beautiful?' Melissa breathed.

'Gorgeous,' Imogen agreed.

'Come on then, let's have 'em!' Nick made to bend down, but Luca caught him by the elbow. For a moment I thought there might be an actual scuffle.

'Ah ah!' Luca chastised, 'First we *identify*!'

'Indeed,' Nick said, smiling through gritted teeth as he removed his elbow from Luca's grip, 'indeed.'

We all gathered round and Luca took out a penknife, cropped a mushroom with great ceremony and held it aloft.

The cap was a delicate shade of oyster, the stem a striking violet, the gills folded in on each other like origami.

'What's it called?' I asked. Luca leaned his face close to mine so that I could smell the faint eggy scent of his breath and rotated the mushroom as if hypnotized by its beauty.

'*Prugn*olo,' he murmured. 'Because of the purple on the trunk, you see?'

'*Stalk*, darling,' Melissa corrected him, her tone decidedly chilly.

'Do we know its English name?' Imogen wondered aloud.

'Wood blewit,' Nick said. Everyone turned in surprise.

'Get you!' Imogen sounded impressed.

'Oh, I'm not just a pretty face, you know,' Nick smirked.

'So now, please…' Luca wafted his hand graciously towards the forest floor. 'But remember, just some, not all.'

Soon Imogen and Nick were scrabbling around among the leaf mould, while Melissa knelt behind them, handmaiden-like, ready to brush the dirt off each new specimen, before laying it reverently in her trug. I had picked the only two mushrooms I could find and had been standing for some time, peering over the others' shoulders, when Luca took my elbow.

'Come,' he whispered, starting to lead me down a woodland path, 'I have a surprise for you.'

'OK,' I whispered back (I didn't know why we were whispering), 'but shouldn't we wait for them?'

'Something tell me they are not going to miss us…' Luca said wryly and turning back I saw what he meant. Nick had one hand resting proprietarily on Imogen's back while he regaled Melissa with some hilarious mushroom-related anecdote. Melissa's face shone with rapt attention, while Imogen's wore the secret smirk of one who has nothing to prove. A month ago, even a week ago, I'd have died inside seeing this; the jealousy, the sheer gut-wrenching humiliation would have floored me. Now I felt... what? Detachment, disdain... maybe even amusement, had it not been so depressing watching two grown females compete for an alpha male, like something off *Life on Earth*. Luca tugged my hand.

'Come!' he said. 'Come!'

It was a circuitous route through knee-deep bracken, tangled brambles and fallen saplings. As the woodland became denser and the path steeper, the faint rumble of Nick's baritone and the ingratiating laughter of the women died away and I began to feel a little uneasy.

'Shouldn't we tell them where we're going?' I called, but Luca crashed on through the undergrowth as if he hadn't heard. We were far from the footpath now. The trees were tall and sepulchral, the light diffuse.

'Luca,' I called, 'what if they find another variety and they need to check with you?'

He didn't seem to hear me, leading me instead to the densest part of the copse, where he stopped suddenly.

'What?' I said warily. He didn't reply, but circled his finger above our heads.

I craned my neck upwards.

'Trees?' I said.

He looked at me in amused reproach.

'Abete rosso,' he announced, 'I don't know in English.'

'Spruce?' I suggested.

'Spruce, yes,' he said, happily, 'and where there is spruce we find…' He pointed down towards our feet and made the same circling motion with his finger. I looked down.

'Wow!' I said. 'What kind are they?'

In among the soil and pine needles and leaf litter were several clusters of squat pebble-like mushrooms, pitted with craters of white where insects and slugs had taken chunks out of them.

'Porcini,' he said as proudly as if he had grown them himself. 'Did I save the best for you or what?'

'Shouldn't we…?' I gestured behind me. 'What about the others?'

'Not yet,' he said, taking my hand and pulling me gently towards the centre of the glade. I made to stoop down and start gathering the mushrooms, but Luca caught my elbow and turned me to face him. Clutching my hands between his, he stared into my face, through his half-misted spectacles. He was almost hyperventilating.

'You have to hear me this time, Karen. You have to listen to what I'm going to say to you. What I've wanted to say since we met…'

'Oh no, Luca, please…' I looked everywhere but into his eyes – at his dirt-filled fingernails, at the dew glistening on his stupid mop of hair, at the frayed edge of his linen scarf, at the spittle gathered at the corner of his too-pink lips.

I might have felt sorry for him if I'd been on home turf, if the others were still within earshot, if *anyone* was in earshot, but instead I felt angry and a little afraid. He had planned this, I realized. Not just the speech he seemed determined to make, whether I wanted to hear it or not; the whole thing. The route through the wood, the Blewits...

'Luca,' I said, plaintively at first and then, when his hands remained clamped, vice-like on mine, more stridently, '*Luca!*'

'Melissa doesn't care, you saw that for yourself. She's more into your husband than she's into me. And your *husband's* into Imogen. You know that, don't you? I've seen them together in your husband's car. They are not very discreet. We've nothing to lose, you see, you and I.'

The faint sulphur smell of his breath was nauseating. I turned my face away in disgust, but he was too carried away with his own seduction plan to bother reading signals. He shuffled me backwards, palms clamped around my wrists, thighs propelling mine, needily, insistently, until my back met a tree and there was nowhere else to go.

'He doesn't deserve you, Karen, a man like that. He doesn't *know* you like I do. When something's right it's right!'

As he lunged towards me, lips puckered, eyes closed, something in me snapped.

26

'Luca can't make it,' Nick mouthed at me, one hand clamped round his mobile, the other poking the risotto with a wooden spoon. 'Migraine.'

I tilted my head to one side and made a sympathetic face. I would have been surprised if Luca could *stand* after the force with which my knee had met his crotch, but it was a relief, nevertheless, to know I wouldn't have to endure an evening in his company. Even with my record of polite acquiescence, I didn't think I'd be able to stomach that after what he'd done. I'd been thinking of feigning sickness myself.

'That's too bad,' Nick was saying into his mobile. 'Yeah, yeah. No, of course *you* should still come, Melissa. I've made enough to feed an army and you can always take some back for when he's better. Yeah, soon as you like. Ciao.'

They had found porcini of their own. They were all over the woods, apparently, not just in Luca's sacred spot. chanterelles, too, and fieldcap and something called Slippery Jack – all identified by Nick. Who knew? He got a bit cagey when I expressed surprise at his hidden talent for mycology. Just shrugged and said it'd teach Luca to be a cocky little sod. I could only imagine what he'd have done if he'd found out what the cocky little sod had tried next. No need to go into that now, though. Much better glossed over. I had dealt with it myself. I was rather proud of that, in retrospect. I'd felt empowered... once I'd stopped shaking, anyway.

'You look nice.'

Nick slipped the phone back into the pocket of his butcher's apron and made to kiss me. I allowed his lips to graze my cheek before pulling away.

'Thanks,' I said.

'Did I buy you that top?'

I looked down vaguely – it was a floppy pleated thing with a tie-neck that I would never have picked out, but which, when I remembered to wear it, always looked better on than I expected.

'No, Jude did.'

He tilted his head regretfully.

'Well, I should have done. You look fucking hot. I'm going to buy you more clothes in future. We should go to London. Have a spree in Selfridges.'

I stretched my lips into a smile, but inside I was recoiling. Is that all you think it takes? I wanted to say, a blank cheque in Selfridges and a few lazy compliments? I came here to heal myself and mend our marriage. I came here thinking you were a changed man who had finally seen the error of his ways but you are the same vain egotist you always were.

'What time are they coming?' I said.

'I told them seven for seven thirty, but knowing the Gaineses, I wouldn't hold your breath. In fact…' He hooked a finger through the belt loops on each side of my jeans and jerked me playfully towards him. 'We've probably got time for a quickie…'

I stretched my neck away from his puckered lips and removed his hands from my hips.

'Bit chancy,' I said. 'Shall I make a salad?'

'All done,' he said breezily. No sign of hurt feelings, I noted.

'I haven't bothered with starters,' he went on, 'just got some nice olives and nibbles from the farmers' market. You don't mind, do you?'

'Why should I mind?'

He turned back to the stove and ladled some more stock into the pan, before bending over it to inhale the fragrance.

'You are going to love this risotto.'

I wandered into the living room. The table looked beautiful – a sprig of rose hips for a centrepiece, a slender candle at either end. Nick had served the 'nibbles' in my hand-thrown pebble bowls, usually left gathering dust at the back of the cupboard in favour of plain white china. The overall effect was artier than he usually went for – less urban.

The fireside looked bright and inviting, too, the cushions

not so plumped as to indicate effort, but not sagging either, the coffee table just off centre on the rug, a handful of arty brochures left casually arrayed. I caught my reflection in the blue-black sheen of the window and thought in my Nick-approved top with my hair freshly washed, I might almost be mistaken, from the outside looking in, for someone who belonged here.

I glanced down at the window ledge and noticed, nestling among the flowers and candles, a family photograph I hadn't seen in years. It had been a favourite of mine, taken for us by a genial Italian waiter in – where had we been? – Sienna? Ravenna? Somewhere like that. Unusually, both boys were in it – adolescent Gabe, raising his half glass of wine triumphantly towards the camera, in celebration of his father's indulgence; little Ethan, sitting ram-rod straight behind a glassful of breadsticks, his face covered in Bolognese sauce, giving a cheery thumbs up to the camera. Nick, with his arm around me, and his face tilted down, so the lens only caught the corner of his laughing mouth, and me looking – what *was* that look on my face? Ah yes, happiness.

I had forgotten this relic from the past, and was surprised to see it enjoying such a prominent position on the window ledge. Nick was known for a slash and burn approach to memorabilia and the last time I had seen this picture in its cheap IKEA frame, we'd been having a clear-out at Trenchard Street and Nick had dumped it with a pile of stuff destined for the attic. That he had given it pride of place this evening struck me as odd. Could this be his idea of an apology? His subtle way of telling me that he wanted us to be a family after all? I glanced up from the photo and caught my breath. His face was just behind mine, reflected in the darkened glass. How long had he been standing there? Seconds? Minutes? Before I could read the expression in his eyes, however, he had stepped closer, put his hands on my waist and with a light kiss to my hair, propelled me towards the front door with a proprietorial slap to the bottom.

'Wake up, silly, they're here!'

'Sorry,' I said, opening the door, 'I didn't hear you knock.'

'We didn't quite like to!' Douglas said, giving me a brief but friendly hug. 'Looked like you were having a moment.'

'Oh no, we were just...'

But he had already handed me on to Imogen who grazed my cheek with hers so that all I got was an expensive whiff of lilies and lemon. Douglas glanced around the cottage with indulgent curiosity.

'So, here we all are. All's well that ends well,' he said jovially.

I frowned at him.

'After your little... escapade... on the mushroom hunt.'

'I got lost,' I said tartly.

'Along with Luca,' said Imogen, with a smirk. 'Our so-called guide. I shall look forward to hearing his explanation later.'

'Ah well, you won't, sadly,' Nick said, taking his apron

off and tossing it ostentatiously back through the kitchen door. He strolled over to his guests and clasped each of them to him in turn.

'Why's that then?' said Douglas. I closed my eyes briefly against an unwelcome rush of memory. Luca's greedy wet lips on mine, my knee jerking upward, a deathless groan, then running, running... undergrowth, brambles... chest panting... feet thudding, blood singing... stile... stumbling... barbed wire... ouch! Up again... running, slowing, daylight, cows... limping, heart slowing... safe.

'Melissa just rang,' Nick told him. 'Luca's got a migraine. She's still going to come though.'

'Oh no, what a shame!' Imogen said. 'About Luca, I mean,' she added hastily. 'Not that Melissa's coming.'

Douglas pulled a sympathetic face.

'Dreadful pity to miss out, especially when it was his thing, as it were.'

'Ah well,' said Nick, his tone suggesting he could live with the disappointment.

'We shall drink a toast to his recovery and send some risotto home in a doggy bag. Now, what's everyone drinking? Shall I open this baby?' he indicated the bottle that Douglas had just put in his hand.

'Might need to breathe,' Douglas said.

Nick perused the label and gave a low whistle.

'Oh yes, I see what you mean. Bit of a show-stopper. Now, what have I got that won't ruin our palates for it in the meantime...?'

I don't know when my husband had become a connoisseur of fine wines – when he'd been schmoozing clients on the company credit card, I supposed – Tesco's Finest had been good enough at home. Douglas followed him into the kitchen. Imogen perched on the sofa and I sat down on Nick's leather chair. The air between us fairly bristled with ill will.

'So cosy,' she said, looking around our living room, 'I sometimes think it would be nice to live somewhere a bit more...'

'Cramped?'

'No, *no*...' Imogen laughed uncomfortably. 'Somewhere a bit homelier, I meant.'

'Well, *you* could,' I said, 'you could sell Walford House and buy yourself half a dozen *homes*. That's what everyone's doing in London now.'

There was a brief silence and then Imogen tried again.

'Do you miss it? London, I mean...'

I felt a stab of something like grief. In the few months since I'd moved here, I had never allowed myself to ask that question, still less answer it.

'I suppose I do a bit... I don't imagine *you* hanker after the city life, though?'

'Oh, I'm there almost as often as I'm here,' she said, airily. 'Twice a month in term-time for my teaching commitments and then for various openings and private views and so-on.'

The shrill of the doorbell made us both jump.

'Don't worry, I'll get it,' said Imogen, who by virtue of being on the sofa was a whole yard nearer the door.

'Melissa-a-a!' they embraced insincerely. Melissa shrugged off a fur-trimmed parka to reveal a slim denim shirt-dress fastened from mid-thigh to throat with small pearl-faced press-studs. I noticed Imogen give her the once-over, before sitting down and smoothing her own velvet pinafore across her knees.

'*Such* a shame about Luca,' said Imogen.

'I kn-o-o-ow,' said Melissa, 'I wanted to stay home and nurse him, but he wouldn't have it. He insisted I come and sample the mushrooms.'

I bet he did, I thought.

A cork popped loudly in the kitchen and all three of us turned our heads.

Douglas came in and sat down between Melissa and Imogen on the sofa and Nick followed, carrying a tray of champagne flutes, the spume still fizzing up their sides.

'Ooh, lovely!' said Melissa, leaning forward to take one.

When we each had a glass in our hands, Nick stood and raised his in the air.

'Now this is not a speech...' he began, to amused groans from his guests, 'no, really. I just want to say a few heartfelt words of thanks. To you, Douglas and Imogen... oh, and *Melissa* of course, for welcoming us into this really rather wonderful community and for the huge generosity of spirit and resilience you showed on Saturday night in the face of... well... let's not go there. I never went to Eton – my alma mater was Harlesden Comp – but I still know backbone when I see it and the way you people rallied round after that display of thuggery, well...'

Nick paused and dipped his chin, as if almost too moved to go on.

Douglas mumbled modestly and Imogen flapped her hand to stem imaginary tears.

'... Anyway,' Nick rallied, 'the less said about that the better. Decency prevailed in the end...'

We all raised our glasses, expecting to drink a toast to decency, but Nick appeared to have had an afterthought.

'... While I'm on my feet, no... indulge me, indulge me...' he grinned and we lowered our glasses again, some of us less tolerantly than others, 'I might as well just say...' he turned towards me and my heart sank, 'how proud I am of my missus. Not only of her prodigious talents – as a potter, as a wife, as a *parent* – a talent I'm afraid I conspicuously lack – but well, just of her. Of who she is. If we're talking resilience, folks, this one wrote the guidebook.'

'Shut up, Nick,' I said quietly.

'... No, love, honestly, I know you're not one for the limelight, but I do just need to say...'

I looked up at the ceiling. A harvest spider was weaving a cobweb on the underside of the lampshade. I watched it wave its tiny legs in the air, to no discernible effect, before resuming its journey between the copper rim of the shade and the Edison bulb. I wondered how long the web would last when the light was switched on. It seemed a precarious spot to have made a home. Then again, it wasn't a home, was it? It was a trap.

'… And for that I shall be forever grateful,' Nick finished, his eyes glassy with tears.

'I'm speechless,' I said with a shrug and everyone laughed with relief.

'Well, that was first class. Absolutely delicious,' Douglas said, tossing his napkin down beside his empty plate. 'Whose recipe did you use in the end? Jamie's? No Carluccio's, I bet. Tasted authentic anyway…'

'It was just one I found online,' said Nick. 'I think it's the Vermouth that gives it the depth of flavour. That and a really good stock.'

'So nothing to do with the freshly foraged local mushrooms then?' said Melissa blinking at him in faux innocence. Everybody laughed.

Douglas's wine really had been something special, even I could tell. It had complemented the dinner perfectly – it was earthy yet smooth, *complex*, I think they call it, and yes, I suppose you'd have to say mushroom-y. We'd had another bottle after that – perhaps not quite as good, but I was not really in a position to judge by then.

They all had brandy too, except for Melissa who was driving.

I vaguely remember their faces looming towards me, smelling of perfume and alcohol and garlic; I remember a lot of goodbyes and thank yous and I remember trying to say that I hadn't done anything. I remember hanging onto Nick from behind as he stood at the sink washing up, and imploring him to leave it till tomorrow and come to bed. I'd felt terribly sentimental, suddenly; maudlin even. I suppose it was the drink, but I felt like I'd been too hasty; as though I should give him a second chance; maybe I just wanted him to fuck me. Either way, my seduction technique was found wanting. He just glanced over his shoulder and said rather coldly, 'You're drunk.'

A little harsh, I thought, considering his sentimental speechifying only a couple of hours before. I steadied myself on the doorjamb and then started up the stairs.

I had only got halfway when the staircase seemed to swing violently to one side, like the stairs in the Crazy House, and suddenly there were two flights instead of one, neither of them leading where I wanted to go.

'Oof!' I said, grabbing onto a wooden tread to steady myself and watching my hand go in and out of focus.

By the time Nick got me into bed, I had vomited twice, once on the bathroom floor and once all over him as I staggered towards the toilet and decided at the last moment that emptying my bowels must take priority. Now I lay, sweating and panting, the room closing in around me like the shutter of a Box Brownie. 'You're burning up,' he said and the touch of his hand on my skin was agony. He pulled the duvet up and it was as though he was hauling back the earth and laying it over me. I wanted it to stop. I wanted not to feel this. I wanted not to be here.

27

It's like looking through the wrong end of a telescope. Everything is so far away. I can see people in the distance but I can't tell who they are and when they speak it's as though they're talking from the bottom of a bucket. It's faint and yet it hurts my ears. They touch me, but I can't tell which part of me they're touching. Sometimes they're saying my name. I know it's my name, even though it sounds tinny and far away... even though it's not really what I'm called. When they say it, I try to open my eyes, because if I don't, how will they know I'm not dead? I try and try, but all I can see is the red scribbles. I think they're sewn shut. That's what the Egyptians do. I don't mind really. I think it'll be fine.

Jesus came once, disguised as Ethan. I saw him through my eyelids. They went transparent while he was there, and then when he'd gone, they went cloudy again and the sewing happened. That's how I know he was Jesus.

Night times are the worst. They bring the chariots then. They're not what I was expecting. Kind of open-plan, but the wheels go twice as fast as normal ones. Sometimes when they're coming and they're waiting round the corner, it's like they're actually already inside my head and they're going to burst out all at once and make my brain into clouds.

It's dark in the wood and the men are here. You are with them.

They're talking about me. I want to say, 'I can hear you, you know,' but actually I can't. I just know they're talking about me because who else would they be talking about?

They're trying to blow me up. Not blow me up like dynamite, blow me up like a balloon. It's in my arm and they send the air through it and when it comes in I get bigger and bigger and you stroke me with velvet so I don't know I'm going to explode.

The men look at me through the knotholes. They have carved my name into one of the trees. I don't know which one.

A crow is here. It's pretending to be a crow but really it's you. You are very close, so close that you're ruffling my feathers. No, they're your feathers. I don't have feathers. You're looking at me with your beady eye and your eye smells of death.

'Hello.'

'Thank God! Oh, sweet Jesus, thank you!'

You have gone back into a man. You are pressing your fist into your beak... into your *mouth*, and you're crying.

'Nurse! Matron! What are you meant to call them? Fuck it! Where's the buzzer? Can somebody—? Yeah... in here. She just opened her eyes.'

Stroking, stroking, stroking; if I tell him to stop, he'll know I know, so I put up with it, even though it's making my hand go on fire.

'I love you,' he says. 'Christ. I never even knew how much... when I was waiting for the ambulance to come... Jesus.'

Tears in his eyes; crocodile tears. He was in the wood with the men. I saw him.

'It's OK,' I say, 'I'm going to get better...'

Watch him; watch for the sign, but he gives nothing away. He's good.

I wonder how he did it, so it was only me and no one else. I couldn't tell from the taste.

'I'm going to dedicate my life to you. I am going to make it how you want it. I'm going to fix it with Ethan. I'm going to give up work. We can manage. We don't need the money. Anyway, once you get better and you finish your pots, you're going to be huge. Cath told me about them. She says it's an installation. She says it's serious art, not just pots. I like Cath. I know I was mean about her, but she's a good person. I can see why you like her. We're going to be so happy, you and me...'

The light flickered on and there was a scraping sound as the nurse pulled the curtain back.

'She's only really supposed to have two visitors at a time,' she was saying, 'but I'll turn a blind eye if you keep it down.'

A face loomed over mine, worried, hopeful.

'Jude,' the word formed on my lips, but no sound came.

I could see a second dark shape behind her. I frowned and winced into the light. Was it...?

'Yep. I've brought Dave with me,' she said. 'I thought – you know – kill or cure...'

I tried for a smile but everything went blurry.

'Hey, hey. Come on,' Dave's voice, panicky, humorous, 'no need to get sentimental. We're not back together or anything. We're just saving on the petrol. Next time you have a life-threatening illness, can you try and have it a bit nearer London?'

There was laughter, then an awkward pause.

'Right, well,' it was Nick's voice, 'I might just pop to the canteen. Leave you guys to catch up. Coming, Dave...?'

'No, I'm all right, ta. You can bring me a coffee though. What...? Oh, right-o. We're going to the canteen apparently. See you in a bit, ladies.'

I heard their feet squeak across the lino and then it

was quiet again except for the tick of the drip. I tried to turn my head but it lay stubborn in the pillow like a watermelon.

'What the fuck, Karen?' There was a wobble of real emotion behind Jude's humorous tone. 'Are you trying to turn this into the worst year of my entire life?'

'Sorry,' I whispered.

'I'm kidding. Hey, I'm *kidding*!' She touched my cheek tremulously with her finger and I felt a tear brim over the edge of my eyelid and trickle down my face.

'Jude,' I said and it came out like the last gasp of air from a beach ball.

She leaned close and, fishing for my hand on the blanket, took it gingerly in hers so as not to disturb the drip.

'I want... to go... home...'

'Of course you do, honey,' Jude said. 'And you will. You just have to get your strength back first. Nick's going to spoil you rotten once you get out of...'

It felt like an earthquake but it was just me shaking my head.

'No,' I croaked urgently, 'not there. I don't want to go there with him...'

'Shhh,' she said, patting my arm, 'don't upset yourself. You're off your tits with the drugs...'

He was reading a book. The room was dim, except for the pool of light around his pages. He looked across at me and smiled.

'Have they gone?' I asked.

'Who?'

'Jude and Dave.'

He smiled indulgently.

'That was yesterday,' he said. 'Go back to sleep.'

I was tap dancing in my dream like Danny Kaye in *Singin'
in the Rain* and the rain was made of milk and the umbrella
was a big spotty toadstool, dripping poison.

I opened my eyes and the brightness made me wince.

'Hello,' he said, reaching for my hand and pressing it to
his lips. It felt different. Freer than before. 'Big day today!'
he said. 'You're off the drip.'

I turned my head. The walls of the room had receded.
There was a sense of light and space and precariousness, as
if my bed had been wheeled onto a cliff-top.

'It's a general ward,' Nick explained. 'You're out of
intensive care. We've won!'

He lifted my free arm off the bed and waggled it in a
feeble victory gesture.

'They said you'll need another round of antibiotics to see
off any last traces of infection, but the good news is, these
ones can be taken orally so once they've dotted the "i"s and
crossed the "t"s, I get to take you home!'

'*Infection*...?' I frowned and shook my head. 'What do
you mean? I thought it was...?'

'What?' Nick smiled at me in puzzlement.

'Oh no, only…' I hesitated, 'I thought it might have been… something I ate.'

'What, you mean the…?' Nick's face contorted in genuine horror as my meaning hit home.

'Jesus Christ, Karen! Do you honestly think I'd be that fucking irresponsible?'

'No, but I just thought… maybe by mistake… one of them was… a bad one might have slipped through…'

'It was sepsis,' he said and his quiet tone spoke of his hurt. 'It was from a scratch on your leg. You should have told me about it. If it had been properly cleaned and bandaged we'd have had none of this.'

I winced at the memory of a tearing pain as I'd hurled myself over a barbed wire fence in my flight from Luca. It had left a nasty gash, but I had showered afterwards, had noticed nothing amiss…

'Yeah. Bloody good job they caught it when they did. It's a killer. Surprisingly common apparently,' he shook his head regretfully. 'I blame myself… should never have let you out of my sight on that mushroom hunt. I knew you'd get yourself in a pickle.'

He looked at me and he shook his head, his eyes full of regret and admonishment and love.

My mouth was dry and tasted of pear drops. I tried to reach for the cup of water on the bedside locker and accidentally knocked a forest of 'get well' cards onto the floor.

'Hey, Missus!' Nick chastised me. 'You tell me when you want something. That's what I'm here for.'

He hauled me up against the pillows and I felt frail in his arms, like something badly super-glued. He handed me the water and then set about picking up the cards, grunting and squeaking his chair legs with the effort of reaching them all.

'You've not seen these, have you?' he said, pleased; it seemed to provide a focus for our conversation. He started to show me each card in turn, first the picture on the front, then the words inside, as if I were a child.

'"*A heartfelt wish for your recovery. From Min and Ray, with love. Kiss kiss.*"'

'"*To Karen, Get well soon from all at The Fleece,*" oh… you're going to like this one…'

He tilted the picture towards me – a blue teddy holding a magic wand, the words, 'WISHING YOU WELL' embossed in a silver arc above it.

'Ta da!' he opened it to reveal the dedication.

'*To Mum, Get well soon, luv Ethan and Sally xx*'

The 'u' of luv was a biro heart.

'Was he here? Was Ethan here?' I grasped his hand urgently, my heart lifting with hope.

''Course he was! He brought his new lady friend. Nice girl, actually. He's done all right there, I reckon.'

'Oh!' I said. 'That's good.'

I tilted my head up at the ceiling and blinked hard. Nick patted the back of my hand sympathetically and then reached for the next card.

'This one's from my work mates, this one's from Jude – no mention of Dave, sorry to say. This one... Linda somebody?' He showed me the handwriting and I shrugged, none the wiser. He was getting bored now, rattling through them in perfunctory fashion, until he came to the last one.

'Ah, now, *this* one's very you.'

I knew it was from Cath straight away. The front showed a photo of a modernist sculpture, a hollowed-out metal sphere set on a plinth in a sunny garden – it was a lovely image, un-showy, yet uplifting in its quiet way. Nick flipped the card open and read portentously:

'"*Nil carborundum illigitimus.*" That's a joke, it means don't let the...'

'I know what it means,' I said.

'She's got it wrong though,' Nick added smugly. 'Should be illigitim*i*. Bastards plural.'

I took the card from him and ran my finger over the dedication, carefully written in what looked like fountain pen.

'If you say so,' I said.

'She brought you some flowers too,' he added, 'but the Gestapo confiscated them. Breeding ground for germs apparently...'

'When was she here?' I asked, aware that my voice sounded petulant, accusing even. 'You should have woken me.'

'Monday... I think,' Nick said vaguely, 'I've lost track. It's like a time warp in this place. You were well out of it anyway. Don't worry, you'll see her soon enough.' He glanced at his watch. 'That's if the doctor gets her skates on.'

It was early afternoon by the time the doctor came with the lab results. She was very apologetic for keeping us so long. She advised bed rest and reassured Nick in a low voice that although the side-effects of the antibiotics sometimes resembled the illness itself – bloating, nausea, diarrhoea – they would not be discharging me were they not completely satisfied that the bacterium had been eradicated and my immune system returned to normal function. She congratulated him on his decisive action in calling an ambulance and added sotto voce that it was not an exaggeration to say he had saved my life. Then her pager went off and she wished us well and hurried away.

'Fucking state of me…' said Nick, wiping tears from his cheeks with the back of his hand. He laughed and a bubble of snot ballooned out of his nose, so that he had to snatch a tissue from the box on the night stand and honk into it loudly. I smiled at him, feeling nothing.

A cheerful orderly called Basil conveyed me to the reception area in a wheelchair, transferred me to a moulded plastic chair with great ceremony, and then haughtily refused Nick's proffered tip. Nick settled me with a copy of *Closer* magazine and went to fetch the car. I sat in a daze, the magazine unopened in my lap, and watched people shuffle through the revolving doors, stopping to gaze at the signs, before moving off purposefully towards Radiography or Orthopaedics, Coronary Care or Oncology. What might confront them at their destinations, I wondered; perhaps, if they were lucky, a bed-bound relative recovering from a hernia operation; if less so, a sober oncologist with a sinister-looking X-ray. *This* was where Death stalked his victims, not on the lonely country road or in the dark wood; here under the strip lights, between the Costa Coffee franchise and the hexagonal fish tank. He was not coming for me this time, but he would come soon enough. Would I be ready when the time came? Would I be able to say that I had lived?

We exited the car park, rumbled over speed bumps, joined slip roads, gradually eased onto dual carriageways. Nick turned the radio on. An art critic was pontificating about the Turner Prize shortlist.

'Pretentious bollocks,' Nick muttered, reaching out to change the channel, before remembering himself.

'Unless…?'

I shrugged indifferently and he flicked to an easy listening channel instead. A caller was explaining to a DJ why 'Kiss Me' by Sixpence None the Richer would always be special to her and her boyfriend. As she came to the end of her story the chorus of the song swelled behind her voice and then took over.

'*Kiss me down by the broken tree-house*
Swing me upon its hanging tyre…'

'Christ,' Nick rolled his eyes but he didn't switch it off, instead gripping the steering wheel with both hands and after a few moments, throwing me a brief, tight-lipped smile.

A faint buzzing noise came from the back seat. I glanced over my shoulder, recognizing it as my ringtone, but just the thought of unfastening my seatbelt and reaching back into the depths of my holdall exhausted me, so I let it ring.

I must have dozed off after that. When I woke up again, we were driving towards our hamlet. In the few days of my absence, the drab taupe of early autumn had given way to a riot of russet and yellow, pink and gold. Burnished by a low autumn sun, the valley was ablaze.

Nick noticed me noticing and patted my thigh. 'Not bad eh?' he said as if he had laid on the show himself. 'And to think we used to get excited about a few crappy Japanese maples in Clissold Park...'

I smiled wanly. The only recollection I had of Clissold Park was his shouting at Ethan for walking in dog shit.

'I was serious, you know,' he added, after a pause. 'About giving up work. I've done a few sums and if I sell my shares in the company, we can manage pretty well, even after I've sorted Ethan for his deposit.'

'What does Ethan need a deposit for?'

'Promise you won't get mad?' Nick threw me a tentative glance. 'He's jacking in his course. Going in on a basement flat in Rivington with Sal.'

Sal? It was *Sal* now? And *me* not getting mad? That was rich. And deposits on basement flats? Subbed by a father who less than a week ago had suspected Ethan of drug dealing, GBH and God knows what else...

He must have caught the expression on my face.

'Well,' he said, and he seemed, for the first time in twenty years to have successfully read my mind, 'if you will marry an immature prick who doesn't know what's important until fate gives him a fucking big kick up the arse.'

As we descended into the hamlet, Nick announced our return with a celebratory volley of toots on his horn and disturbed a crow, which had been perched on the gate of Prospect Cottage. It squawked indignantly and took off, revealing its iridescent under-wing as it swooped across the windscreen and soared away.

28

'There you go,' he said, applying the hand brake decisively. The car lurched back, making my empty stomach heave.

'Thank you,' I said.

He nodded meaningfully out of the window, and I noticed a makeshift banner hoist above the gate.

'WELCOME HOME, KAREN,' it said, in blue poster paint, the letters surrounded by multicoloured hearts and flowers.

'That's sweet of you.'

'Team effort,' Nick said. 'My idea, Cath's handiwork. Min and Ray supplied the paints. This is what you get when you live in a proper community. Can you imagine anyone bothering in London?'

I climbed down gingerly from the passenger seat and Nick hurried round to assist me as if I were royalty.

'Can I carry you over the threshold?' Nick said. 'Go on, let me carry you over the threshold.'

'I might just walk if it's OK with you.'

He installed me on the couch with a blanket over my knees and pointed out the three bouquets I'd been sent – none of them, this time, anonymous.

'Right, I'll put Madam's washing on,' he said, brandishing the holdall. I smiled at him.

'Oh, Nick…' I remembered, 'my phone's in there…'

He scrabbled in the bag and handed it to me.

'You're not to start *doing* stuff on it,' he said sternly. He flicked on the TV.

'There you go – Netflix.' He handed me the remote.

When I thought he was safely out of the way, I picked the phone up and scanned the screen. Three missed calls all from the same London number. My thumb hovered over the playback button.

'Er…' He popped his head round the kitchen door, jokily admonishing.

I grinned, put the phone down and picked up the remote again.

'The Gaineses send their love,' Nick called above the sound of water thundering into the kettle. 'Frieda's recovering well you'll be pleased to know…'

Frieda? Frieda…? I couldn't think who… oh yes, the blessed dog.

'Cath said she'd drop round later. She and Min are helping Jean's daughter with the funeral arrangements.'

'Mmmm?' I said vaguely. It didn't sink in at first. I was too busy scrutinizing Ethan's card.

'Whose funeral arrangements? Nick?' I threw off the

blanket and started towards the kitchen, panic rising in me; desperate to be told I'd got it wrong, but the cold feeling of dread in my stomach told me I hadn't. I remembered the pale bruise on Jean's cadaverous face, the way she had cringed in fear as Gordon and Nick had marched her back towards the cottage. She may or may not have met a violent death but my allowing her to be returned to that morgue, that benighted *prison* of a house, to which even her own children had long since stopped coming, had been an act of betrayal.

'Nick…?' I said again, but he had his back to me, fishing in the teabag jar and I was no longer in the kitchen; I was back on the lane and it was no longer the squeal of a boiling kettle, but the sound of Jean's keening.

'Karen!'

My body jerked like a marionette as he caught me under the arms, one of my fists thwacking the doorframe as I passed out.

'Now stay put,' he said with pretend sternness when he'd laid me in the bed, and pulled up the duvet around me. 'I'll bring your tea up in a minute. And how about a nice bit of toast?'

He looked at me, then shook his head in self-reproach. 'I knew I should have carried you.'

'It wasn't that,' I protested, 'it was what you said about the funer—'

He raised his hand.

'Don't even go there. It's not for you to be worrying about. If you're better, fine, but if not… we hardly knew them and there's plenty of people rallying round… the daughter's here and the son's flying in from Dubai.'

He paused for a moment, and, resting his hand on the door handle, added wistfully, 'You'd hope your kids'd visit *before* you popped your clogs, really, wouldn't you?'

Then he left the room.

I was probably still a bit unhinged. I was certainly light-headed and Nick was right, I needed something to eat, but the thought of Jean's death tormented me. I kept thinking back to the hunted look on her face when we had found her wandering in the lane, her resistance to being led back to the cottage. No wonder. No wonder…

Nick brought the toast, cut into four dainty triangles and watched me force down two of them. I handed him the plate and he narrowed his eyes and took it away with a grudging smile. Later he brought home-made broth and fed it to me, spoon by spoon, laughing when the vermicelli noodles slithered down my front and making a game of retrieving them with the spoon. I must have slept after that. When I woke, the room was grey with dawn and I could see him, cheek propped on palm, face silhouetted above me, eyes grave with concern.

I finished the course of antibiotics, but my body was rebelling by the end. Food was passing straight through me and the one time I attempted to make it to the bathroom by myself, I collapsed and Nick got mad at me for 'trying to be a hero'. But it was that or feel mollycoddled – claustrophobic. He'd bought a smoothie maker, on the basis that I was finding solids tricky, and kept appearing by my bedside with large unappetising glasses of gloop, one time with a stick of celery for a swizzle stick. It was touching, I suppose, but it wasn't really helping. In fact, with each day that passed, I found Nick's devotion a little more irksome. Perverse, perhaps, considering I had spent the twenty years of our marriage yearning for such behaviour.

Suddenly, I was flavour of the month. He couldn't get enough of me. He perched on the bed, pretending to lose at Scrabble while he told me about his plans for a family Christmas and a winter holiday – maybe Spain again for the art. He planned kohlrabi in the veggie patch come spring, he told me, and a Trivial Pursuit night with the pub quiz team when I was properly better, just to limber up, so we didn't get trounced a second time. He plumped my pillows and laid his cool palm across my forehead and looked at me as though he were seeing me for the very first time.

Once, I woke late in the evening to hear the familiar burr of Cath's voice downstairs. I sat up in bed and called her name, but my sleepy croak couldn't compete with *Newsnight* on the telly and Nick holding forth and I was halfway out of bed when he caught me.

'Hey, young lady, where d'you think you're going?'

'Cath's here!' I said.

'Yes,' he agreed,' taking my elbow and steering me back to bed again, 'and she'd be mortified if she thought she'd disturbed you. She just called in because she's got nothing to wear for the funeral tomorrow and she wondered if we had anything she could borrow.'

'She can have my grey pashmina,' I said, breaking free of him and struggling with the catch on the wardrobe door. 'It's got sequins round the edge, but I don't think that'll...'

'Not a problem, hen,' Cath's voice called up the stairs. 'Your man's lent me a very smart fedora. Just the job. Now, you get some rest and don't be showing your face tomorrow unless you're a hundred per cent, you hear?'

Before I could get near the landing, her footsteps were receding, the front door pulled shut behind her.

29

It was a nothing sort of day, neither indecently sunny nor portentously gloomy; the sky was white, the trees drooped under yellowing, but still fairly substantial leaf cover and the birds tweeted blithely as if to signal their indifference to the occasion. Black-clad figures milled about on the lane, their faces turning expectantly our way as Nick led me down the path. He was wearing his good suit, its cut so sharp, his shirt so white, his tie so immaculately knotted, that it was just as well he had lent his black fedora to Cath, or he would have looked like a Mafioso; meanwhile I was sweating unbecomingly in my grey linen dress and an old Hobbs coat, wishing that the only un-laddered tights I'd been able to find had been less than eighty denier. Nick opened the garden gate for me with exaggerated courtesy, flinging aside my welcome home banner, which had come adrift and snagged on the garden wall so that only the legend 'ME KAREN' was visible.

Cath was chatting to a woman I didn't recognize. Seeing me, she squeezed the woman's arm apologetically and hurried over to give me a consoling hug. I succumbed briefly, but then, feeling my composure start to wobble, stepped back. Cath seemed about to say something, but before she could, Ray descended, resplendent in an Edwardian-style frock coat.

'Bloody hell, young Karen, you scared the life out of us.'

'Ray,' Min chastised him, with an apologetic glance over her shoulder at the other mourners.

'You *did*, though,' she confirmed quietly, giving my arm a friendly squeeze. 'Lying there on that drip like a poor little ghost…' She shuddered. I mumbled something vaguely apologetic and then tried to find a way to steer the conversation back to the circumstances of Jean's demise, but before I'd got very far at all, the funeral cortege was spotted making its way along the main road towards the hamlet. Everyone turned and conversations trailed off, as the shiny black roofs of the hearse and an accompanying limo flickered in the distance. An awkward hush fell, followed, once people realized that it would be another five minutes before it reached the hamlet, by a shuffling of feet and a renewed outbreak of sombre platitudinizing. Imogen and Douglas had by now emerged from Walford House and taking this as our signal, as surely as if they had still been the Lord and Lady of the Manor, we turned and started moving as one down the lane.

Heads swivelled and hats were doffed as we passed Prospect Cottage, but the house was blank, not so much as a flicker of its closed curtains betraying the presence within of the funeral party. It would, I supposed, be a tight-lipped little gathering anyway, in view of what Jean had told me about the strained relations between Gordon and his children. Always assuming they had come at all; I hoped for Jean's sake that they had.

Rounding the corner, we met the cortege head-on and shrunk back into the hedgerow to let it pass. The casket was an old-fashioned mahogany monstrosity, ornately carved and adorned with a single cross of white carnations. It looked so unsuited both in its bulk and grandiosity, either to Jean's physical frailty or her mercurial persona as to seem an insult to her memory. As others bowed their heads or crossed themselves, I looked away, fighting a rising sense of indignation, of *fury* really, on behalf of the old woman.

As we reached the junction with the main road and forked right into the village, it occurred to me how little the walk there from the hamlet must have changed in Jean's lifetime. The scene must have varied more according to the season than the decade. Had she and Gordon married in the little sandstone church? I wondered. Had their children been christened here? How many times must she have walked beneath this same arch of trees, past these same cottages, gone by the school house and the pub and then through the lychgate and up the winding path through the church-yard where she was now to be buried? Had she been a churchgoer? I didn't know, any more than I knew which star sign she'd been born under or which way (if any) she had voted, what books she'd read or whether she liked dogs or cats or neither, had had a best friend, or an unrequited love. I didn't know and now I never would and my ignorance felt both a loss and a betrayal.

The vicar stood outside the church porch, greeting the mourners with sad benevolence.

'Hello, welcome to St Aloysius. Good morning and welcome...'

Next to him, a female funeral attendant in a top hat was handing out orders of service. Nick took one and we went inside, pausing for a moment for our eyes to adjust to the dim interior. It was a small plain church with whitewashed walls. A single aisle led between rows of dark wood pews to a simple altar beneath a triptych of stained-glass windows. As mere acquaintances of the deceased, I had expected to squeeze in inconspicuously at the back, and was surprised to find the church barely a third full, and to be ushered forward, along with the other residents of the hamlet, to fill up the gaps in the foremost pews. Catching Cath's eye I gave her a puzzled look and she shrugged back, a little insouciantly it seemed to me, but before I had a chance to comment to Nick on the poor turnout, the organ's mournful tootling had come to an abrupt halt and the meagre congregation had risen to its feet.

There was a brief expectant silence, some shuffling and coughing at the back of the church and then a gusty off-key organ note heralded the start of the funeral march. It was almost too pathetic to bear, the half-empty church, the generic lugubrious music, the sombre faces of the hired pall-bearers, who though advancing now with downcast eyes, would be laughing and joking in their civvies in an hour or two. Surely Jean's life had been worth more than this?

As the coffin was lowered onto the aluminium bier, and the chief mourners drew level with our pew, I took a surreptitious sidelong glance at them. There was a plumpish woman of about my age, wearing a navy mac and a bouffant hair-do, whom I took to be the estranged daughter, and a suntanned man in a flash double-breasted suit, looking every inch Dubai. But between them, where I would have expected to see Gordon, tall and prideful, keeping his upper lip characteristically stiff, there was only a smallish elderly figure – a female relative, I assumed, although the daughter's bulk prevented me from seeing her clearly. I nudged Nick, jerked my head towards them and furrowed my brow, enquiringly, but he didn't seem to catch my drift.

I was staring up at the stained-glass window, thinking back to the strange premonition I had had about Jean when we first met and wondering if something other than my own self-absorption had prevented me from acting on it, when the vicar stepped forward, pink sausage fingers clasped piously in front of his cassock and began to intone with the sing-song, counter-intuitive cadences beloved of the clergy, 'We are gathered here today to say farewell to Gordon Victor Anthony Naylor and to commit him into the hands of God.'

The service had long finished and the mourners were mingling in the churchyard before the scale of my misapprehension had even begun to sink in. I sat on a bench and stared nonplussed at the order of service – an A5 pamphlet, the cover bearing a silver crucifix, beneath which was printed:

A SERVICE OF THANKSGIVING
FOR THE LIFE OF
GORDON VICTOR ANTHONY NAYLOR
1925–2018

On the inside page was an oval sepia photograph of a handsome but rather arrogant-looking young airman, with a supercilious half-smile playing about his lips, the legend beneath, 'Gordon "Spider" Naylor semper fidelis.'

I didn't have the courage to admit to Nick that I'd thought it was Jean who was dead. Clearly I *had* been told, and if I'd been too far gone at the time to digest the information, I was not inclined to cite my illness in mitigation. This was supposed to be the new me, the strong me, the sane me. Besides, it would have felt unseemly, for Jean was standing, large as life, just feet away from me, her dress smart, her posture erect, her hair neatly coiffed beneath a half-veiled pill-box hat. Given the scale of the transformation she appeared to have undergone since the last time I'd seen her, distressed and vulnerable on the lane, I felt I could be forgiven for not having recognized her.

'... And this is my son Peter,' she was saying to Douglas Gaines. 'Come over special from Dubai.'

Nick was worried the wake would tire me out, but I was determined to go. I wanted to express my – condolences would be the wrong word – sympathies, I suppose, euphemistic enough to cover it. I also wanted to lay the ghost of Prospect Cottage once and for all to rest. I needed to satisfy myself that it was not the ghoulish mausoleum of my imaginings, but, as Nick had always insisted, a dreary little house blighted by nothing more sinister than a coal-effect gas fire and some flock wallpaper.

In fact, for the home of two reclusive pensioners tricked out for a wake, it had a surprisingly jaunty air about it. The curtains were now half-open, one window stood ajar and some ugly yellow chrysanthemums on the ledge had attracted the attention of a late, lazy wasp. The small front parlour was crammed with furniture – two wing-backed armchairs stood either side of the fireplace, a glass-fronted china cabinet took up one alcove and a TV the other, whilst the only free wall was dominated by a bulky sideboard, covered in crocheted doilies and laden with enough sandwiches and sausage rolls to feed an army. Recalling Gordon's abstemiousness on the night of our party, I was surprised to see a cluster of tumblers and an array of hard liquor on offer as well.

I watched Nick work the room – clasping shoulders, shaking hands, pitching his comments perfectly between sombreness and cheer while I hovered awkwardly by the refreshments. I was still trying to take in the scale of my misapprehension about the funeral.

'Excuse me, love, you couldn't top me up, could you?'

It was the plump woman from the church, still wearing her navy coat and looking as much a fish out of water as me. I obliged and she tilted her sherry glass towards me with a wary smile.

'Cheers,' she said, taking a sip. 'I'm Pat, by the way. The daughter, for my sins...'

'Karen,' I said, offering her my hand, 'I live just up the lane. I'm sorry for your loss.'

She gave me a slightly pained smile and I recalled my conversation with Jean at our housewarming: 'she and Gordon don't see eye to eye'. Something of an understatement, judging by the unease this poor woman clearly felt in what had been her childhood home.

'Your mum seems to be coping well,' I ventured. We both looked across to where Jean was sitting in a high-backed chair, chatting animatedly to the vicar, a glass of whiskey in one hand and a sausage roll in the other.

Pat gave me a look as if to say, 'Well wouldn't you?' But I didn't dare let on how much I knew – as objectionable an old tyrant as Gordon had been, I was conscious I was still at his wake.

'I suppose... she... her... circumstances will change now...' I added, delicately. 'It's a lot of house to deal with on her own.'

The knots in which English people will tie themselves, to avoid saying the obvious: your mother is old and frail. What are you going to do about it?

But Pat didn't turn a hair.

'She'll not want to budge from here,' she said. 'Believe you me, I've tried.'

'So what will... happen then?'

But Jean had tired of making small talk with the vicar and was making her way over to us. Perhaps she had risen to the occasion, perhaps she just brushed up well, but she seemed much more the woman I had first encountered – erect and beady, than the one Nick and I had found wandering unhinged and vulnerable that night on the lane.

'I see you've met our Pat,' she said, giving me what seemed a smile of recognition. 'Pat, this is... no, don't tell me...' She clasped my hand to silence me and I held my breath.

'... *Karen*. She and her husband bought the Marsdens' old place two doors along. You remember the Marsdens, Pat?'

I could have punched the air. Not only did Jean remember who I was, she was a person again, cogent and engaged.

'Yes, Mother, I remember the Marsdens,' said Pat tolerantly, then turning to me in an undertone. 'What did you pay for it, if you don't mind me asking?'

'Oh gosh, I'm afraid I don't… my husband dealt with all that… why are you…? Is your mother thinking of selling…?'

'No, I am not!' Jean interjected in an indignant tone. There was nothing much wrong with her hearing either, it seemed.

'Well now, Mum, let's see how you go,' Pat said. 'I've a lot on my plate. I'll be over when I can but I'll not be able to drop everything if you fall and hurt yourself again.'

'You cheeky wotnot!' Jean said, mock indignation scarcely concealing her obvious delight that Pat would once again be back in her life, in however limited a capacity.

'There are all sorts of modifications you can make, anyway,' I said brightly. 'Walk-in showers and stair-lifts and so forth.'

'Oh, I don't think that'll be necessary,' Jean said a little huffily and I felt myself blushing. 'I shan't be rushing into anything and besides…'

She looked over at the chimneybreast, where a framed wedding photo of her and Gordon took pride of place and for a horrible moment I thought she was about to wax lyrical about the home they had shared together.

'My top priority will be getting rid of that horrible wallpaper.'

30

'Well, that was fucking grim,' Nick said. 'I tell you what, when my time comes, I want you all to have a bloody big party. Hire a DJ, get rat-arsed and let your hair down.'

'What makes you think *I'll* be there to organize it?' I said.

'Oh, you'll outlive me for sure,' Nick said. 'What with my lousy genes and my misspent youth, I'll be lucky to see sixty-five. You did brilliantly, by the way,' he added, turning my face towards him and bestowing a kiss on my forehead.

'It was a funeral, not a school play,' I said, taking off my coat and tossing it over the back of the sofa.

'She put a brave face on it, didn't she? The Old Dear.'

'I'm not sure she needed to...'

Nick gave me a funny look.

'What, you think she's *glad*...?'

He looked faintly shocked and I thought, were you there, that night? When she had to be manhandled back through her own front door? When she flinched from her husband's touch as if he were her jailor? Did that look like a happy marriage to you?

'Well, I think there might have been an element of...'

remembering that Gordon was still warm in the ground, I deployed all the tact I could muster, '*relief* on her part.'

'Christ,' he said, shaking his head. 'Bleak.'

I looked at him then and it struck me how unobservant he had always been about other people and their relationships – bit-players, as they were, in the drama of his life.

'Well,' I said with a shrug, 'relationships are tough, aren't they? Christ, you of all people should know that...'

He looked bewildered, as though the fact he had one failed marriage and a string of infidelities under his belt had enlightened him not one whit.

I watched him scoop my coat fastidiously off the back of the sofa and hang it on the hook next to his. He undid the top button of his shirt, loosened his tie, ran his fingers through his hair – just as he used to do every night when he got home from work, oblivious to the aphrodisiac effect it had on me. Used to have.

He saw me watching him and tilted his head on one side indulgently.

'Well,' he said, 'wake up call for me. Our marriage is my top priority now.'

'Right, well,' I said briskly, '*my* top priority's a cup of tea. I'm spitting feathers here.'

'I'll get it...' he said. 'You take the weight off your—'

'Nick!' I snapped. 'I think I can make a cup of tea.'

I marched into the kitchen, filled the kettle noisily and put it on the stove, then scooped the used teabags out of the pot and rinsed it out under the mixer tap, the faintly rust-tinged water reminding me, with a shudder, of the trace of fox blood I had washed away that first night. Had it really only been six months ago?

I glanced over my shoulder. Nick was leaning against the doorjamb, regarding me thoughtfully; hands in his pockets.

'I've got a confession to make,' he said.

'Oh?'

My first thought was Imogen. He'd slept with her. I waited for the trapdoor to open beneath me but I felt… nothing. No, not nothing… I felt a little lift, a sense of possibility, a chink of light.

'So… when you were in hospital,' he continued, 'and I was sitting around looking at you, at your lovely face and realizing how lucky I am to have you and what a fucking prick I've been…'

'Yes…' I said warily. I would need to make this look good.

'Well, your phone kept going off…'

I frowned. It was only then it dawned on me that he was confessing some other misdemeanour altogether. I thought of the buzzing I had heard coming from my holdall on the return journey from the hospital, the three missed calls I had not yet got round to checking.

'And…?' I said.

'… And, well, I suppose I thought, if someone's *this* keen to get hold of you, I'd maybe better… have a listen…'

'Right.'

'… Which I know is an invasion of your privacy and not

335

my place, *yadda yadda*, but I figured, under the circumstances... Anyway, it was this gallery in Mayfair...'

As soon as he said it, it was as though I had always known it. Those low atonal buzzes coming from my holdall on the back seat had been my future calling me.

He gave me his jokey hangdog look and I realized that it was impossible for him to conceive of a predicament which he couldn't either charm his way out of, or somehow turn to his own advantage.

'You're not mad at me, are you?'

I kept my voice matter-of-fact. 'What did they say?'

'Well, it was a bit hard to follow, but essentially this guy, Tom Hayden-something or other knew your work from before and he'd bumped into someone from round here at a private view, and whoever it was, was bigging up your new project. My money's on Luca...'

'It won't be Luca,' I said with a bitter laugh.

'Well, whoever it was, this geezer – super posh, terribly RP, wants to set up a meeting with your people...' he sketched inverted commas humorously in the air, 'with a view to maybe giving you a show.'

'Ha,' I said, 'wait till he finds out I don't have any people.'

'Ah...' said Nick looking at me significantly, 'but you do!'

I smiled at him, but my heart was sinking.

'It's a no-brainer!' Nick said. 'Your work's in demand, I'm stepping back from mine. You need time and space to get on with your new project, I need a little enterprise to keep me out of trouble...'

He came up to me then and looped his arms around my waist, pushing his cheek insistently against mine, as certain as ever of his power to endear, to prevail.

'Look at us!' he said, indicating our shadowy twins, reflected in the dusk-darkened windows behind the sink. 'We've got it all now. You've got your studio and your talent and with a bit of a leg up from Tom Doo-Dah Whatsit, a lucrative future ahead of you. We've got this place. We've got a community. But more than anything else,' he leaned his head against mine so that our two reflections became one, 'we've got each other.'

In the dusk-darkened glass, my smile could almost have been mistaken for the real thing.

We took the tea up to bed and sipped it, side by side, like two old fogeys and then Nick snuggled down, his palms clasped tightly around my upper arm, his limpet lips only relaxing away from my flesh as sleep took hold. I sat propped against the pillows in our exquisite little bedroom, with its rustic charm and its imaginative storage solutions, and watched the achingly tasteful linen blind turn slowly from grey, to charcoal, to black.

When I woke the blind was grey again and just discernible against the darker recess of the window frame. I hadn't set an alarm. I hadn't needed to. I lifted the duvet up as gingerly as if it were rigged with explosives, but Nick didn't stir, just lay spread-eagled on his back, his chest rising and falling in the deep untroubled sleep of one who has made his accommodation with the world. I took my phone off the bedside table, gathered yesterday's clothes off the chair in the corner of the room and slipped outside to put them on. Tiptoeing downstairs, I instinctively avoided the one creaky stair and, moving through the living room like a ghost, collected my handbag from beside the sofa and my car keys from the window ledge.

I pulled the door of the Renault shut as quietly as I could, put on my seatbelt and let out the hand brake, grateful for the slight decline on the lane that meant I didn't have to start the ignition right outside the cottage. Coasting down the hill, I let the car drift to a standstill by itself and was about to start the engine when I was struck by the silence and stillness in the little hollow. I sat for a moment, taking in the scene for the last time. The hedgerow, thick with Old Man's Beard, seemed to glow in the dawn light beneath it clumps of nettles rose like spires. I started in shock as two bright animal eyes locked on mine through the mist. I shuddered and looked away, remembering the sickening thud as I had swung round this same bend heading into the hamlet all those months ago. Was this a haunting? Some fox ancestor, come back to jinx my departure as its forebear had jinxed my arrival? I looked again, half expecting the apparition to have gone, but it was still there, its pupils beady and unblinking. And then the creature sprang out onto the road and it was no fox but a young doe, body all angles, tail erect, torso steaming in the chill dawn. She stood there for a second, regarding me, head cocked and I sat mesmerized. Holding my breath, I turned the key in the ignition, but at the first stutter of the engine, she skittered off up the lane. I followed her for a few yards, keeping my distance. She glanced back once, as if in valediction, and then with a flick of her hind legs veered off up the bank and was gone.

The sun was up by the time I reached the junction. I held the car on the hand brake and took one last look down the valley. I had never felt so calm and resolute, so unburdened by doubt. I let the brake out and the engine roared as I pulled out into the empty road and headed for London.

Acknowledgements

I am very grateful to the following people:

For their encouragement, invaluable editorial input, kindness and enthusiasm, my agent Sallyanne Sweeney and editor Kate Mills.

For their inspiration and constructive criticism, members, past and present of The Little George Writers' Group and Stroud Writers' Circle.

For their patience and attention to detail as first readers, Julie Bull, Polly Jameson, Petrina Dorrington, Martha Everett and Thea Everett.

Above all, for his unstinting love and support as well as for truly constructive and tactful criticism, and for helping me see the wood for the trees, Adam Goulcher.

ONE PLACE. MANY STORIES

Bold, innovative and
empowering publishing.

FOLLOW US ON:

@HQStories